All I Need

Book 4 of the Rocky Creek Series

KATHRYN ASCHER

North Carolina

Published in the United States by BQB Publishing
(an imprint of Boutique of Quality Books Publishing Company)
www.bqbpublishing.com

979-8-88633-014-4 (p)
979-8-88633-015-1 (e)

Library of Congress Control Number: 2023944457

Book design by Robin Krauss, www.bookformatters.com
Cover design by Rebecca Lown, www.rebeccalowndesign.com

First editor: Allison Itterly
Second editor: Andrea Vande Vorde

Acknowledgments

Writing may be a solitary endeavor, but I couldn't have done it without a few people pushing me along, motivating me to keep going, and helping me with feedback every step of the way.

First, my writing buddy, Connie, thank you for all your constructive criticism, and especially the advice I didn't necessarily like at the time. You always help me see things in a different light.

For Mary, thank you for your edits and being one of the first set of eyes on the finished draft. I hope you go far in whatever you do.

For my mom, thanks for being my biggest fan.

And for Matt, your cheerleading keeps me going.

One

Hannah Murphy stared at the short tumbler of muddy, pale-yellow liquid in front of her, then up at the man who had placed it on the table. He gave her a cocky half grin.

"You looked thirsty," he said.

"You could tell that from across the room?" Hannah fought to keep her disdain from showing on her face. She lifted her eyebrows innocently and kept the habitual polite smile from her lips.

Not smiling was probably the easiest thing to do this evening.

"That's pretty impressive, Eric," she continued casually.

Eric's half grin split into a full smile as he leaned his elbows on the high-top table and peered at her. Hannah folded her arms and backed as far away from him as possible.

"You look lonely too," Eric said. His green eyes glinted with something that made her stomach turn.

She refrained from curling her lip as she held his stare. "Your powers of observation are simply astounding," she said flatly.

He inched closer. "So, how about you and me get out of here?"

Hannah blew out a long breath and barely resisted the urge to roll her eyes. Her fiancé's friends never had much interest in socializing with her, even when he was around. But tonight, every single one of them had approached her with offers similar to Eric's. They hadn't spoken to her at all in the past year, and she struggled to imagine the reason behind their sudden interest in her. While they had never been the sharpest group of guys when it came to intelligence, Eric was clearly the dullest tool in the box. At least Adam and Will had picked up on her sarcasm and left her alone. She didn't drink, and she had no intention of starting with this offering.

Eric bobbed his head toward the door. "So? You wanna get out of here?"

"No," she answered. Then, because she couldn't avoid it, "Thank you."

He stood and shrugged. "Hey, whatever, babe. I'm just here because Tori suggested it." He turned and walked toward a group of young women at a nearby table, who giggled as he approached.

Hannah shook her head. Victoria "Tori" Davis had been a party girl since they were twelve. At fifteen, she'd been the first in their class to lose her virginity. In the nine years since, she hadn't slowed down in her partying or her conquests, and she couldn't understand that not everyone lived by her rules. Tori seemed to have forgotten the reason why they were all gathered at Finnigan's Pub. At the party that Tori had arranged.

Against Hannah's wishes.

It looked like Hannah would be having a lengthy, unpleasant conversation with her "friend" later.

Hannah grabbed the glass and made her way through the double swinging doors and into the restaurant. Walking up to the bar, she smiled at Jim, the old bartender. He returned her grin with one of his own, his white teeth gleaming against his dark skin.

"Hey, Jim." Hannah placed the glass on the wooden bar top and eased herself onto one of the emerald-green leather stools.

"Another one, heh?" He chuckled as he took the drink from her and dumped it into the sink in front of him.

"It's not funny," Hannah whined, sounding like one of her third graders. She looked around the room. "I've been in here how many times in the last month? You couldn't have warned me about this little get-together?" Although, Tori's increased insistence over the last six weeks that she and Hannah have dinner at Finnigan's Pub now made more sense.

"Now, what fun would that have been?" Jim winked as he placed a glass of water in front of her. "The party girl said you wouldn't be happy about it."

"Well, she was right." Hannah took a sip of water. "I asked her not to do this. I told her it wasn't necessary." She took a deep breath. "I'm not even sure it's in good taste."

Jim's eyes darkened. "It's never poor taste to honor someone you loved."

Hannah's heart dropped to her stomach. "He was my fiancé, not hers."

"He was her friend." Jim raised an eyebrow. "Maybe she just needs this for closure and thought you could too," he said softly.

Hannah frowned. She guessed there could be a deeper reason behind this party, a memorial to her fiancé, Carter Elliot, who had died a year ago in a helicopter training accident off the coast of Rhode Island. Two men in uniform had come to her house to tell her the awful news. There were no survivors, and his body had never been recovered. It was a tragedy. At twenty-three, Carter had had his whole life ahead of him, and Hannah was supposed to be a part of that future.

When Tori approached her last month about throwing a memorial party in Carter's honor, Hannah had immediately dismissed the idea and asked her not to. Hannah and Carter had been a couple for three years, engaged for two. She'd known him better than anyone at this party. She'd accepted his death and moved on, so why couldn't everyone else do the same? Maybe her reluctance to have a party in his honor had been a bit selfish. Just because she didn't need it didn't mean others couldn't use it for closure.

"There you are," came a high-pitched voice as fingers wrapped themselves around Hannah's upper arm.

Hannah turned to find Tori, blue eyes bright, blonde hair draping over her shoulders, tugging her toward the party room.

"I'm about to make a speech and thought you might want to say something about Carter," Tori said in a cheerful tone.

Hannah tried to dig in her heels and protest as they approached the swinging doors, but she found herself blinded by the bright room and in the center of the party. Compared to the pub, the room was small with pale grayish-white walls. High-top tables with chairs were spaced along the edge of the walls. The doors that separated the party room from the game room, also attached to the pub, were open to make room for the crowd of at least thirty, most of them former classmates.

Tori cleared her throat and called for silence. "Hi everyone," she began in her typical singsong tone. "Thank you so much for coming here tonight to honor and remember one of our dearest friends. Carter was a hero to so many of us, even before he upped his game and joined the Navy."

Hannah lowered her gaze to the floor. Carter Elliot was liked by everyone in Rocky Creek. His father, Darren, was a successful and highly respected local builder, and his mother, Sylvia, was an arrogant woman who looked down on anyone who was below her class. In high school, Carter was captain of the football and baseball teams, and he was homecoming king. Every year, he was voted the most popular in his class. He'd always had a smile for his friends or admirers. He had been attractive in a movie-star kind of way, even first thing in the morning, and on occasion he would show a softer side of himself when sweet-talking the older women in the community or volunteering with Hannah at the food bank when they were in college.

It was obvious why he was a hero to so many.

After almost four years together, Hannah had seen the darker sides of him as well. When he was with his high school friends, he was often arrogant, selfish, and inconsiderate, characteristics he most definitely inherited from his mother. He could be subtly condescending, and his wit had been quick, if not always sharp, but cut just the same. Hannah would wager that most of this crowd didn't know that side of him, and those who did didn't care. He had never shown that side of himself to the general public, only to his closest friends, who were more than likely to join him in his haughtiness.

But there were good times too. Enough for her to say yes when he'd proposed to her. She had looked forward to becoming his wife, but then he unexpectedly joined the Navy without consulting her. Looking back, she wondered if he'd ever truly loved her. In the months before Carter died, she'd started to doubt if they would ever make it down the aisle.

Tori squeezed her arm, and Hannah shook her thoughts away. She hadn't realized Tori had stopped talking.

"What?" Hannah's gaze left Tori's perfect small face and skimmed the room. All eyes were on her. Heat crept up her spine, and her cheeks flamed under the scrutiny.

"I asked if there was anything you'd like to add." Tori's smile made Hannah want to crawl under the nearest table. Tori was one of the prettiest women in Rocky Creek, Virginia, and Hannah had never felt attractive next to her. She ran a hand over her own blonde hair. They probably wouldn't have been friends at all if it hadn't been for Carter. She wasn't really sure why they were still friends now that he was gone.

Hannah looked away. "No. You've said it all." She winced. She had no idea what Tori had said. It was probably nothing like what Hannah had been thinking, but Hannah couldn't really share her thoughts.

Tori's smile softened, and pity filled her eyes as she tipped her head sideways. She turned to the crowd. "So, thank you for coming. Let's mingle and share."

"Share?" Hannah parroted.

"Memories," Tori answered. She released Hannah's arm and moved to stand in front of her. "I know this is hard on you, and you are holding up so well. But don't you think it's time to move on? I mean, you're only twenty-four. You're in the prime of your life. You should be having fun, exploring all your options. I'm more than happy to fix you up."

Hannah blinked. "I noticed," she said, her jaw surprisingly tight.

Tori blushed. "Well . . ." she stammered. "I just thought—"

"I know what you thought," Hannah snapped. "But my love life is none of your business. And for the record, I'm not interested in dating any of Carter's friends."

Tori laughed lightly. "Honey, most of the single men in this town are Carter's friends. Who do you plan on dating?"

Hannah fell back a step and scowled. "Again, that's really none of your concern."

Tori's expression sobered. They stood motionless in a silent showdown until Tori was called away by someone on the other side of the room. Hannah turned on her heel and marched toward her empty table in the corner of the room. She wasn't sure what infuriated her more: that Tori had put her on the spot, or that Tori assumed to know what was best for her.

Hannah had moved on from Carter. Almost immediately, in fact. She hadn't dated anyone since Carter's death, but as Tori had pointed out, most of the eligible bachelors in Rocky Creek had been friends with Carter.

"You look like you want to get out of here," Phillip Mercer said. He was the most persistent and worst behaved of Tori's directed suitors. His brown eyes were heavy lidded, and one corner of his mouth lifted in a way he clearly thought was sexy. He reached across the table and placed his hand on hers, giving it a gentle squeeze as he lifted it to his lips. "That was so wrong of Tori to put you on the spot like that. Everyone knows how much you hate the spotlight. I say we get out of here and find something else to do. Something a little more enjoyable." His eyebrows lifted and fell a few times.

She yanked her hand away. "No thanks, Phillip. I'm still not interested in going out with you." Phillip was always making moves on her, sometimes right in front of Carter. Of course, Carter never stood up for her or came to her defense and instead would laugh along, as if it were some kind of inside joke.

"I was suggesting we stay in," he replied seductively. "Maybe a little horizontal tango, if you know what I mean."

"An even less appealing idea," she scoffed. Although she had to admit, his idea of getting out of here was tempting, and as he came around the table toward her, she grabbed her purse and bolted around the opposite side, through the swinging doors, and back into the main area of the pub.

Resisting the urge to run, she snaked around high tables as she moved toward the front door of the bar. She turned to wave to Jim and saw Phillip sauntering toward her with a smirk that made her skin crawl.

Crap. Where could she go? She could slip into the bathroom, but she couldn't guarantee that Phillip wouldn't be waiting for her. Tori had driven her here and she had no car. She pushed the heavy door open and slipped into the early September night, quietly praying Phillip had given up his pursuit.

As the door closed behind her, she heard him call her name, but she kept moving toward the parking lot. There were stores she could duck into. Across the parking lot was a grocery store and a fast-food place on the main street. Her stomach grumbled, and she suddenly had the urge for something cold and sweet.

"Hey, Hannah."

She turned toward the friendly voice and smiled. "Quinn," she said, surprised to see him. Her eyes skimmed his familiar features. His brown hair, darker than usual in the dim light, was parted on the left side of his crown and swept up to the right. His eyes were shadowed, but she could feel the steeliness of his blue gaze focused on her.

"Hannah, baby, wait!" Phillip called out behind her.

Shit.

Without thinking, she launched herself into Quinn's arms and pressed her mouth to his.

Her heart raced the moment their lips collided. His strong arms wrapped around her waist and pulled her closer, even as he fell back a step. His lips softened as they moved against hers, encouraging and soothing. His breath was warm and sent a shiver down her spine.

What am I doing?

She quickly pulled away. "I'm . . . um . . ." she stammered in a small, shaky voice. "Is he gone?"

She'd never done anything so impulsive in her life. She liked having a plan. She liked order. She liked calm. This kiss was spontaneous, chaotic, and a little wild.

She liked it.

"Yeah, he's gone," Quinn said.

"Thank goodness." She backed away and stumbled over her own feet. He gripped her elbows to steady her. Warmth filled her cheeks as her breath caught in her throat.

The look in his blue eyes had an edge of protectiveness to it. She'd known Quinn Taylor since they were five years old. They'd met in church and became friends, and they were on the same academic teams in middle school, but nothing had ever progressed beyond a casual friendship. Their paths diverged once they reached high school—he took an athletic route, while she stuck with academics—and they'd stopped talking altogether by the end of their senior year.

She focused on her breathing—in through her nose, out through her mouth—in hopes of getting her heart rate to slow down. She was clearly still caught up in whatever impulse had forced her to kiss him.

"What just happened?" he asked.

She giggled, not sure how to answer his question. "It's called a kiss," she teased, choosing to believe he was just as shocked as she was and not offended. "Has it been that long for you?"

His eyes narrowed as his lips twitched, then widened in a smile. "That's not what I meant," he said. "And no."

She adjusted the thin strap of her purse and hooked her fingers around the leather.

"Why did you just kiss me?" He looked at the door of the pub. "Was it because of Phillip?" His gaze returned to her, and all humor drained from his face.

Her smile fell. "Yes," she muttered, not really sure Phillip was the real reason. She'd have to figure that out later. "Sorry."

He waved the apology away. "What did he do?"

"Nothing," she said slowly. "He just didn't want to take no for an answer."

"Did he hurt you?" His tone was gruff.

She shook her head. "No, nothing like that. It's more that Tori convinced him to ask me out, and he was aggressive in his attempts to get me to say yes."

Quinn narrowed his eyes.

"Not physically. Just verbally." Hannah tilted her head and laid a hand on his arm. "I'm fine, really."

He held her wide-eyed stare for a few moments, then nodded. "Were you headed home?"

The corner of her lip quirked up. "No, I can't. Tori drove me." She laughed lightly. "I was heading over there to get some ice cream." She pointed to the fast-food restaurant under the golden arches. "Want to come with me? I feel like I owe you a sundae."

"For what?" he chuckled.

"For coming to my rescue, of course."

Quinn smiled. "Hot fudge?"

Her grin widened. "Is there any other kind?"

Two

Hannah and Quinn sat in the back booth of the fast-food restaurant near the window with their sundaes. She couldn't believe she was sitting across from Quinn Taylor, a person from her past. And she'd kissed him. *What was I thinking?* This evening was getting stranger by the second.

As she studied him, she realized how much time had changed him. His cheekbones were more prominent than she remembered, and his chiseled jaw was dabbled with stubble. His nose was slim and straight at the bridge, and his blue eyes were framed in long lashes. She'd forgotten how handsome he was and felt an overwhelming need to rebuild the friendship they once had.

She stuck her spoon in her dessert, lost in thought, trying to make sense of things.

"You look like you could use something a little stronger," he said with a chuckle, his deep voice vibrating down her spine, causing her heart to flutter. Unlike the guys at the pub, she knew he was only teasing.

"Possibly, but this will have to do for now," she said. He watched the spoon as she lifted it to her mouth. As she savored the cool, sweet cream on her tongue, his Adam's apple bobbed once, and he quickly looked down. But not before she saw the desire in his dark blue eyes.

Maybe being with him right now was a mistake. Especially after that kiss. She still couldn't think straight.

"How was the party?" he asked.

She took a deep breath. The last thing she wanted to talk about was this debacle of a night. Or the reason for it. She wanted to close the door on that part of her life, but every time she thought she had, something—or someone—reopened it.

"Surprising," she answered with a shrug, and pushed the hot fudge around with her spoon.

"Surprising good?" he drawled. "Or surprising bad?"

She gave him half a smile. "Just surprising." She spooned more ice cream into her mouth, then tried not to laugh at his curious expression. "I didn't know about it until I got there."

He frowned. "Tori didn't tell you."

Hannah shook her head. "Did you know about it?"

"I got my invitation a month ago," Quinn said. "Sorry I was running late. I was hung up with a class project."

Hannah tipped her head and studied him. He had a good job with Charlie Dodd's renovation company, and she'd forgotten he had gone back to school to study architecture. She worked with his sister, Rachel, at the elementary school, who spoke of him often. "You're graduating soon, aren't you?"

"December." He took a bite of his ice cream, then pointed at her with his spoon. "And you're trying to change the subject."

She stared at the white laminate tabletop and tried to find a pattern in the black specks. "I would never." She glanced up at him.

He chuckled. "Why didn't Tori tell you about the party?"

"Probably because I asked her not to throw it in the first place."

"Of course. That's how she is." His eyes filled with pity, and she immediately regretted her answer. "Is it still hard . . . you know, with everything that happened?" he asked.

Dealing with Carter's loss?

He didn't say the words, but he may as well have. She knew what he was asking. In the past year, every time she'd seen someone in town for the first time in a while, they'd asked the same thing.

She nodded once.

She was sad when Carter died. Any loss of life was sad, but in hindsight, she'd never really felt grief over him. She'd mourned for their relationship when he'd left her and joined the Navy, but that truth felt far worse than letting Quinn think she was still mourning the death of her fiancé.

They sat in silence, each taking a few bites of their sundaes. She was swirling the dark and sticky fudge around the melted cream when he cleared his throat.

"You want to tell me what really happened?" Quinn's tone was serious and commanding. She froze mid-swirl. His steely expression matched his tone, and she swallowed hard.

"It really was nothing," she mumbled.

"Okay," he said. "So, tell me about it."

She pushed her cup away and folded her forearms on the table but remained silent.

His eyes narrowed, and he leaned forward. "Has Phillip been pursuing you for long?"

Hannah shook her head. "No. It's nothing like that."

"Would you like me to say something to him?"

She broke into a smile. "No, I don't think it will be a problem after tonight."

He opened his mouth, but she held up her hand to stop him. It was probably best if she explained what happened rather than allow him to continue with his misplaced chivalry.

"Tori put him up to it," she confessed. "And Eric, and Adam, and Will."

Quinn tipped his ear toward her, as if he hadn't heard her. "What?"

"Tori encouraged all of Carter's gang to ask me out," Hannah explained. "Phillip was first. Then Adam, then Will, then Phillip again. Then Eric and Phillip one more time. Because he can't resist, I guess."

"He is persistent," Quinn mumbled. "Are you sure she put them up to it?"

Hannah nodded.

"Why would she do that? Does she think you need help finding dates?" he asked.

"No." A mischievous smile tugged at her lips as she held his stare. "She thinks I need to get laid."

Quinn choked on his ice cream and covered his mouth with a napkin. She leaned back in the booth and laughed.

"Do you agree?" he sputtered as he set his napkin on the table, his eyes sparkling with amusement.

She tried to maintain her calm, neutral expression. "My love life is none of Tori's business," she said.

"That's not an answer." He grinned.

"That's all the answer you're getting."

He laughed quietly. "Fair enough."

Hannah covered her mouth to hide her laughter. Quinn was always easy to talk to, and his teasing was never meant to be cruel. Unlike Carter's friends, who knew their target's weaknesses and would exploit them when the mood struck. She'd always thought Carter was the same until she'd gotten to know him. In high school, he'd been just as obnoxious as the crew that had harassed her tonight. But when it was just the two of them in college, when he was away from his friends, he was a much better person. Most of the time, he was fun to be around.

"So, given that Tori is trying to fix you up, I guess she thinks you've mourned long enough?"

"She wouldn't encourage me to date if she didn't."

He raised a skeptical eyebrow and she shrugged.

"You know how she is. She's not happy unless she has a man on her arm, and she thinks everyone else feels the same." Hannah inhaled deeply. "And since she's never been in a long-term relationship, I guess she's determined I've had long enough to get over it." It was true, of course, but she wasn't sure anyone needed to know that. Hannah wasn't currently dating because there was no one who interested her, not because she was still grieving Carter's death.

She put her napkin in her cup and slid to the end of the booth.

Quinn did the same. "Can I give you a ride home?"

Hannah smiled. "That would be nice. Thank you."

Three

During the first song of the church service, Quinn slipped along the wall and slid into the pew to sit next to his sister, Rachel. He took out the hymnal and opened it to the song the congregation was singing.

Rachel leaned over. "How did the party go?" she asked just loud enough for him to hear over the music.

"I don't know," he replied out of the side of his mouth. He didn't have to look to see his sister give him a confused look. He could feel her blue-eyed stare on the side of his face. "Something came up at the last minute," he added.

Rachel moved closer to him. "He was one of your friends."

"For a while." Quinn hadn't talked to Carter in years, but they'd been friends in high school, which was the only reason he'd received the invitation in the first place.

She looked back at the hymnal in her hands, leaving him to think in peace.

He hadn't been able to get that kiss off his mind. He replayed his conversation with Hannah several times and found himself hung up on the questions she hadn't really answered.

After the chorus, Rachel leaned over again, her light-brown hair brushing his shoulder. "You could have at least gone to the party for Hannah. She was your friend too."

Hannah had always been more of a friend than Carter. In middle school, they'd competed on the school's academic teams, the Odyssey of the Mind and the Quiz Bowl. Even though they went their separate ways in high school, he always appreciated their conversations.

Quinn's friendship with Carter was complicated. The Elliots were rich and well-known in Rocky Creek. Quinn's family was poor, and the kids would tease him for being nerdy and pudgy, and they made fun of his second-hand clothing.

In eighth grade, Carter's grades had begun to slip, which jeopardized his positions on the baseball and football teams. Their math teacher, Mr. Waddy, had threatened to fail Carter if he didn't get his grades up, so he'd assigned Quinn to tutor him. They met at Carter's house three times a week for tutoring. Carter was nice enough, and he seemed eager to learn, if not a bit distracted. One day, they took a break from studying and went outside to throw around the football.

"Dude, you ever think about joining the team?" Carter had asked. "We could use someone big like you. All the heavy guys play defense. I'll talk to Coach Taylor."

A backhanded compliment, for sure. Quinn was on the heavier side and had some bulk, so he'd never thought about playing sports. But to his surprise, Quinn decided to venture out of his comfort zone and try out for the team. Carter may have helped get him on the football team, but Quinn's skills landed him a position as a defensive tackle. It was enough to keep Carter's friends from making fun of Quinn for his intellect and slight pudge.

Others saw Quinn and Carter's relationship as a friendship, but Quinn knew the truth and simply didn't correct them. Theirs was a more symbiotic relationship, as both of them got something out of it: Carter was able to keep his grades up with the private tutoring, and Quinn was able to hang out with Carter and his friends and be treated like one of the popular kids. That was when he and Hannah had drifted apart.

"I saw Hannah," he said and felt his sister's stare again.

"You said you didn't make it to the party."

"I didn't. I saw her as she was leaving."

Rachel's eyes filled with pity. "Poor thing."

After their conversation, Quinn wasn't completely sure Hannah would appreciate the pity. He hadn't missed the way she avoided his questions or the lack of emotion when he'd asked about Carter.

"She said she didn't know about the party," Quinn said. In his peripheral vision, he saw his sister's eyes widen. "She had asked Tori not to throw it."

"Figures." The word was laced with disapproval.

As the pastor made announcements, Quinn looked around the sanctuary. His brother-in-law, Seth Bremner, sat with the choir at the front of the church. Seth's gaze was fixed on their four-year-old daughter, Lily, who was sitting in the second pew on the other side of the church with Quinn and Rachel's parents.

Hannah's family sat on the same side as his parents, a few rows behind him. He couldn't remember the last time he'd seen Hannah in church. Her father, mother, and sister still came to church every Sunday despite Mrs. Murphy's current fight with breast cancer and her treatments. She always wore a different scarf wrapped around her head. Today's scarf was pale yellow, not very different from the natural hair color she and her daughters shared. Hannah's eyes were a pale honey brown, more like her father's. She and her sister, Kailee, shared the same straight nose and full lips.

Music started for the next hymn, and he opened to the correct song in the hymnal.

"When was the last time Hannah came to church?" Quinn asked as soon as the congregation started singing.

Rachel shrugged. "Probably a year ago. Maybe more. Why?"

"No reason," he answered.

They sang a verse and the chorus before Rachel turned to face him. "Why are you asking so many questions about Hannah?"

"I'm just curious."

Her eyes narrowed. "Why?"

He looked at the words on the page, trying to follow along with the song. "She seemed a little odd last night. I'm just trying to figure out why."

"Mm-hmm," Rachel said. "Probably upset about the party. She hates being the center of attention."

"I'm sure Tori was the center of attention," Quinn replied. If there was one thing he knew about Tori, it was how much she loved being the focus of any event.

Rachel rolled her eyes. "Sounds like Tori. Maybe it was the theme of the party that got Hannah down."

Quinn wasn't sure he'd say she was "down." It was more of a cool indifference.

"Does she ever talk about Carter?" he whispered as the music came to an end.

The pastor called the children up to the front for their little story. Rachel grinned as she gazed at her daughter. That look on her face always made Quinn smile too.

Lily was sitting unusually still on the step next to the pastor, smiling at her grandparents then at her mother. A red headband kept her bright-blonde hair out of her face. Quinn and Rachel both had hair that color when they were younger. Rachel's had darkened to a light brown, while his was more of a milk-chocolate color.

"What is she doing?" Rachel muttered under her breath.

Lily's hand slowly reached out for the bow on the braid of the little girl in front of her. Rachel shook her head at her daughter. A smiling Lily mimicked her mother and eased her hand to her lap. The pastor finished his story, and the children were dismissed back to their parents before any real chaos erupted. With a group of about ten children between two and five years old, the pastor had learned to tell stories as quickly as possible.

Rachel growled softly, "She knows better."

Quinn laughed silently as his mother handed his niece a lollipop as she slipped back into the pew with his parents. The laugh almost became audible when Lily looked directly at Rachel as she slid the lollipop into her mouth.

"I'm revoking her grandma privileges for a month." Rachel sat back in the pew.

Quinn, still chuckling, watched Seth scowl at his mother-in-law. He was sure the day would come when his mother would be bribing his own child with candy to keep him or her quiet in church. But for now, he'd enjoy how his mother's behavior tortured his sister.

"You know," Rachel whispered. "I don't think you've talked about a woman this much since Alexa."

Quinn scowled. She knew better than to bring up that name. "I don't know what you mean," he hissed.

The corner of her mouth quirked up. "I'm just saying. Someone who doesn't know you might think you were suddenly interested in Hannah Murphy."

He leaned away and faced the front of the church. "Then I guess it's a good thing you know me."

Four

"You did what?" Dani Prescott-Johnson screeched as Hannah strolled past her, pitchfork in hand, into the next stall of the barn.

Hannah cringed at the question. She and Dani had been mucking horse stalls for the better part of an hour, talking about anything but the party the night before. As far as Hannah knew, Dani hadn't been invited. No surprise, since Dani wasn't Tori's biggest fan. Hannah didn't want to bring it up, but she couldn't hold in her excitement any longer.

"I . . . kissed Quinn."

The wheelbarrow appeared in the open doorway of the stall before Dani did, her grin wide and beaming. "Quinn?"

Hannah leaned against the upright pitchfork handle and tilted her head.

"Quinn Taylor?" Dani continued in an absurd tone. "Rachel's brother? Quinn, the best looking, most well-rounded guy to come out of our graduating class?"

Hannah's cheeks burned as she turned her back to Dani and began scooping straw and tossing it into the wheelbarrow. "I didn't kiss him because of that," she ground out. But it certainly didn't hurt that he had brains, brawn, and looks.

"You needed a reason?" Dani walked into the stall with a pitchfork and followed Hannah's lead.

"There's always a reason," Hannah said.

"So, what was yours?" The flecks of green in Dani's gray eyes danced with an amusement Hannah didn't like. She hated feeling like she was being laughed at, even if it was her best friend since middle school doing the laughing.

Hannah stuck the tines of her pitchfork into the dirt floor and hugged the handle.

Dani's face sobered. "Don't be mad. You can't just drop a bombshell like that and not expect me to ask questions."

"It was hardly a bombshell."

Dani laughed as she tossed a pile of dirty straw into the wheelbarrow. "You haven't so much as looked at a man in over a year, and you think a kiss isn't a big deal?"

Hannah opened her mouth to argue but quickly closed it.

"It's not a bad thing," Dani said softly. "It's been a year. You should feel free to move on."

Hannah sighed. "I'm not afraid to move on. I welcome the chance." She scooped up the straw with her pitchfork. "It's just . . . I may have used Quinn last night." She still didn't know what had come over her. It was as if there was a magnetic force pulling her toward Quinn, and she'd been powerless over her actions. Never in her life had she done anything remotely spontaneous like that.

Dani went back to work as well. "So, why did you kiss him?"

"To get away from Phillip," Hannah said quickly, convincing herself that Philip was the reason for her actions.

"Phillip Mercer?" Dani's upper lip curled. "Where were you that you were running from Phillip and into Quinn's arms?"

"Don't be so dramatic," Hannah muttered. "I was at the pub."

"Why were you at the pub?"

Hannah had made it clear many times that while she didn't mind an occasional dinner at Finnigan's, she didn't really enjoy going by herself. It was one of Carter's favorite hangouts, and he had dragged her there almost every night when he was home between trainings.

"A party," Hannah answered quickly.

"And I wasn't invited?" Dani's tone was lighthearted and teasing.

"I didn't know about it until we got there." Hannah scrunched her face, waiting for the reaction.

All humor was gone from Dani's face, and her expression had become that of the stern schoolteacher she was during the week. "Tori?" Her tone was as cold as her steely eyes.

Hannah nodded. Dani returned to the task at hand in silence, and Hannah followed her lead. They finished the stall, and Hannah moved to the final stall as Dani pushed the wheelbarrow out of the barn to dump it. Hannah paused for a moment to watch the horses graze in the field where she and Dani had herded them earlier this morning. She'd been helping Dani on her horse farm for the last few months. Dani's husband, Chas, had just shown up at her barn one day and asked for a divorce. Six months prior to the proclamation, she'd suffered a miscarriage and was desperate for another pregnancy. She'd thought she and Chas were on the same page and was blindsided by the separation.

A mild breeze blew through the open upper half of the barn's wall, and Hannah closed her eyes to soak it in. It was much more refreshing than the hot, humid breezes of summer, and it whispered of the coming fall and cooler temperatures.

A squeaky wheel pulled her out of her reverie. Dani's expression had softened, almost back to normal, and her eyes had lost some of their hardness. "Why did Tori throw you a surprise party?"

Hannah stabbed the pitchfork into the ground between her spread feet. She placed her hands on the handle and rested her chin on top of them. "It wasn't for me. It was for Carter."

"Whoa," Dani said as her brow creased.

"It's the one-year anniversary," Hannah said somberly. "And it was a surprise. I had asked her not to throw a party in his memory."

Dani's face darkened. "And she didn't listen. Surprise, surprise."

"You're not being fair." Hannah moved to the outer wall. The breeze ruffled the hair on the back of her head.

"You're not being realistic. Tori threw that party for one reason and one reason only: so she could take the credit for it and get all the attention," Dani hissed.

"Dani." Hannah shook her head. "In most cases, I would agree. And yes, she did this against my wishes—"

"*You* were his fiancée, Hannah. Not her. If you didn't want the memorial, then it never should have happened." Dani folded her arms across her chest.

"Maybe she needed it for closure," Hannah argued. It did seem like a logical argument.

Dani rolled her eyes. "I seriously doubt she's thought of him that much in the last year. She only thinks of herself, and she only does things to make herself look good."

Hannah lowered her gaze to the straw-covered ground. Most of the women their age in Rocky Creek who had gone to their high school disliked Tori. Aside from her promiscuity, she'd been a notorious flirt since they were teenagers and had been a distraction for half of the male population in their high school. Dani, however, had the most legitimate reason to hate Tori. She'd caught her soon-to-be-ex-husband, Chas, with Tori at the pub on the same night he'd asked for a divorce. Dani had been overly critical of Tori ever since.

Hannah knew otherwise. Despite her inclination to flirt, and despite what others thought of her, Tori hated infidelity. Hannah had seen Tori suddenly stop flirting with a man as soon as he flashed a wedding ring or mentioned a wife. When Dani had seen Tori and Chas at the pub, Tori had been under the impression that the couple was already separated. Tori cried to Hannah for hours about how sorry she was to have hurt Dani so badly. As often as Hannah tried, she couldn't convince Dani to hear her out.

"Why didn't you want the party?"

"I'm tired of the pity." Hannah sighed. For the past year, she felt as if she'd been handled with kid gloves. Everyone she spoke to on the street, at her father's store, and at the school always had the same sympathetic look in their eyes when they asked how she was. She was tired of it.

Even worse . . . she didn't deserve it.

By the time Carter had died, she no longer wanted to marry him.

"You could just be honest with people," Dani stated, and not for the first time. "Just tell them the truth."

Hannah raised an eyebrow. "What truth would that be?"

"As much of it as you need to tell them." Dani shrugged. "Until they leave you alone."

Hannah rejected the idea. Nothing good would come from her being honest.

"You're too nice, Hannah." Dani's voice was stern but sympathetic.

"What happens if I tell people I didn't mourn him the way everyone else did? What happens if I tell people I was sorry he was gone but I don't really miss him? Everyone in town holds him in such high regard, and they'll all think I'm a horrible person."

"Then tell them the truth about your relationship." Dani looked out into the field where the horses played. "Tell them how he joined the Navy to get out of marrying you. How he continued to find ways to stay away because he would rather string you along than break up."

Hannah cringed. "That makes me sound weak."

"You were," Dani responded softly. "But so was I."

"You were in love with your husband," Hannah said. She could say the same for her and Carter, but she was no longer in love with him by the time he died.

She had missed him at first, the fun they'd had together when it was just the two of them. He could be fairly sweet when he wanted to be. Even though they'd gone to the senior prom together, they didn't start dating until college. She'd gone away to college, about two hours away from home, and was incredibly homesick. She'd bumped into him on campus in the spring of her freshman year and was so happy to see a familiar face.

Carter became her anchor to Rocky Creek, and they'd bonded over their hometown connection. He began joining her in the things she did, from her volunteer work to her book clubs or study groups, and he made them all more enjoyable. While still handsome and charming, he wasn't the big shot on campus like he was in high school, and somehow they fell for each other and started dating their sophomore year. Before Carter came along, she had spent most of her free time in her dorm. Being an extrovert, he often encouraged her to stretch her comfort zone, and would take her to off-campus parties with people she didn't know. Even though she stayed on the edge of the crowd, she wouldn't have been there at all if it hadn't been for him. Beyond the parties, he had exposed her to experiences she knew she never would have had without him in her life.

For two years, things were going well in their relationship. Hannah had brought out a softer side of his personality, and he always made her laugh. In their senior year of college, Carter had proposed, and they made plans to move back to Rocky Creek. But then he'd joined the Navy without discussing it with her first. She'd gone along with his plan, as she usually did. When they graduated and moved back to Rocky Creek, as they'd discussed, she was happy to be home and near her family.

When Carter left for basic training, she was angry and hurt. When he came home from basic training and told her he was going to Officer Candidate School, she let go of the anger and focused on her actual feelings, only to discover there wasn't much left. Something in her began to change, and she'd chalked it up to his absence. After he'd flunked the first round of OCS and announced he was going to try OCS again—another decision he didn't consult her on—she'd given up on their marriage plans altogether. In his absence, she realized that she preferred living without him. She never had the chance to tell him that she no longer wanted to be his wife.

As a result, the entire community viewed her as a grieving widow and treated her accordingly.

"It would tarnish his reputation if I told people he deserted me," Hannah said.

"He's dead. It won't hurt him," Dani replied bluntly.

Hannah decided to ignore the comment. The only thing that bothered her more than ruining her reputation was ruining his. At least she could defend herself.

"And if I tell people how I really feel, they'll look down on me."

"That's on them, not you," Dani said.

"Maybe," Hannah said. "But I have to live with that. And I have to teach their children. How can I do that successfully if the parents don't respect me?"

"Is it better to live with their pity?" Dani asked.

"It's better than their condescension."

Dani faced the window to look outside again, her long, jet-black hair brushing her shoulders. Hannah directed her gaze to the horses as well.

Dani and Hannah had been best friends since the sixth grade. Dani always loved horses and the outdoors, while Hannah tended to hang out at her father's convenience store and pursue academic interests. They approached things differently. Hannah was cautious and always aware of what others might think. She was more concerned with the well-being of those around her than with her own happiness. Dani was more carefree and easily lived in the moment, and while she did care about those around her, she was less concerned with their opinions of her.

Even though their colleges were in completely different parts of Virginia, they both loved Rocky Creek, and they taught at the same elementary school. Hannah appreciated the way Dani was honest with her without being critical. She also knew Dani would be there for her, no matter what.

"I'm willing to bet Tori had something to do with Phillip chasing you too," Dani said.

The corner of Hannah's lip quirked up. "What makes you say that?"

"Because the only thing that interests her more than herself is sex." Dani had a glint of mischief in her gray-green eyes.

Hannah tried not to laugh.

"And I've never met anyone more concerned with other people's love lives than Tori," Dani added, and they both laughed.

"Sadly, you'd win that bet," Hannah said, still chuckling. "And Phillip wasn't the only one."

Dani's eyes rounded. "No," she breathed. "Who else?"

Hannah listed the other guys who had asked her out.

"Almost all of Carter's friends," Dani murmured. "Except Quinn?"

"He wasn't at the party. He was coming in as I was going out." Hannah grabbed her pitchfork and began scooping straw again. She focused on her work to hide the questions in her eyes.

"Did you enjoy the kiss?" Dani asked once the stall was clean.

The heat in Hannah's cheeks flared again. "Dani!"

"What?" Her eyes were dancing. "It's an honest question."

"Not one that deserves an answer," Hannah hissed. "Besides, I told you that I feel like I used him."

"There are worse ways to use a man." Dani tipped her head back and laughed. "I'm sure he's not complaining."

"That's not the point," Hannah replied with a sigh.

"Then what is the point?" Dani asked. "From what little you've said, I get the impression that Tori was trying to set you up last night, and I have a feeling it wasn't for a date."

Hannah mumbled an acknowledgment of her accurate assessment.

"Your need for a good time with a man is probably the only thing I agree with Tori on." Dani shook her head as if to shake the stigma of that statement away. "And in spite of her best effort, you managed to find one of the few good men left in this dinky little community and made a move yourself."

"No," Hannah snapped. "That's not why I did it. I was only trying to shake Phillip, who seemed determined to make me go out with him."

Dani grinned. "Regardless of why you did it, my question was if you enjoyed it."

Hannah pulled her lower lip between her teeth, trying to hide her smile.

"I'll take that as a yes." Dani laughed. "So the next question is, will you do it again?"

Hannah shrugged. She certainly hoped so.

Five

Charlie Dodd's contracting office was on the corner of the town's two main streets. Neither street was ever really busy. Most of the traffic usually came in the form of the town's annual Christmas parade, but that was three and a half months away. Today was quiet as usual.

Quinn paused with his hand on the door and turned his face to the warm sun, which peeked out from behind the courthouse across the street. Adjusting the strap on his satchel, he pushed in the glass door and stepped into the empty foyer of the office. To his right was a small arrangement of chairs with a glass-topped coffee table littered with magazines you might find at a hardware store. To his left was a large corner desk with one side against the wall and the other extended into the room.

When he first started working for Charlie a little more than a year ago, the desk was always piled high with papers that covered nearly the entire surface. The only thing that had been visible at the time was the computer screen that sat on the desk in the corner against the wall. Almost as soon as Kerri Dodd, Charlie's sister, started working as his office manager, the mess had disappeared. She now kept neat stacks in an organizer on the open side of the desk. The rest of the piles resided in a filing cabinet she'd made her brother buy.

Kerri came down the hallway, her long black hair swinging in a high ponytail, and gave him a wide smile.

"Good morning, Quinn," she said as she sat at the desk. "How was your weekend?"

Surprising. "Not bad," he answered. "Yours?"

"Busy," she answered happily. "Wedding stuff. I can't wait to just be done with it."

"How much longer?" Quinn asked.

"Just under six weeks." Her eyes narrowed on his face. "Which reminds me, we haven't gotten your RSVP yet. Will you be able to come?"

He shrugged. "Maybe."

Her smile fell a fraction.

"Probably," he amended.

She nodded. "Good. We didn't invite too many people, mostly just family and close friends. Right now, Jackson's side of the church is a little heavy. I need to balance it out or Charlie will start inviting clients or business connections." She laughed lightly. "Are you bringing a plus-one?"

Hannah's face immediately came to mind. Would she want to join him? He hadn't been able to stop thinking about her. He couldn't think of anyone else he'd like to bring. The real question was whether she would want to go to a wedding, considering she'd been planning her own when her fiancé died.

"May I make a suggestion?" Kerri must have sensed his hesitation. "Find a plus-one. Otherwise, Olivia will find one for you."

Quinn's eyes rounded and he blinked.

"I'm serious," she said with a laugh. "You were going to be my plus-one to her wedding."

"You were dating Jackson at the time," Quinn argued, bringing more laughter.

"True." She tipped her head from side to side. "But she made the threat before Jackson and I started dating."

Quinn had no idea. Not that it would have mattered. He would have refused if Olivia, Kerri's sister-in-law, had asked him. At that time, he was on the verge of proposing to Alexa. No one had known he was dating her. In hindsight, he understood her desire to keep their relationship private. As much as he hated doing it at the time, he was now thankful he had. He'd only told Rachel about Alexa, so he was saved the embarrassment of having to tell people about Alexa's infidelity.

And even worse, that he'd been the other guy.

He'd really dodged a bullet with Alexa and learned a valuable lesson. Never again would he keep a relationship secret, and he'd never play second fiddle. He would walk away before he begged a woman to choose him over another.

"I'll bring a plus-one," Quinn said without thinking. It couldn't hurt to ask Hannah. And if she said no, maybe he could ask Rachel.

Kerri's grin widened. "Did you need something?" she asked as she wrote in a small notebook.

"Is Charlie in?"

She shook her head. "He's in consults all day." She slid to her computer. "Today and tomorrow, I believe." She typed something on the keyboard, and her face scrunched as she studied the screen. "Three additions, one interior remodel, and four outdoor spaces. At least Jackson will be happy."

"Any kitchens?" Quinn asked. He set down his bag on the desk and leaned over to look at the screen.

"Doesn't look like it." She scrolled the screen so he could read along with her. "But you know you're his go-to kitchen guy, especially after what you accomplished at Finnigan's."

"I know," he replied. "But that's not why I'm here."

The remodeling project at the pub was his most difficult job yet, not just physically but emotionally as well. Finnigan's Pub had been a staple in the community for his entire life. When Mr. Finnigan died suddenly due to the pub's roof partially collapsing on him, Quinn had been the one chosen to put it back together. He'd worked with Claire, the oldest Finnigan child, who was two years his junior, to streamline and modernize the kitchen. The budget had started out tight but had grown with a fundraising event. The timeline was short, but they'd done the job and he'd finally made a name for himself in the area of kitchen design.

If only that were enough.

"I have an interview this week and was hoping Charlie could look over my design portfolio." Quinn opened his bag and pulled out his binder.

"An interview?" Kerri asked. "How long until you graduate?"

"December."

He was currently taking online courses, working toward a degree in architecture. He hadn't told many people. He'd graduated in the top five percent of his high school class, but even with scholarships, he couldn't afford college and hadn't wanted to take out loans when he hadn't really known what he wanted to major in.

Instead, he turned his part-time job with a local cabinetmaker into a full-time job and apprenticeship. Through that, he discovered a talent for woodworking and kitchen remodeling. He became so successful with his designs that he ventured out on his own after a few years of practice under his belt. He started taking classes, more or less to boost his knowledge, and the pub job with Charlie's firm had allowed him to put some of those lessons to good use while he built his savings.

"I have a few interviews lined up in the next few weeks," Quinn said.

"When's the first?" Kerri flipped through his binder, studying his designs from every angle.

His heart skipped with a sense of pride. "Wednesday."

"That's in two days," she said.

"Right," he answered with a smirk. "And I have to leave tomorrow afternoon."

"Where's the interview?"

"Boston."

"Wow, that far?" she murmured. "Jackson and I were hoping you'd stay close and start your own firm. You could make Charlie work for you for a change."

Quinn laughed. "Why would I do that?"

"To keep my brother humble." She looked down at the binder. "You want to leave this here? I'll make sure he goes through it tonight and gives it back to you tomorrow."

"I can do that." Quinn slung the strap of his bag over his shoulder. "You'll let me know if there are any kitchen projects?"

She grinned. "You know I will. I may go drum up some business for you just to keep you around."

"If you must." He walked toward the door, then turned to face her. "It won't help."

He had bigger plans. He wanted to design large office spaces or family homes from the ground up, not remodeling tight kitchen spaces in older homes or following other people's designs. He was ready for something different. He was ready for a challenge.

He was ready for a change.

Six

Hannah strolled through her father's convenience store and smiled at the clerk behind the counter. The gas station and convenience store had been in her family since her grandfather bought it forty years ago. It had been his deepest wish for the store to stay in the family for as long as possible. While Hannah's father followed in his father's wishes and ran the store, both of her uncles had pursued careers in other fields and in other parts of Virginia. They always visited the store when they were in town. Her cousin Colin was the only one out of her six cousins who had ever shown any interest in the business.

Colin was a year older than Hannah and the oldest of their generation. He'd always been her favorite. After graduating with a business degree, he pursued a career in investment banking with a large investment firm in Richmond. But with all of her cousins employed elsewhere or still in school, the responsibility of running the family business fell to Hannah or her sixteen-year-old sister, Kailee. Hannah chuckled to herself at the idea. Kailee rarely set a toe inside the store to shop, let alone take an eager interest in how things were run.

"Good afternoon, Donna," Hannah said with a smile. She edged around the counter and moved toward the coolers. Donna Harper had been an employee of the store for as long as Hannah could remember. Donna's children were around Hannah's age, and Hannah had fond memories of playing in the storage area and office with the Harper kids and Colin on school holidays when they had nowhere else to go.

"Hi, Hannah. Good to see you," Donna replied. "How was your weekend?"

Hannah grabbed a bottle of water from the cooler, then moved to the chip aisle. "Interesting question," she muttered as she grabbed a bag of pretzels and made her way to the register. She set the items on the counter for Donna to scan. "My weekend wasn't bad," she said.

The corner of Donna's mouth turned up a little. "I heard about that party on Saturday night."

Hannah's mouth fell open. "How did you hear?"

"Oh, honey." Donna laughed. "The whole town knows. It was all anyone could talk about yesterday."

"Why does that not surprise me?" She was almost certain Tori single-handedly made sure her party was the talk of the town. "What did you hear?"

"That it was the best party of the year and everyone had a fabulous time." Donna slid the items across the counter to Hannah as the bell on the door jingled.

"Really?" Hannah was disgusted by the fact that everyone seemed more focused on the party and not the reason for it.

"No one mentioned why they were there?" A shrill voice cut through the air, and a chill ran down Hannah's spine. "The party was to celebrate the anniversary of my son's death."

Hannah groaned inwardly and slowly turned to face the woman who might have been her mother-in-law. "Hello, Sylvia," she muttered.

Sylvia Elliot lifted her chin and looked down her sharp nose at Hannah, raising a dark eyebrow as her brown eyes narrowed. After scrutinizing her long enough to make Hannah's skin crawl, Sylvia harrumphed under her breath and looked away.

"I suppose you thought a party was a good idea," Sylvia said haughtily.

Hannah opened her mouth to argue, but Sylvia didn't give her the chance to speak.

"You never treated Carter right when he was alive." Sylvia shifted her purse from one arm to the other. "Why should I expect any differently now that he's gone."

Even though Sylvia had never been anything resembling kind toward her, Hannah bristled at her rudeness and tripped over her own thoughts. Hannah had done so well over the past year to avoid Sylvia whenever possible. Whenever she saw Sylvia in town, at the grocery store or while running errands, Hannah did what she needed to do as quickly as possible so she could avoid making a scene.

"I . . . I . . ." Hannah stammered. "I had nothing to—"

Sylvia turned her hawkish gaze back on Hannah. "My son was too good for you, and it doesn't surprise me one bit that you would do something so tacky."

The words slapped her across the face. She'd said the same thing to Tori, that a memorial party felt a little tacky to her. Her blood simmered at the thought that this woman believed Hannah would condone such a thing.

"If you're not going to buy anything, I think you should leave," Donna said.

"I had nothing to do with the party," Hannah spat, surprising herself with her own vehemence. "That was all Tori—"

"Spare me your excuses." Sylvia's eyes narrowed to dangerous slits. "Victoria has always been such a good girl. She would never dream of doing something so horrid. And it disgusts me that you want to use her as your scapegoat." Sylvia tucked her purse under her arm. "You could probably learn a thing or two from Victoria." She gave Hannah a once-over and shrugged. "Then again, it's probably too late for you. You can put lipstick on a pig, but it's still a pig."

Hannah's blood turned icy as Sylvia sailed through the doors of the store, her chin tipped upward, her shoulders back. Hannah watched her climb into her Mercedes SUV and race out of the small parking lot, not even slowing down as she pulled onto the highway.

Hannah felt dizzy and her legs felt weak. She gripped the counter for support. Her vision blurred as she was transported to another time and place: the day she'd found out that Carter was dead.

Two men in uniform had knocked on the door and stood on her porch.

"Hannah Murphy?" asked the shorter man. The top of his white cover was level with her eyes.

"Yes," she'd answered, letting her eyes travel over both men's uniforms, Navy dress blues. One man, the blond, had four silver buttons on his abdomen, while the other man with the darker hair had six gold in the same place. Neither had any other ornamentation. Their shirts were crisp white, just showing over the blue collar of their jackets.

"May we come in?" the taller one asked.

Something in the back of her mind screamed at her. Something was wrong. With a nod, she'd stepped back and motioned the men inside. She sat at the dining table and folded her arms in front of her. The men sat across from her and set their covers in their laps.

Hannah watched them, waiting for whatever it was they'd come to tell her. "Is there something I can do for you?" she asked in a small voice.

"Miss Murphy." The man with the dark hair frowned at her. "I have been asked to inform you that your fiancé, Carter Elliot, has been reported dead in Newport, Rhode Island, at 1632 hours on September ninth. On the behalf of the Secretary of the Navy, I extend to you and your family my deepest sympathy in your great loss."

Hannah stopped breathing. Her heart rate slowed almost to a stop as she stared at the men.

Carter was dead.

"How?" Hannah heard herself asking as her thoughts slogged through the molasses of her mind.

"A training accident off the coast of Rhode Island." The man with blond hair reached across the table and laid his hand over hers.

Her brow furrowed. "What kind of training accident?"

"It was a helicopter crash. The chopper went down over the water, and we haven't been able to recover his body. We will keep searching, but we have to assume it was lost at sea," the dark-haired man said, and the blond gave her hand a squeeze.

She shook her head. None of this made sense. Carter had made it through all the basic training. She thought Officer Candidate School would be safer.

"Are they sure he's dead?" Hannah slipped her hand free and pushed her chair away from the table. Wrapping her arms around her middle, she lowered her stare to her knees as she rocked back and forth.

"They have found the wreckage and there are no survivors."

She blinked furiously against tears that wouldn't come and forced her eyes to focus on the denim of her jeans until the lines in the fabric sharpened. Her fiancé was dead, and all she felt was a numbing chill through her body.

"Ma'am?"

She looked up at the men. Concern laced their features; sadness filled their stares.

"Yes?" Lowering her hands to her lap, she pulled her shoulders up.

"Are you okay?" the blond asked.

Hannah stood and walked toward the door. Was she okay? They'd just told her the man she'd planned to spend her life with was dead.

Her limbs felt weak and her thoughts were muddled. How could he be gone? He'd been healthy and happy, strong and so excited about his future in the Navy. She opened the door and looked at the men.

"I'm fine." She bobbed her head once. "Thank you for letting me know."

They slowly rose to their feet, not taking their eyes off her.

"Would you like to call someone? We can stay until they arrive," the dark-haired man said.

"No," Hannah reassured them, and herself "I'm fine, thank you."

The men exchanged a look, then walked out the door. Hannah watched them stroll toward their dark car at the end of the sidewalk. Once they were on their way, Hannah closed the door and pressed her back to the cold wood. A heaviness settled in the pit of her stomach.

She looked down at her left hand, at her empty ring finger. She'd stopped wearing her engagement ring months ago, after Carter had gone through basic training and told her he'd decided to do OCS the first time. The only time she'd worn the ring had been during his visits, and those had been few and far between. She'd taken most of his knickknacks off the shelves. None of the furniture in her townhouse had been chosen by him. There was nothing in her home that would tell anyone it was Carter's home too. She'd decided their engagement was over after he'd decided to try Officer Candidate School again. She simply hadn't had the chance to tell him yet.

Now he was gone.

She stared at the floor, waiting for the tears to come. Her legs were numb, her body cold. She should be crumpled on the floor in tears right now. All she felt was empty.

"Hannah? You okay?" Donna muttered, pulling Hannah from her thoughts.

"Yeah ... I just felt a little dizzy," she said. She shook off her confrontation with Sylvia. Her heart rate slowed to a calmer pace, but her stomach was still in knots. She had a sudden need for something chocolatey and dashed down the candy aisle. When she returned to the register, she slid two candy bars and a bag of M&Ms on the counter.

"That woman is a nightmare," Donna muttered. "Was she always that bad?" Her tone and eyes were filled with pity.

"Not always," Hannah answered softly. "She never liked me, but she didn't get that bad until after Carter proposed."

"Let me guess," Donna scoffed. "Just never in his presence."

"Quite often in his presence," Hannah said.

"And he never said anything to her about it?" Donna's pity turned to irritation.

"No."

Hannah took the paper receipt from Donna. Her father didn't mind if she took a snack from the store but always insisted on a paper trail for bookkeeping and inventory purposes.

Donna's smile was sad. "Sounds like you dodged a bullet."

Hannah shrugged, hating to admit how often she thought the same thing. The more time Carter spent away from his mother and friends, the better his behavior became, and she could have lived with it. But she always dreaded having to visit his mother and often wondered just how the kinder, gentler Mr. Elliot could live with her.

"And for the record," Donna continued, "you don't need to take any lessons from Victoria Davis. If anything, she could stand to learn a thing or two from you." She tipped her chin up and laughed.

"Thank you, Donna," Hannah said, giggling with her. "I'm not sure Tori would agree with you."

The bell on the door rang as a customer came in, ending their conversation.

"He still here?" Hannah asked after her father, certain she knew the answer but wanting to verify.

"No, he left half an hour ago," Donna answered. "He says he left a list but figures you probably know what to do."

"I should hope so." Hannah walked toward the office. After a lifetime in the store, Hannah had a feeling she knew almost as much as her father did when it came to running things. Just the same, she really appreciated her father's lists. He always left little notes of encouragement in the margins, and his organization, something she'd inherited tenfold, helped her stay focused.

Between Sylvia's appearance and the fact that she couldn't get Quinn off her mind, she could use all the help she could get.

Seven

The squeal in the hallway could only mean one thing: Lily was here.

Hannah smiled as she glanced at the stack of papers she was grading. The last of the students had left on their bus fifteen minutes ago, but the teachers couldn't leave for another half hour. Most of the time she would wander the halls or loiter in either Dani's or Rachel's classrooms and chat as they counted down the minutes until they could leave. Today, however, she decided to catch up on grading papers.

For two reasons.

Hannah spent every other Saturday fixing meals for her family to freeze, so she would need to go grocery shopping to meal prep for the week. Her mother had chemotherapy every other Wednesday, and freezer meals were easier to fix when her mom wasn't up for cooking or if they were short on time.

Second, Dani had been in a teasing mood all week, mostly about the kiss with Quinn, and Hannah was tired of hearing about it. She didn't regret kissing Quinn; she regretted telling Dani about it.

It didn't help that she hadn't stopped thinking about the kiss all week. She'd spent a lot of time reflecting on their childhood friendship. She remembered times at church events—potlucks, youth group meetings, fundraisers, and festivals—with amusement. On the bus rides to the Quiz Bowl competitions, she and Quinn would have lengthy conversations about so many topics, some of which would last for weeks when they'd meet up at church and continue them.

Her dreams this week had also been filled with those memories, but they'd taken on a more erotic undercurrent. One that had never been there. They left her feeling off-balance, and as a result, she was trying to avoid any conversation with Dani that might lead to talking about Quinn. She also didn't even want to picture Dani's reaction if she told her about her encounter with Sylvia at the store.

"Lily's here." Dani strolled into the classroom and leaned her hip against Hannah's desk.

"I heard." Hannah tried not to laugh. Lily was always here on Friday.

Rachel's commute home from school was about an hour, not including the time it took to pick Lily up from preschool, so Rachel's mother would pick Lily up and bring her to the school to give Rachel a head-start on her weekend.

"Guess who brought her." Dani had an impish smile.

Hannah's heart skipped a beat, but instead of giving the answer she was sure Dani wanted, she shrugged. "Seth?" she said as she looked down at the papers in front of her, hoping to hide the flush of heat creeping up her neck.

"Seriously?" Dani scoffed.

"That would be logical. He is her father." Hannah marked up the paper with her red pen.

"That would be tremendously less exciting." Dani rolled her eyes.

"Her grandfather?" Hannah said.

The mischievous smile was back in place. "Her sexy uncle." Dani's eyebrows jumped up and down, and Hannah couldn't help but laugh.

Still smiling, trying to hide the skipping in her heart, Hannah set down her red pen on the stack of papers and folded her hands over it. "And?" It was the same tone she often used with her students when they'd done something wrong but were trying to blame another child for it. It was one that always got to the truth, even if it took a while.

Dani's grin stretched and she shrugged, showing her immunity to that tone. "Just thought you'd like to know," she replied in a singsong voice, laughing as she left the room.

Shaking her head, Hannah rose from her chair and walked over to the door. It wasn't the first time Quinn had brought his niece to school, so it was ridiculous for Dani to think this time was so "tremendously exciting."

Hannah stood in the hallway and watched Dani stroll into her own classroom a few doors down. Behind her, she could hear the rumble of a familiar male voice and felt it vibrate up her spine. She looked toward Rachel's classroom, the next door down from hers.

Quinn wasn't here to see her, was he? *Probably not.* He was just here to help his sister. Nothing unusual about that.

And she shouldn't seek him out. Why would she? She had never made the effort in the past. If they'd passed in the hallway when he was here to see his sister, they'd exchanged a few kind words. But that had always been the extent of their interactions.

Besides, what would she say to him? Sure, they'd shared a kiss and ate ice cream together. But nothing else had really changed in their relationship. They were more strangers now than friends. It would just be awkward for her to try to force a conversation.

She almost wished Dani had stuck around a little longer to give her some advice. Hannah had never been very good at approaching her crushes in high school, and she hadn't needed to practice because she'd been with Carter all through college. Kissing Quinn had awakened some need deep inside her, and now that a small part of her wanted to approach a guy, she had no idea where to start.

"Miss Murphy," Principal Anthony Keller said as he strolled down the hallway toward her with a large grin on his face.

"Mr. Keller," she said, pasting on a friendly grin. "What can I do for you?"

"Several things actually." He stopped a few inches from her. "First, we need to set the date for the yearbook pictures. You can go ahead and put out the call for volunteers to help you with the yearbook this year."

Hannah took a small step backward. "I hadn't thought about asking for volunteers yet. We usually have such a poor turnout from students and parents. I thought I'd handpick a few this year instead."

The dark hair on the sides of his head was short, while the hair on top was longer and brushed his smooth forehead. He had a nice smile with dimples. "I completely understand. But we should at least get the official picture date on the calendar." He took a step closer, and she struggled to keep her kind smile from faltering. He towered over her, and while he had the demeanor of a golden retriever, his height alone was intimidating. "Next, are we ready to start OM for the season? Given the competitions are less than six months away, we should probably start that soon."

"I just got the packet this week," she answered as she inched back, her arm skimming along the wall. Hannah had been the Odyssey of the Mind coach since she began teaching two years ago. She'd been on OM teams every year since the sixth grade. The worldwide problem-solving competition had always been a mental challenge and one that stretched her creativity. "I was just about to go through this year's long-term problems to see if I could gauge interest and ability."

"Great! Maybe you'd like me to help? I'd love to see what they're asking for this year." His smile widened. She'd heard other teachers comment on how handsome they thought Mr. Keller was, but he wasn't her type. Besides, she worked with the man on a daily basis and could never even consider dating a coworker. Hannah had never been one to giggle and fawn over him the way some of her coworkers did.

"It's just the usual problems. A drama, a balsa wood challenge, and a few others," Hannah said. "Nothing I need help with until we know what the kids will want to do."

He nodded, and they each moved in unison, him forward, her backward. Hannah suddenly felt a presence behind her.

"Of course." Mr. Keller smiled. "So, do you know when we'll invite the students to join?"

Hannah shook her head, too distracted by whoever was behind her to notice Mr. Keller's further encroachment into her personal space. "I can let you know next week."

Mr. Keller lifted his gaze from her face to over her shoulder, and his smile faltered a fraction. He stepped backward. "Great. I'll meet with you next week and we'll work on all of that."

"Sounds good," Hannah agreed as she caught a whiff of fresh cedar she immediately recognized, and her shoulders relaxed.

"Have a good weekend," Mr. Keller said, then turned and hurried back up the hall.

Hannah sighed in relief as a true smile touched her lips. She turned to the man standing behind her. "What, exactly, did you just do?"

Quinn shrugged. "What do you mean? I just walked over."

"I've never seen him move so fast," Hannah said with a laugh.

"I think you owe me another ice cream," Quinn said.

Her pulse quickened. "For what?"

He leaned closer. "I just saved you from another would-be suitor." Laughter filled his blue eyes, and her heart somersaulted in her chest.

"You're kidding, right?" she scoffed as she turned and glided into her classroom. As she'd hoped, he followed her. "Mr. Keller is not interested in dating me." At least, that was what she told herself.

"Could have fooled me," Quinn retorted. "I saw the way he kept creeping closer."

Hannah leaned her hips against the edge of her desk. "He does that with everyone. He doesn't understand personal space."

Quinn raised a curious brow. "Hm."

Her classroom was arranged so her students' desks all faced the whiteboard at the front. Her desk was to the right, and a black Formica counter ran the length of the wall, with a shallow stainless sink at one end and laminated pine cabinets along the bottom. Quinn jumped up and sat on the counter.

"You're sure about that?" he said.

"Yes." Hannah laughed uncomfortably. "He's not interested in me." Believing he wasn't interested was easier to accept than the awkwardness of rejecting her boss. If she could pretend not to notice his advances, she didn't risk their working relationship or her job. Besides, she had seen him encroach into other teachers' personal space with completely harmless intent. It wasn't out of the realm of possibility he was doing the same with her.

Quinn folded his arms over his broad chest and tilted his head to the side, silently scrutinizing her. She looked toward the door.

"He's not interested in me," she repeated. Whether Quinn believed her or not was up to him.

Her cheeks blushed with embarrassment. Carter was the first, and only, guy to ask her out. She wasn't the kind of girl that guys fell over themselves to ask out. When Carter asked her to the senior prom, her initial response had been a resounding no. She'd suspected it was a joke, and she wasn't about to set herself up to be laughed at. Her friends had thought she was crazy—no one was supposed to turn down the school's star athlete. She'd thought that would be the end of it, but when he'd asked a second time with a bouquet of flowers, then a third time with her favorite candies, she'd finally agreed. He'd made her feel special. Carter was a lot of things, and he was really good at being charming. But even back then, they were a mismatched pair, as different as oil and water. He was athletic and handsome; she was nerdy and plain. And even a year after his death, she still struggled to figure out why he'd stuck around.

"Anyway, I came to see if you were free this weekend," Quinn said with a boyish grin.

His eyes shone with excitement, and she hated that her answer might extinguish that. "I can't. I'll be at my parents' house most of the day tomorrow," she said. "But I'm free next week." She rushed through her words, afraid he might notice how nervous she was. Or worse, leave the room.

The corner of his mouth turned up and he moved closer. "Then maybe we could go out next Saturday?"

Butterflies fought to burst from her stomach, and she swallowed hard to tamp them down. She could only nod. She couldn't remember the last time she'd been this nervous with a man. Sure, Carter had made her feel tongue-tied when they'd first started dating, but this bubble of nerves was new.

"I think we can do that," she answered.

He beamed as he blew out a long, slow breath, as if he were as nervous as she was. "Good," he said quietly as he took one of her hands in his. "Great." He lifted her hand to his lips. "That's great." Holding her gaze, he pressed a kiss to her knuckles, and heat from his lips spread throughout her body.

"Quinn!"

Rachel's voice echoed into Hannah's classroom from the hallway, and Quinn released her hand.

"In here," he answered as he hurried toward the door.

Hannah fumbled to straighten the papers on top of her desk.

"Oh," Rachel said, nearly bumping into him as she entered the room. "I wondered where you disappeared to."

Hannah gave her friend a slight smile. Rachel's pale-blue eyes narrowed a fraction, but a grin played at the corners of her mouth.

"Did you need something?" Quinn asked calmly as Lily stepped around her mother and slid her hand into his.

"We're ready to go. You coming with us?" Rachel adjusted the strap of her bag over her shoulder and took her daughter's other hand.

"Sure." Looking down at Lily, he added, "To grandmother's house we go." The little girl giggled and smiled at her uncle.

Hannah stacked her papers and shoved them into her bag, still feeling a bit flustered.

"Bye, Hannah, see you on Monday," Rachel said as she led her daughter into the hallway.

"Bright and early," Hannah replied. She looked up in time to see Quinn glance over his shoulder and smile just before he disappeared.

Eight

Quinn took out his tape measure and checked the distance between the counters for the third time in the last thirty minutes. It was precisely as large as it was supposed to be, exactly as he'd expected when he ordered the new stove. His crew had gotten it right, as usual.

He looked at the invoice again. He'd ordered the correct size, so why didn't the stove fit in the space? He handed the paper back to his foreman, Doug.

"They sent the wrong stove." Quinn shrugged. There was no other answer for it.

"We triple checked before we left the warehouse," Doug said. "They didn't have any other special orders in stock."

Quinn nodded as he paced the narrow kitchen, tapping the end of the extended tape measure against his shin.

One of the things he'd grown to love about cabinetmaking and kitchen remodeling was the creativity. When he'd started making cabinets, he enjoyed getting artistic with the basic design. His mentor had given him the freedom to create different designs on the cabinet doors. He had taken his cabinets beyond the basic square bevel and added layers, curves, and even wooden ornamentation.

Kitchen remodeling simply took his imagination to the next level and stretched his artistry even further. When he had large spaces, he could always come up with three or four different designs, and he always had wiggle room in case something didn't go right.

This kitchen was small and unforgiving. He'd determined on his first visit that there was only one logical way to lay out the major appliances, and there was no room for error. Now the special-ordered stove had arrived and it was too large for the space allotted to it, and he had to figure out a way to make it fit.

When he'd first started working for Charlie's firm, he enjoyed puzzles like this. Now it just affirmed he was on the right track. He would much rather build kitchens and houses from the ground up. It would be so much easier to have a completely clean slate to work with instead of fitting his design ideas into kitchen footprints that had been built decades before he was even born.

"How's it going in here?" Charlie's voice echoed through the bare house. The crew working on the living and dining rooms had yet to put the drywall back up.

"Could be better," Quinn called out as Charlie strolled into the kitchen between two of the floor-to-ceiling studs that separated the kitchen from the living room. "Are you sure they won't allow us any extra space?"

Charlie frowned. "You were at the meetings with me. The couple would prefer a larger living room since they spend more time there."

Quinn threw his arms out to the side. The walls only extended a foot on either side of the tips of his fingers. "This isn't practical."

"It's what we have to work with." Charlie pinned Quinn with a resigned look.

"I know," Quinn mumbled and walked back toward the opening for the stove. They only needed another quarter of an inch to slide the stove into position. It didn't seem like much, but he could find a way to make it work by sanding or planing the side of the cabinet. That would be better than the alternative of pulling them out and remaking them entirely.

"How did the interviews go?" Charlie's question pulled Quinn out of his contemplation.

"I don't think I'll be moving to Boston any time soon." Quinn rested against the frame of the counter.

"They aren't offering you a job?"

"They haven't yet." And even if they did, he wasn't sure he'd accept. Quinn had liked the city well enough, but it didn't feel like somewhere he could call home.

Charlie folded his arms over his chest and squared his feet. "And Philly?"

Quinn had interviewed in Philadelphia yesterday. He'd flown up on Sunday night and caught the red-eye home early this morning. The question served as a reminder of his lack of sleep. Maybe that was adding to his frustration.

"If I had to guess, I would say that's a no." The company had looked good on paper, but when he'd reached the office and seen the projects lining the wall, he realized it probably wasn't the company for him. Most of their projects dealt with high-rises and large offices. While those would be a challenge, Quinn preferred to focus on residential buildings and single-family homes.

"You could always stay here," Charlie suggested, drawing Quinn's full focus. "We could always restructure the company and redirect our attention to new builds instead of remodels."

Quinn considered Charlie's words. On the surface, it sounded like a great idea. He could continue to work for a company he liked. Charlie gave him the freedom to do as he pleased as long as he met the customers' requirements. If they focused on building from the ground up, that would give him even more freedom and he wouldn't just be building kitchens. His degree in architecture would allow him to fully design homes.

But Rocky Creek was still just a small community in Virginia tucked into the foothills of the Blue Ridge Mountains. The cost of living would never be as high as a large city, so the income could never be as large. Sure, he could live comfortably, but he could never really make a name for himself in such a small market.

"I appreciate the offer, and I'll keep it in mind," Quinn said. "But I think I'd like to spread my wings a little and give the big city a shot. At the very least, I could get some good builds on the outskirts of the city."

Charlie chuckled. "I understand. But the offer still stands." He stared at the stove. "Now, let's figure out this small problem."

Nine

It was a cloudy Thursday morning, and Hannah dropped her phone into her purse and snatched the keys from the hook on her way out the door. Her mother's reaction to her latest chemotherapy treatment had been worse than usual, and Hannah had tossed and turned all night, worrying. Her phone call with her father to check in for an update had her running behind. She hated being late.

Outside, she fell back a step when she saw Sylvia gliding toward her house with her signature scowl on her face. Keys in hand, Hannah gritted her teeth.

"Why is my son's name still on your lease?" Sylvia stood on the sidewalk, her eyebrows nearly disappearing into her hairline.

Hannah schooled her features as she met Sylvia's stare. "I just haven't removed it." It had always been in the back of her mind that it needed to be done, but it never felt like a high priority. The lease automatically renewed, so whether his name was on the lease didn't really affect her living arrangements.

"Surprising. Given your obvious disdain for his memory, I would have thought that was one of the first things you would have taken care of." Sylvia lifted her chin to look down her nose at Hannah even though she stood below her.

"Why are you here, Sylvia? I'm sure it's not to discuss my living arrangements, and I'm late for work." As if to prove her point, Hannah hit the button on her key fob to unlock her car door.

Sylvia rolled her eyes, then opened her oversized handbag and pulled out a cigar box. "I was honoring my son in a dignified way when I came across these pictures stashed in his room. I would have kept them, but they're tainted with your image. I thought you might like them, even if you are the reason he's dead."

Hannah's stomach knotted as she blinked back the sudden tears. She shook her head as if she could shake the words away. "It's not my fault he died. I didn't ask him to join the Navy," she said through gritted teeth.

"You drove him to it just the same." Sylvia's upper lip curled. "You were always trying to change him. You made him think he needed to prove something to you." She took a step closer and thrust the box into Hannah's hand. "If you hadn't forced him toward marriage, he'd still be alive today."

Hannah forced herself to breathe deeply as she opened the lid of the box and glanced at the contents. Sitting on top was a picture of her and Carter at their prom. A lump formed in her throat as she looked at her smiling face. That had been a happy night, the first of many to come, but she looked at it with a bittersweet remembrance.

"I suggest you remove my son's name from your lease as soon as possible. I can promise you, if you can't make your payments, we will not step in to help in his stead." With that, she turned on her heel and walked away.

Hannah really had to find a way to not let Sylvia always have the last word. Releasing a low growl, she turned and went back inside her townhouse. As much as she wanted to flip through whatever was in the box, she'd have to get to it later.

The school day went by in a blur. The kids had all left, and Hannah was supposed to be getting ready to go home for the day. Instead, she was slumped over her desk with her fingers clamped around the phone at her ear. She pressed her free palm to her forehead, closed her eyes, and counted to ten.

"Hannah, please," her sister Kailee whined. "It won't take you that long."

"Kailee." Hannah's teeth were clenched, and she was doing her best to keep her voice down. "It won't take you that long either, and you live there."

It was the third call Hannah had received from her sister since the students had left. Not counting the call at lunch, the three texts, and the two voicemails that had been waiting for her when the classroom had emptied.

Hannah really should talk to her parents about revoking her sister's cell phone privileges if she was going to abuse it so much during the school day.

"I know, but I have plans for tonight." Kailee's whine was replaced with the arrogance of a teenager who thought the world revolved around her.

"On a school night?" Hannah scoffed as she raised her fingers to her throbbing temple. "I doubt that."

"Seriously, Hannah. Quit being so selfish." Kailee's tone was now bordering on an angry scream. "Come over and fix dinner for us. I don't know how."

Hannah closed her eyes. Had she been this moody as a teen? Kailee's moodiness had only gotten worse after their mother's cancer diagnosis, but still. The selfishness had always been there. And the manipulation.

"No," Hannah replied. "I fixed several casseroles on Saturday."

"I don't want a casserole."

"Then get one of the pasta dishes. There are several to choose from." Hannah heard a throat clear and looked up to see Mr. Keller standing next to her desk. She groaned in silence.

"I don't know how to cook them," Kailee answered, sounding confident that she'd finally won the argument.

"The proper time and temperature for the oven is written on the foil cover for each of them," Hannah answered smoothly, holding up a finger to her principal. "You can do this, Kailee. I have to go."

Without waiting for a response, Hannah ended the call and dropped her phone onto her desk. The pounding in her head had started as a slight twinge when she arrived at school but had grown progressively worse as the day had worn on, despite taking two separate doses of ibuprofen. She wanted nothing more than to go home to her blissfully dark bedroom and crawl into her bed.

"Did you need something?" she asked Mr. Keller, hoping her tone wasn't as short as she wanted it to be.

"Yes." He placed a stack of papers on the desk in front of her. "These are all wrong. I need you to fix them before tomorrow."

Hannah looked down at the flyers she'd worked on with him every afternoon this week, and she'd done exactly as he asked.

"What's wrong with them?" She picked up the save-the-date yearbook picture notice. They'd agreed on the date with the photographer. The clip art was what he'd asked for. She held it up to him. "It's exactly what you wanted."

"I think there should be more emphasis on the importance of appropriate attire for the pictures." His arrogance caused her mouth to fall open. He couldn't possibly be serious.

"You do realize we can't dictate what the kids wear to school, right?" she asked.

"Yes, of course." His tone was as dismissive as the wave of his hand. "But I think parents should be encouraged to find nice clothing for their kids. I'd like that added to the flyer before it goes out on Monday."

She narrowed her eyes, partly out of aggravation but mostly because of her migraine. She picked up the Odyssey of the Mind handout and stared at it. Without invitation, Mr. Keller moved to stand behind her and leaned over her shoulder.

"I don't know if I like that picture." He pointed to an animated robot, then to the skyscraper. "I don't like that one either." Leaning closer, he pointed to a picture of a raccoon. "And this one bothers me as well. It just doesn't seem to fit."

Hannah closed her eyes and pinched the bridge of her nose.

"Each of those pictures represents one of the long puzzles offered this year." She pointed to the robot. "The students are supposed to build a robot that learns from watching others." She pointed to the skyscraper. "This is the balsa-wood building challenge they have every year." She pointed to the raccoon. "And this is the mascot and a part of the time travel challenge. They all fit, they're all appropriate, and we agreed on this two days ago," she said slowly through clenched teeth. Her migraine was gradually worsening. Soon, the nausea would become full blown with results beyond her control. Then the room would start spinning. Nothing would help at that point.

"Are you feeling okay?" Mr. Keller asked, and she sensed him backing up. "You look kind of green."

Great.

"No, not really." She may as well be honest even though it wouldn't change anything.

"Oh." His voice was fading.

She opened her eyes and saw he was halfway to the door.

"Well, if you could get those changes made by tomorrow, that would be great." He left the room, and she felt relieved.

She looked down at the flyers again. They were perfectly fine. She'd probably change one word, bring it in tomorrow, and he'd think it was perfect. It was the same thing every time they worked together.

Her phone rang again, and her sister's face filled the screen. She let it ring as she slowly stacked the papers on her desk and searched for her bag. The ringing stopped as she spotted her bag on the floor beside her desk. She reached down to grab it and the room started to spin.

Oh no.

Sitting back up, she put her elbows on the desk and rested her forehead in her hands, squeezing her eyes shut tight against the wave of nausea. The phone rang again, and she answered it without looking.

"What," she snapped.

"Excuse me?" Kailee scoffed.

"I'm not coming over," Hannah said. At this point, she wasn't sure how she was getting home.

"You have to. I have things to do."

"No you don't. I will call Dad to make sure of it if I have to." Hannah forced herself to take long, slow breaths to keep herself stable.

"Look, just because you weren't popular in high school doesn't mean I have to suffer." Kailee's words were laced with condescension. "I'm going out with my friends tonight, and you can't stop me."

"That sounds like a challenge," Hannah growled. "I really don't care what you do tonight, but you *will* fix dinner and have it ready before Dad gets home."

"And if I don't?"

"Then I guess you'll starve." Hannah ended the call again and slammed her phone down on her desk.

"Whoa."

Hannah opened her eyes and turned her head. Dani was squatting next to the desk, concern softening her steely eyes.

"Let me guess," Dani said. "The brat doesn't want to warm up the dinner you slaved over on Saturday."

Hannah nodded, then groaned as a wave of nausea rolled through her again.

"And your headache's gotten worse?"

"How'd you guess?" Hannah answered, moving her mouth as little as possible.

"Let me help." Dani picked up the bag and slipped the neatly stacked papers into it.

Hannah's phone rang again, and she glanced at the screen. With a groan, she picked it up and lifted her arm to throw it across the room.

"Not so fast," Dani said as she took it from her and answered the call.

Whatever Dani said was lost to the roar in Hannah's ears as she slid from the chair and hung her head over the trash can.

Quinn strolled into the school, not entirely sure what he would say if he was asked why he was there. All he knew was that he had to see Hannah. His week so far had been more than frustrating. After the disastrous job interview in Philadelphia on Monday, the rest of the week had been consumed with coursework, on-site work, or consultations with Charlie. The only thing that had kept him going was the thought of his date with Hannah on Saturday night. He couldn't remember the last time he'd been this excited for a date. Maybe his first date with Alexa, but that was so long ago. Given the way their relationship had ended, he didn't really want to think about it.

Quinn walked into his sister's classroom only to find it empty. He checked his watch to make sure he would catch her in time before she left, then realized the door was still open, which meant Rachel was still in the building. Not that it mattered. He wasn't here to see his sister. He left her room and wandered down the hallway toward Hannah's classroom and stopped short at the sight in front of him.

Dani was pacing in the front of the room, a phone to her ear, her face red as she punctuated her words with her finger pointing at the air. Hannah was sitting on the floor with her back against the lower cabinets, her face pale and damp as she hugged a trash can. Rachel squatted beside her, holding a towel to her forehead and murmuring something in the soothing tone she used when she consoled Lily.

He rushed into the room and crouched down next to Hannah. "What's going on?" he asked, laying his hand on her knee.

Hannah opened her eyes, and they widened briefly on his face before she closed them again. A hint of color returned to her cheeks as she slowly breathed in through her nose and out through her mouth.

"She has a migraine," Rachel answered softly. "And nausea and vertigo."

Quinn looked at Hannah's pale face, and he was overcome with the desire to scoop her up in his arms and hold her until she felt better.

"Good times," Hannah muttered, almost inaudibly, and Rachel smiled slightly.

"Who's Dani talking to?" Quinn asked as Dani's voice grew louder behind him.

"Kailee."

Hannah's upper lip curled. "Little brat."

"Here." Rachel handed him the cool cloth. "Hold this to her forehead." She stood and stretched, and he slid closer to Hannah and placed the towel to her head. "Hannah, where is your lesson plan for tomorrow?"

"I think . . . it's in . . . my bag," Hannah said between breaths.

Quinn watched his sister sift through the black messenger bag. Dani finished her call and sat on Hannah's other side at her feet. She peeked at the trash can and scrunched her nose.

"I called your dad and ratted on your sister," Dani confessed.

"You didn't tell him . . . about this, did you?" Hannah asked slowly.

"No," Dani answered with a roll of her eyes. "Although I don't know why you don't want him to know."

"Because . . ." Hannah opened one eye and looked at Dani. "He's got enough to worry about . . . with Mom." She closed her eyes and leaned her head back against the cabinet. "I wish you hadn't called him about Kailee."

"I tried not to, but she was determined to have you fix dinner tonight." Dani met Quinn's stare. "It was all I could do to keep myself from telling the little bitch off."

"Dani," Hannah slowly reprimanded.

"Sorry." Dani shrugged but looked unapologetic. "What sub do you want us to call?"

Quinn ran the cool cloth along Hannah's forehead and cheeks, his concern growing with every passing second.

After a slow exhale, Hannah opened one eye again and looked at Dani. "Mrs. Miller. She's always good with the students, and they seem to like her." She looked at Quinn and gave him a small smile.

His chest constricted, and he wanted to do anything to make her feel better. "What can I do?"

"Can you take her home?" Dani asked.

"No," Hannah protested as a deep furrow appeared in her brow.

"You can't stay here. You need to go home and get a good night's rest," Rachel said. "Quinn can take you home and we'll follow with your car."

"No." Hannah opened her eyes and looked at him.

"You can't drive, can you?" Quinn removed the cloth from her face and tossed it toward the sink behind her.

"She can't even walk right now," Dani answered.

"I meant, no," Hannah said slowly, holding his stare as he slid an arm around her back. "I'm not riding in your truck. I don't want to risk getting sick in it."

He smiled. "I don't care about that."

"I do." She closed her eyes. "Please."

"Okay," he agreed. He slipped his other arm under her knees, then eased to his feet. Hannah slowly rested her head on his shoulder, and he tightened her against his body.

"Easy, Quinn," Rachel warned as she put Hannah's sunglasses over her eyes.

Quinn stared down at Hannah. A small crease formed above the bridge of her nose with every step he took. He eased his stride until the crinkle faded and she snuggled against him. Her warmth seeped through his body, and he pulled her closer.

"I'll sign her out and request the sub. You can lead him out to her car."

Dani moved around them and toward the door. "You want to drive his truck? I can follow in mine and bring you back here."

Rachel glanced at Quinn. "If that's okay with you."

"That's fine," he said with a nod. "I'll give you the keys outside."

"I'll meet you out there, then." Dani left the room.

As Quinn followed his sister to the parking lot, Hannah whimpered with each jarring step he took. He slowed down, doing his best not to jostle her and cause more discomfort. He glanced down at her pale face, surprised to see that her eyes were open behind the sunglasses.

"I'm sorry," she murmured.

He frowned. "For what?"

"I'm not sure we'll make it out on Saturday night."

He gently pressed his lips to her forehead. "Just feel better."

They could worry about the rest later.

Ten

Quinn got Hannah home without any problems. She rode the whole way with her eyes closed and the window down, and he was able to carry her inside and up the stairs toward her bedroom before the nausea became too much for her to handle.

Now that she was tucked into bed, he wandered the living room downstairs, debating whether he should go home. She had assured him she would be fine in the morning, but that wasn't as comforting to him as she'd probably meant it to be. While he debated, he figured he could take a look around her home, hoping he could learn more about the woman she'd become.

As expected, her townhouse was perfectly cleaned and organized. Her living room was sparsely furnished. A large black entertainment center sat against the wall below the stairs that led up to the two bedrooms. There was a plush beige sofa, a small wooden coffee table, and a beige glider rocking chair in the corner. There was a tall wooden bookcase: the top two shelves were filled with photos and tchotchkes made of ceramic and glass, and the lower three with books. A tall dracaena palm plant was tucked in the corner behind the chair.

As he looked around, it wasn't at all what he expected. She told him that she and Carter had signed the lease on this place before he'd gone to basic training. Quinn had created a picture in his head of what her home would look like: expensive furniture, top-of-the-line electronics, and over-the-top decor to match Carter's tastes.

This was anything but. There was almost no sign of Carter at all in this house.

Quinn wandered over to the bookshelf. There were photographs of

Hannah and her family, one or two appeared to be vacation photos from her childhood. He chuckled at the picture of her, Dani, and Rachel dressed up as Dr. Seuss characters at school.

There were no pictures of Hannah with Carter, for which he was surprisingly relieved. He looked around the room again. Not a single thing in this room said that Hannah had ever lived here with a man, let alone one she'd planned to marry.

Quinn let his gaze lower to the books on the shelves, an assortment of fiction and some nonfiction reference books. None of which surprised him or struck him as something Carter would read. He slowly circled the room again, then into the kitchen and dining room.

On the table was a cigar box, and Quinn wondered if this was finally a sign of the man who had once lived here. He lifted the lid and saw a picture of Hannah and Carter at the prom sitting on top of a stack of photos. He lowered himself to a chair and pulled the box toward him. He cast a quick glance toward the stairs. Would Hannah mind if he skimmed through the photos? He hoped not.

He thumbed through the stack of photos. They were all of Carter and Hannah, always smiling regardless of what they were doing. Mini golf. Horseback riding. At a football game. He couldn't shake the uneasiness that her smile caused him. They made an attractive couple. On the surface, they looked perfect together. He wondered how deep that perfection had run. He didn't know how they'd gotten together in college, but he knew the truth of why Carter had asked Hannah to the prom. It was all because of a dare.

He remembered that day vividly. It was senior year, and they were all sitting in the cafeteria. Quinn's stomach was in knots as he stared at Hannah across the cafeteria, silently considering how he would ask her to prom. He'd been contemplating it for several weeks but hadn't had the chance to get her alone after church to ask. Plus, he hadn't wanted to make a big show of it in front of their family and other churchgoers. She wouldn't like being the center of attention, and he wasn't sure he was prepared for a possible rejection.

The sun streaming in through the window had caused her blonde hair to glint like gold. Quinn had smiled at the sight and wondered what color dress she might wear to the prom.

"What are you smiling at?" Carter's voice had cut through Quinn's thoughts.

"Nothing." He turned his attention back to the tray of food in front of him. He poked at the mashed potatoes with his fork as Tori slipped into the seat next to him. At least if Hannah agreed to go to prom with him, he wouldn't have to go with this bunch of miscreants. When he'd first agreed to tutor Carter in the eighth grade, he hadn't realized it would require they hang out all the time.

While Carter had an arrogant attitude, he was tolerable for the most part. But his gang of friends was horrible, and they brought out the worst in him. Sometimes, Quinn didn't know why he hung out with them. Being more active and playing sports had helped Quinn finally get rid of the "baby fat," which in turn had stopped Carter's friends from teasing him for being overweight. But they had just turned their teasing to other things about him: his lack of wealth, his level of intelligence, his interests outside of sports, whatever they could find that set him apart from themselves.

Just before his eighteenth birthday at the end of the football season the previous fall, Quinn had finally grown tired of them. He was the oldest of the bunch, only by a couple of months, but apparently still the only virgin among them. They'd teased him about it since he was sixteen, and their ribbing was wearing thin. He'd never been foolish enough to think Phillip, Eric, Adam, or even Carter were truly his friends; he just hadn't found a way to remove himself from their circle. Part of him liked being part of the gang. Popularity had advantages he'd never gotten as a chubby bookworm.

"So, I've been thinking about prom," Tori had said as she slipped her arm around Quinn's shoulders. "I think it would be so much fun if we just went as a group."

Phillip scoffed. "You would like that, wouldn't you? Five dates, just for you."

She squeezed Quinn's shoulder. "Well, of course that would be my preference. I hate sharing," she had said with a laugh. "But I suppose, if you each wanted dates, I could find a few appropriate girls for each of you."

Carter looked at Tori. "Appropriate? By what standards?"

"That they'll put out?" Phillip asked.

"They'll be drop-dead gorgeous?" Eric added.

Will smirked. "We won't have to talk to them?"

Tori laughed lightly at each question. "What about you, Quinn? Any requests?"

Quinn shook his head.

"Carter?" Tori's expression became distinctly feline as her hand slipped down Quinn's back. "Any requirements?"

Carter chuckled. "No, too many girls would be more than happy to fill those requirements for me."

"Oh really?" Tori laid her forearms on the table and leaned over them. "I'll bet there's at least one girl in this room who wouldn't."

Quinn looked at Tori and then Carter. Why did he get the sinking feeling that she was up to something?

"Every girl wants to go out with Carter," Eric said. "Why do you think we hang out with him? We get the castoffs."

Everyone at the table laughed except for Quinn. He couldn't stomach the way they ridiculed people they deemed beneath them, and it seemed the smarter the student, the harsher the comments. Hannah was one of the smartest people he knew, and he did everything he could to protect her from their notice. He hadn't wanted to tell any of his friends about wanting to take Hannah to prom. But earlier in the week, Tori had badgered him about who he wanted to ask to the dance. He'd done everything he could to dodge the question, but she wouldn't accept his non-answers. When he finally told Tori the truth, he'd sworn her to secrecy, and she'd agreed to keep it between them.

Tori narrowed her eyes. "What about her?" Her long, perfectly manicured finger pointed in Hannah's direction.

"Who? Dani, the horse whisperer?" Eric turned up his lip. "She's pretty enough, I guess."

"No, not Danielle." Tori rolled her eyes. "Hannah, the blonde sitting beside her."

Quinn's nostrils flared and his muscles tightened with anger.

Carter's eyes traveled over Hannah, and Quinn could tell he was considering Tori's suggestion.

"She's such a know-it-all." Will laughed. "Think you could actually have a conversation with her?"

Carter's stare remained fixed on Hannah. "I think we could manage."

"She probably won't put out," Phillip said with a mouthful of food.

Quinn's fist clenched under the table. If it weren't for the fact that he'd helped Carter pass almost all of his classes, he would have ditched these people years ago.

"She's almost as cute as her friend," Eric laughed. "But still, pretty much a nobody. I don't think she'd go out with you if you asked."

"I don't know why you'd want to," Phillip added.

"Guys, that's enough," Quinn said. They'd made stupid dares before, but they'd never included people outside of their group. "There's no need to bring her into this."

Carter ignored him and addressed the group. "What's in it for me?"

Tori's smile widened. "A hundred bucks. We'll each throw in twenty."

"I'm not throwing anything in." Quinn did his best to keep his tone neutral, even as his blood boiled through his veins. "This is ridiculous. Why don't we stick to the original plan and just go as a group." At this point, he knew he wouldn't be going to prom with them. And if Carter did ask Hannah, he wouldn't be going with her either. If she said no to Carter, Quinn wasn't sure he'd want to hear what they had to say about her.

And if she said yes . . . well, he didn't want to think about *that* at all.

"Fine, the rest of us will throw in twenty-five each." Tori nudged Quinn with her shoulder, and he slid away from her. "One hundred dollars if you ask Hannah Murphy to prom."

Carter looked over his shoulder and his grin widened. "Make it two hundred and I'll take your dare."

"So you pay us if she says no?" Eric asked.

"No, it's a dare, not a bet," Tori said. "We pay him if he takes our dare."

Phillip smirked. "I'll give you another fifty if you try to get to second base."

Quinn had jumped up and snatched his tray from the table. "You're a bunch of assholes." He'd grabbed his backpack off the floor and stomped off as they all laughed.

From that day on, he'd given Carter and the rest of his gang a wide berth. He'd wanted nothing more to do with any of them. The separation had been building, and the dare was the final straw. He never understood why Hannah had agreed to go to prom with Carter, or date him after that. He wondered if Hannah even knew about the dare. He would bet that Carter never told her about it.

Deeper in the stack, Quinn found pictures of Carter without Hannah. Several of them looked like they'd been taken at basic training, but Carter still looked just as happy. A few of the photos had been taken at bars, with Carter surrounded by other men with shaved heads, still smiling and living it up. Quinn couldn't help but grin, even if it was only a small one, as he looked at the pictures. Carter always knew how to have a good time no matter the situation. Quinn studied the pictures for a few more seconds, then shook his head. What was he doing?

He closed the lid on the cigar box. If Hannah had been looking at the pictures recently, then what did that mean? Was she missing Carter and reliving their memories together? Was she over him?

He headed up the stairs. He'd check on her one more time before he left, just to reassure himself.

The first door at the top of the stairs led to the bathroom, and just to the left of that was Hannah's bedroom. He tiptoed up to her door and eased it open so he could peek in. He expected to see her sleeping, but she was propped upright on several pillows, and she slowly turned her head toward him.

"You're still here." She gave him a small smile as she sat up a little more. "I thought you went home."

Quinn leaned his shoulder against the doorframe. "I wanted to make sure you were feeling better."

Her head leaned back against the headboard. "You don't need to stick around. I can handle this on my own. I'll be better by morning and back to normal in a few days."

"You feel this way often?" He entered the room and lowered himself to the edge of the bed at her feet.

"Not as often as I used to," she said faintly.

"Do you know what brings it on?" he asked.

"Sometimes it's stress, sometimes it's the weather. Lack of sleep, too much sleep, too much caffeine, not enough water, too much sugar." She shrugged. "Sometimes it's hard to pinpoint until I feel well enough to go through all the possibilities."

The corners of his lips turned down, and she laughed lightly.

"Don't feel bad. I can usually prevent the headache." She held out her hand and he grabbed her fingers. "The dizziness, however, is harder to predict."

"What do you think caused it today?" He slid toward her until he could hold her palm against his. Her warmth crawled up his arm and settled in his chest, drawing him closer.

"Most likely, it was stress," she whispered.

He watched the rise and fall of her chest as she took several slow breaths. When her eyes opened and met his stare, his heart tripped. His sister always acted like a wounded animal when she felt ill, snapping at him every chance she got. Most of the women he'd dated over the years hadn't behaved much better.

Yet here Hannah sat, perched against her pillows as if they were her throne, calm and collected in the face of discomfort. Her brow furrowed as she closed her eyes, and he wished he could take the distress from her, at least a little.

Hannah sank further into the mattress. Her breathing became steady and slow, and he realized she'd fallen asleep. He pressed a light kiss to her fingertips, then tucked her hand under the sheet.

Slowly, he rose and moved toward the door. He paused and looked at her. He didn't want to leave her until he knew she felt better. Reluctantly, he closed the door and headed downstairs. He couldn't stay by her side all night—he wasn't sure how she'd react to that—so he'd have to settle for the next best thing.

Eleven

Hannah slowly opened her eyes and inhaled deeply. She was on her side, stretched out on the bed. She wasn't sure when she'd flattened out, but the fact that she had boded well for her day. She'd still have to take it easy, but at least the worst seemed to be over. The headache wasn't completely gone, but it had subsided enough that ibuprofen would help ease the remainder of the pain. The dizziness and nausea had passed, but her stomach still felt a little tender.

She eased herself up in bed, then lowered her feet to the floor. After changing out of the clothes she'd slept in the night before, she shuffled to the bathroom. As she washed her hands, she studied her face in the mirror. She was still pale but not as bad as she had been. She'd gotten at least twelve hours of sleep, but the circles under her eyes were dark. She splashed her face with cool water.

Halfway down the steps, she heard a low rumble coming from her living room. A wave of panic rushed through her, and she slowly continued down, stopping when she could squat low enough to see into the living room. Relief washed over her when she caught a glimpse of the man sleeping on her couch. Her heart fluttered as she tiptoed the remainder of the way.

Quinn was fast asleep. She studied his sleeping face. Hannah had always been jealous of his long lashes. Light-brown stubble, lighter than his hair, graced his jawline and softly sharp chin. His features were still familiar to her.

But, at the same time, different.

Gone was the boyishness, replaced with the strength of a man she didn't know. She couldn't remember when she'd last spent time with him—before the kiss outside of the pub, anyway. Her cheeks warmed at the memory.

Suddenly, his blue eyes opened and met her stare. He held her gaze, then he pushed himself up to his elbows and rolled toward her.

"Good morning," she whispered.

"Hannah," he croaked as he sat up completely. He stretched and rubbed his eyes with the back of his hand.

She gave him a soft smile. "I thought you went home."

"I wanted to make sure you were okay."

She bobbed her head once, then winced at the dull ache that rolled through her temple.

"How are you feeling?" he asked.

"Better," she answered with a sigh. His intense stare, full of kindness and concern, caused another kind of ache to roll through her and squeeze her heart. She noticed his makeshift bed and smirked. "If I'd known you were staying, you could have slept in a more comfortable bed upstairs."

"I didn't want to be presumptuous."

Hannah frowned. "I meant the spare bedroom," she said, aiming for a scolding tone but failing miserably if his raised eyebrows was any indication. "Across the hall from mine."

"Oh," he said, then shrugged. "I wasn't sure if it was prepared for guests, and I didn't want to intrude."

"You didn't look for yourself?"

"No," he answered. "The door to that room was closed, so I didn't snoop."

The slight throb in her temple increased. She needed to get something in her stomach soon so she could take some medication.

He rose to his feet and took her hand. She turned toward the kitchen and he followed, his hand still enveloping hers. She was starting to feel her heartbeat behind her eye and exhaustion coming on.

Quinn pulled out a chair for her at the small, round dining table. "Are you hungry?" he asked. "I can run out and get something for us."

Hannah placed her elbow on the table and leaned her head against her open palm. "Run out?" she asked, and he nodded. "There's plenty of food here."

Another pain speared through her head, and she closed her eyes.

"Besides, I'm not that hungry. I just need something in my stomach to take the ibuprofen."

He laid his hand on her shoulder, his warmth seeping into her. "Do you have crackers?"

"In the cabinet." She pointed to the cabinets over the kitchen counter. "I'd like some ginger ale too. That's in the fridge."

His warmth disappeared, and she heard the opening and closing of the cabinets. She peeled open her eyes and watched him search for what she needed.

"If you see something you want, you're welcome to it," she said. Quinn glanced at her and smiled. "There are biscuits in the freezer."

"What kind?" he asked.

"Sausage."

He pulled out the box of biscuits from the freezer and studied them. "Mustard?" He looked at her.

"Fridge," she answered with a smile. She liked her sausage biscuits with mustard.

He set the box on the countertop, then handed her a sleeve of crackers and a cup of ginger ale. "Where is the medicine?" he asked softly.

She waved over her shoulder. "The bathroom under the stairs. In the cabinet." She opened the sleeve of crackers as he disappeared behind her. "What time are you leaving for work?"

"I need to be there by noon," he answered, his voice slightly muffled by the distance. "Then I have to pick up Lily from preschool after that."

Hannah laughed. "And take her out for ice cream?"

"Of course." He returned a moment later with the ibuprofen.

"You know Rachel hates when you do that." Hannah opened the bottle and shook two pills into her hand.

"Why do you think I do it?" Quinn pulled out a plate from the cabinet, then grabbed two biscuits from the box.

"To drive your sister crazy?" Hannah laughed.

"No. I do it to spend time with Lily." He put the plate of biscuits into the microwave and hit the start button. A mischievous grin filled his face. "It's just a bonus that it drives my sister crazy."

Hannah tried not to laugh as she chewed on some crackers. As much as Rachel complained, she loved that Quinn picked up his niece from school and took her out for ice cream. Rachel often talked about how much Lily loved her uncle, and how much those memories would mean to all of them in the future. Rachel's husband, Seth, was the local Navy recruiter and in the Navy Reserve. He was gone at least one weekend a month, sometimes more, and Rachel appreciated that Quinn was interested in picking up the slack in being a strong male influence in Lily's life.

Quinn sat down at the table with his plate and their gazes met. A pleasant wave rolled down her spine, and she looked down to hide her blush. She stuffed two more crackers into her mouth and chewed slowly.

"You want to talk about it?"

"About what?"

"About what stressed you out so much yesterday." His voice was full of concern, and the fire in her cheeks only deepened.

She hated talking about herself. Almost as much as she hated causing any kind of concern about her. The fact that she couldn't make it home by herself yesterday was beyond embarrassing.

"Why do you want to know?"

"It might help to talk about it. I'm a surprisingly good listener. Just ask Rachel."

Hannah grinned. "Does she burden you with her problems often?"

Quinn chuckled. "More often than I would have liked when we were younger. I didn't mind, though. It was good practice."

"For giving advice?" Hannah asked.

Quinn shook his head. "For listening. All I had to do was listen for thirty minutes and she'd talk herself into a better mood or come up with a solution for her problem."

Hannah laughed, causing a faint throb in her head. She gently rubbed her temples.

Quinn cringed. "Sorry."

Hannah popped the pills into her mouth and chased it with a swallow of ginger ale. "Do you really want to know why I was stressed?" she asked.

"I wouldn't have asked."

"It's kind of stupid," she muttered.

"Not to you," he said. "And that's what matters."

Her chest tightened. In the last year of college, she'd moved in with Carter. The dynamic of their relationship shifted. He rarely noticed when something was bothering her. He always had such an upbeat attitude, and she wasn't sure he ever knew what to do when she was upset. He would always leave her alone for several hours until he figured she'd gotten over it. He'd often trivialize her troubles, but she hadn't really noticed until she'd reflected on their relationship after he was gone. He rarely acknowledged that the problem really mattered, if only to her.

"My mom had chemo on Wednesday," she began with a sigh. "My dad called me on Wednesday night to let me know how she was doing, and I could hear her heaving in the background."

Quinn frowned. "That doesn't sound good."

"It's not always like that after a treatment. Some days are worse than others. And this week wasn't as bad as it has been."

"I'm sorry to hear that," he said.

"I called my dad yesterday morning, and she wasn't much better. I didn't get much sleep the night before. I took some medicine after breakfast, but it didn't really help." Seeing Sylvia before work hadn't helped either. "My dad stayed with her until one of her friends could come over, then he went to work, so I called her twice to check in on her," Hannah said.

"Did she improve throughout the day?" The depth of concern in his voice tugged at something deep inside of her.

"For the most part. She was sleeping both times when I called, but her friend gave me an update."

Quinn popped the last bite of his biscuit in his mouth as she ate another cracker. They chewed in silence for a few moments.

"I'm guessing Kailee didn't make things easier?" Quinn asked.

"That would be a good guess. How did you know?"

"Well, Dani wasn't speaking very highly of her."

She grimaced. "She rarely does. Kailee started calling at lunch to ask me to come home and prepare dinner for them."

Quinn's brow furrowed. "Would you have done it if you were feeling better?"

"No," she answered. "I spend most of my Saturdays at my parents' house preparing meals so Kailee or my dad can heat them up if my mom doesn't feel up to cooking. My dad was going to be late because he'd gone to work later, and all Kailee had to do was put it in the oven."

"She can't do that?"

"She *won't* do that," Hannah corrected. "She has no interest in learning how to cook, and I can never get her to do more than hand me an ingredient when I'm there. She avoids the kitchen as much as she can. So she didn't want to cook yesterday, even if it was just to reheat something I'd already fixed. She called me five or six times between lunch and the end of the day to try to convince me to do it for her. Plus several texts and voicemails."

"Did you tell your sister that you didn't feel well?"

Hannah shook her head. "It wouldn't have mattered. Then in the middle of my conversation with Kailee, Principal Keller came in and asked me to change the OM flyers that he and I had worked on every afternoon this week. That was kind of the last straw."

"Wow, OM is still around?" Quinn said. "I remember those days."

"Those were fun times." She gave him a small smile. "OM is one of my extracurricular activities. I'm the lead teacher for that." While she had help from a couple of teachers for OM, most of the other teachers had families they needed to take care of. "I also head up the yearbook."

She fought the yawn that wanted to escape. She pushed away from the table and rose to her feet, and he stood with her. They went back into the living room, where she plopped down on the couch and leaned her head against the cushions. Quinn sat in the chair next to the sofa.

"You have a lot on your plate right now," he said. "No wonder you got a migraine."

"I also help out at my dad's store two afternoons a week. Usually, I just do inventory or payroll, but it gives my dad a chance to go home early." She sank into the cushions. "Oh, and I help Dani at the stables every Sunday."

"Is that why you don't go to church anymore?" he asked softly.

Hannah sat up, surprised by the question. "More or less."

"I've wondered why I haven't seen you there in a while. Why did you stop going?"

"I just didn't want to go anymore."

It was the only answer she was willing to give him. No one had ever asked her why she'd stopped going to church, which was just as well for her. She wasn't sure how to explain that she was exhausted with all of the pitying stares and questions from her fellow churchgoers. For three months after Carter's death, it took her thirty minutes or more to get from her pew to the door simply because everyone stopped to talk to her.

She hadn't minded at first. Most of the congregants were like family, and their concern came from a place of love. Even if she didn't think she deserved their pity, she appreciated their consideration. But as she'd had more time to reflect on her relationship with Carter, the comments and concerns began to grate on her. No one had anything negative to say about him. They loved reliving his high school athletic accomplishments with her. They asked what his plans had been before he joined the Navy, and if she'd been looking forward to seeing the world with him. They'd spent more time planning her future with Carter than Carter had.

"That's it?" Quinn said.

"You don't believe me?" she asked.

"I didn't say that." Quinn rested his elbows on his knees and leaned forward. "I just remember how much church always meant to you. You always said the members were like a second family."

Her breath caught in her throat. She had told him that at least ten years ago. The church members were like another family, and she still felt that way. They were always there when you needed them. Some of the women at the church had been the first to visit her mother after her surgery.

"Fine," she sighed. "I got tired of the sympathetic comments and pitying looks."

"Really?"

"Yes, really," she said. "Every week, people would come up to me after the service to offer me their sympathies, or tell me how it would get easier, or share a story about Carter that they thought I hadn't heard before."

Quinn remained silent as he studied her.

"I got tired of the weekly barrage of questions, hugs, unsolicited advice, and the I'm-so-sorry's, so I stopped going."

Sure, she'd considered asking them all to stop. She'd considered telling them how she really felt about her absent fiancé. But to keep the peace, she decided it was just better to remove herself from the situation entirely.

Quinn opened his mouth, but she held up a hand. She was done talking about this. She'd told him all the truth she was going to give him for the time being. Anything more would venture into a conversation she didn't want to have. With anyone.

"You don't have to stick around," Hannah said in a sleepy voice. "I'm fine. I'm going to sleep for most of the day."

"I'm still going to hold you to our date when you feel better," Quinn said as he brushed a strand of hair from her face. "You're not getting out of it that easily."

"Deal," she said with a smile.

He stood and hovered over her for a moment. "Is it okay if I check in on you later?"

She grinned. "I think I'd like that." She gave his fingers a squeeze, then tucked her hand under her head as she closed her eyes.

She heard his deep intake of air and his slow exhale. Then he left, closing the door behind him.

Twelve

Quinn held tight to his niece's hand as they climbed the steps into the school. His day on the job had been frustrating, and he was glad when he left to pick up Lily. After a quick stop at the ice cream shop so he could spoil her, he was ready to deliver her to her mother. He pulled the heavy door open and allowed Lily to let go of his hand and scurry into the building.

"Wait for me," he called as she disappeared around the corner toward the hall that ran the entire length of the school. When he turned the corner, he found her staring up at him pouting, with her hands on her tiny hips.

"I know," she huffed with as much indignation as a four-year-old could muster.

He matched her stance and tried not to laugh.

"Now?" She pointed toward her mother's classroom.

"If you walk."

She skipped away before he could say another word. With a shake of his head, he followed at a slower pace. He reached the darkened doorway of Hannah's classroom when Lily squealed her greeting to Rachel. His sister's laugh welcomed him as he walked into her room.

"You took her for ice cream again, didn't you?" Rachel said.

Quinn smirked. "I have to maintain my favorite-uncle status."

"Quinn, you're the only uncle she sees on a regular basis." She pinned him with a stare. "I think your status is safe. At least until you move. You sure you don't want to stick around? I'm sure Charlie could give you a raise or something."

"He actually brought that up again," Quinn said.

Rachel's classroom was laid out identical to Hannah's. The only difference was the back corner where Rachel had set up a little play area for Lily.

Preschool toys and books and a small, brightly colored rug looked a little out of place in a fifth-grade classroom, but it made his niece happy.

"Maybe you should consider whatever he offered." She grinned at him. "If you move, you might lose your favored status."

"I guess I'll have to risk it." Quinn glanced at Lily, who was sitting on the floor, flipping through the pages of her favorite book about a caterpillar.

"I don't know why you're suddenly itching to set down roots somewhere else, Quinn," Rachel said. "You're successful here already, even without your degree. Do you really have to go to a big city to try to prove something to yourself?"

Quinn scowled at her. "Watch it."

"Just to please someone who doesn't even want you in her life?"

"This isn't about Alexa," Quinn grumbled. Maybe in the process of breaking his heart, Alexa had opened his eyes to the possibility that he wasn't living up to his potential. She'd chosen an investment banker with a six-figure income over Quinn. But his choice to move had nothing to do with his ex.

"If you say so." Rachel waved his argument away. "I haven't had the time to call Hannah yet, so have you checked in on her today?"

"I saw her this morning."

"You saw her?" Rachel tilted her head. "You went to her house?"

"I stayed the night." He noticed the disapproval on his sister's face. "It was completely innocent. I slept on the couch."

Quinn watched the questions play across her face.

"Are you serious about pursuing her?" Rachel leaned against her desk and crossed her ankles in front of her.

"We haven't even had a date yet."

"But you've asked her out." It wasn't a question. Whether his sister guessed it or Hannah had told her, he didn't know. He nodded his answer. "So, do you intend to talk to her about your plans?" Rachel asked.

"If they come up," he said. "What are you so worried about?"

"Her," Rachel said, bobbing her foot up and down. "I just don't think it's a good idea for you to start dating anyone when you're planning to move away."

"I don't understand why one should impact the other." He was only hoping to date Hannah; it wasn't like they were getting married. He didn't know what the future held, but if they grew closer and things seemed to be working out, then who said they couldn't make a long-distance relationship work?

"That doesn't surprise me," Rachel said.

"What's that supposed to mean?" Quinn said through gritted teeth.

She averted her eyes. "It means you aren't thinking about anything but what you want."

Ouch. "That's rude," he mumbled.

"Did you or did you not buy a house without any feedback from the woman you'd hoped to marry?" Rachel fisted her hands on her hips. "Even if she hadn't been a gold-digging cheater, she probably wouldn't have appreciated not having any say in the house she lives in."

Quinn's nostrils flared. There was some truth to what Rachel said. Last year, he'd bought a forty-year-old house on the outskirts of town when he was still with Alexa. He thought things were moving in the right direction and that she would move in with him. Every room in the house needed to be updated, but the house had good bones.

"I told you this isn't about Alexa," he snapped.

"No," she said gently. "But I don't want you to make a similar mistake. Don't assume you know what she'll be willing to go along with. Maybe Hannah doesn't want a long-distance relationship."

"And maybe it won't even be an issue," Quinn said as ice slid down his spine. "It's one date."

"So far." Rachel's eyes widened. "But you've been in love with her since you were sixteen."

"No, I haven't," Quinn scoffed.

His sister knew too much. She used to tease him about his friendship with Hannah, so of course she knew that he'd had a crush on her.

"Just reassure me you aren't going to string her along until you move. She's been through enough already." Rachel gave his forearm a squeeze.

"That was never my intent." He slipped away and shoved his hands into his pockets. "I'll talk to you later," he added as he walked out of her classroom.

His sister was overreacting, but he still couldn't shake the sense of foreboding her words brought. He honestly hadn't even considered telling Hannah about a potential move until he knew there was something definite to tell her. While most of their classmates had dreamed of moving away to large cities or faraway places, he and Hannah had often shared their similar goal of staying in Rocky Creek and being a part of their community into their old age. They used to joke about being next-door neighbors with their own families, watching each other's kids grow up, and always rooting for their high school football team. Hannah had assured him she would return home after college, and she did. He just hadn't realized Carter had become a part of their imaginary neighborhood.

But now that Rachel had brought it up, he wondered if things weren't as he assumed. If he and Hannah started dating, would she be willing to move to be with him? He was no longer sure pursuing her was a good idea. He was also no longer sure he couldn't at least try to see if there could be more between them. But the urge to see her again pulled at him, overriding any thoughts of rationality. It was just one date, he told himself.

He pulled out his phone and dialed Hannah's number. He'd offer to bring her dinner, just so he could see her again.

Quinn pulled into the parking lot of Hannah's small complex and parked next to her car. He grabbed the bag of Chinese takeout, climbed out of his truck, and took two steps toward the sidewalk before he heard the running engine on the other side of Hannah's car. He smiled at the driver of the idling vehicle as she rolled her window down.

"Hi, Isobel," Quinn said.

Isobel Finnigan grinned at him through the open window. "Hey."

"Claire gave you the night off?" he asked.

Isobel rolled her eyes but her smile remained.

Even though she was seventeen, Isobel was the only other Finnigan child who worked regular hours, always behind the scenes, at the family's pub. When their father died, Claire, the oldest of the five children, had come home early from college, a semester shy of graduation, to help get everything back up and running. During the rebuild of the kitchen, Quinn had gotten to know Claire's family a little better, and he thought of Claire, and by extension her siblings, like an addition to his family.

"What are you doing here?" Quinn asked.

Isobel's smile fell. "Kailee wanted to see if she could borrow Hannah's car."

Quinn glanced toward the front door. "Why would she need to do that?"

"She doesn't *need* to," Isobel answered. "My car holds enough people."

Quinn peeked into the surprisingly clean minivan. "I should say so."

"But she *wants* to borrow Hannah's car so we can get more people." Isobel sighed as she looked at the building, sounding resigned but not necessarily happy.

"Where are you taking these people?"

Isobel turned her focus to him. "There's a party Kailee wants to go to."

"And you don't?" Quinn chuckled.

Of the five Finnigan children, Isobel, tamer since her father's death, was still the wildest child in the bunch. At least for now. Her ten-year-old sister seemed to be on track to give her a run for her money when she got older.

"No, I do," Isobel answered. "I just don't think we need to bring half the school with us."

"I doubt half the school would fit in these two vehicles." Quinn motioned to Hannah's car, then the van.

Isobel released an exaggerated sigh. "You know what I mean. Besides, by the time she convinces Hannah to let her have the car it'll be past my curfew, so it won't really matter."

"Let me see if I can hurry her along," Quinn said.

"Please do," Isobel said.

"Promise me you'll stay out of trouble?"

"Gah," she huffed. "You're as bad as Claire."

Quinn laughed, considering the comparison to be a compliment even if she hadn't meant it as one. He walked up the two steps to Hannah's front door, hoping her sister's visit didn't cause a relapse.

Hannah was sitting in the kitchen with her elbow propped up on the dining table, her temple resting against the tips of her fingers, her eyes focused on her sister. The opened cigar box was on the table, and a few of the pictures were scattered in front of her. Kailee had her back to him with her hands on her hips.

Hannah's stare flashed at him, then to the bag in his hands.

"You're not being fair," Kailee whined.

One of Hannah's eyebrows quirked upward. "Excuse me?"

"You heard me." Kailee glanced over her shoulder. Her tawny brown eyes glared at him, and her scowl deepened. "What are you doing here?"

"Kailee Dawn," Hannah snapped, and Kailee turned back to her. "*My* guest. Be nice."

"Everything okay?" Quinn asked.

Kailee huffed and rolled her eyes.

Quinn moved further into the kitchen, away from the sisters, to put down the bags on the counter. As they continued to argue, Quinn wasn't sure what to do. Should he leave? He couldn't believe Kailee's attitude. If Hannah had to deal with this on a regular basis, it was no wonder she'd gotten stressed. Kailee's whine alone was enough to give him a headache.

"Why can't I have your car for the night?" Kailee's tone oozed with petulance.

"Because it's mine," Hannah said, surprisingly calm in the face of her sister's attitude. "It's my name on the loan. I'm the only one making payments. I pay for the insurance. Therefore, I can decide who drives it and who does not." She shifted in her seat. "Why are you asking, anyway? Did Dad not let you borrow his car because of what happened the last time you borrowed it?"

"That was not my fault," Kailee argued. "The road was wet. Anyone would have slid into the ditch."

Unfazed, Hannah continued, "Or do they not know you're going to this party?"

Kailee deflated where she stood, her hands fell to her side, and her shoulders drooped.

"That's what I thought," Hannah said quietly.

The sisters stared at each other for a few silent moments before Kailee pulled her shoulders back up and stomped her foot.

"I'm the only popular kid without a car. It's not fair."

Hannah sighed deeply. "I've told you before, popularity isn't everything."

"You say that because you weren't," Kailee snapped. "But that doesn't mean I should be punished for it."

"It doesn't mean you get to drive my car whenever you feel like it either."

Kailee let out an awful screech and stormed toward the door. "I hate you," she screamed as she yanked the door open.

"Yes," Hannah said in a calm tone. "You've told me that."

Kailee repeated the ungodly sound and left the house. Quinn cringed as the door slammed behind her. Hannah's eyes were closed, and her shoulders slowly rose and fell as she rolled her head one way, then the other. When she opened her eyes, she gave him a smile and his heart skipped a beat.

"Are you okay?" he asked.

Hannah nodded. "Thank you."

"For what?"

"For not interfering." She slowly rose to her feet and took a deep breath when she was upright. She had no idea how much he'd wanted to interfere.

"I brought dinner." He waved toward the counter.

Hannah glanced at the bag of food. "Thank you," she said.

She opened the cabinet and retrieved two plates while he pulled the food containers from the bag. The dark circles under her eyes were gone, and her color was back to normal. He was beyond happy that she finally looked like herself again.

He returned his attention to the food, pulling out a few spoons from the drawer and sticking one in each box.

"Is that sesame chicken?" she asked.

"Yes. I didn't think you'd feel like cooking," he said sheepishly. "And I don't know how."

"You can't cook?" The surprise was quickly replaced with amusement, and she covered her mouth with her fingertips, her smile stretching beyond the width of her hand as she laughed.

"No," he said.

"But you remodel kitchens for a living," she said.

His cheeks warmed as he turned his body from hers. "I don't use them. But I would like to learn how to cook."

"Really?" Hannah's honey-colored eyes sparkled.

"Yes," he said.

She glanced at the food, then back at him. "Why don't you come with me to my parents' house next week," she said slowly, as if weighing the words as she said them. "I could show you a few things while I'm preparing the meals for them."

Quinn smiled. Maybe it wasn't an ideal date—her family would be around—but he'd get to spend the day with her. And, as a bonus, maybe he could learn a thing or two about cooking.

"If you don't think they'll mind," he replied, beaming.

She laughed, tossing her head up a little. "I think they'll enjoy the company."

He took a step closer, and the honey tones in her eyes darkened a fraction as she held his gaze. "I'd love to."

She swallowed, then licked her lips. "Great," her voice cracked, and she cleared her throat and took a step backward. "Let's eat. I'm starving."

Despite the fact that she was putting a distance between them, Quinn laughed. "I've been waiting all day to hear you say that."

Thirteen

Holding two fabric bags full of groceries, Hannah closed the car door with her hip and looked up at her childhood home. The planter on the left side of the house stretched from the corner to the small front porch, currently colored with mums in oranges, reds, and yellows. The house had a pale, beige vinyl siding that covered the entirety of the building. The roof of the small porch at the front door was held up by two Greek Doric columns on one side and the short wall of the dining room on the other. The front window spanned almost the entire length of wall facing the street. Hannah's gaze skimmed the wall over the planter, all the way up to the roofline and gables. She inhaled the crisp air as she stepped toward the house.

Once inside, she carried her load straight to the kitchen and set them down on the floor. Behind her, Quinn carried two more, plus the large thermal bag full of the cold items. Her father brought up the rear with the last bag as Hannah slipped past him and into the family room to greet her mother on the couch.

"How are you feeling today?" She bent over to give her mother, Faith, a kiss on the cheek and adjusted the lavender scarf around her mother's bald head. Hannah stared down into those familiar eyes, mostly green with honey-colored and golden-brown flecks.

Her mother looked more exhausted than usual. A cold ball formed in the pit of Hannah's stomach. She worried that the chemotherapy was finally catching up to her mom. For the first time, the fear that her mother may not win her battle with breast cancer gripped and squeezed at Hannah's chest. Since the diagnosis two and a half months ago, her mother had done well. She'd bounced back almost immediately after the partial mastectomy at the beginning of August, and the first chemotherapy treatment hadn't been too bad. But the more treatments she got, the longer it took for her to recover. She only had three treatments left, but after a few weeks for recovery, she'd begin her radiation therapy. If all went well and there weren't any setbacks, she'd be done with treatments by Christmas.

"I look worse than I feel," her mother said, her voice raspy and dry. Her T-shirt seemed to hang from her body, and the rest of her was covered in a thick, cream-colored crocheted blanket. "I promise." Her mother laughed lightly, then began to cough. Hannah reached for the cup of water on the nearby table and held up the straw to her mother's lips. After a long sip, her mother pushed the cup away and her eyes focused on something over Hannah's shoulder. "Quinn Taylor?"

Quinn reached out to meet her mother's outstretched hand, his arm brushing against Hannah's, sending a pleasant shiver throughout her body. As he and Faith locked hands and exchanged greetings, Hannah fought the urge to place her hand on his back, his arm, or his waist. Her fingers tingled to touch him in some way.

"What a surprise to see you." Her mother raised an eyebrow at Hannah. It was the same greeting her father had given him when they'd arrived.

"Hannah promised to teach me how to cook." Quinn's voice held a hint of laughter. "Although I'm not sure how much luck she'll have. Both my mother and sister have tried and failed." He winked at Hannah.

"Hannah's a born teacher. I'm sure she'll have more luck." Her mother's voice was starting to fail.

Hannah reached down to pull the blanket closer to her mother's chin. "Rest, Mom. We'll try to keep the noise down."

"No worries." Her eyelids lowered, and she sank further into the couch cushions.

Hannah gave Quinn a slight push toward the kitchen. As they moved, her hand slowly slid down his arm until her hand was in his. He gave hers a squeeze, and she led him around the island that separated the family room from the kitchen. Her father had emptied the contents of the bags onto the counter and stood on the kitchen side of the island, looking over one of the recipes Hannah had brought with her.

Joseph Murphy, like his wife, wasn't quite fifty, but the silvery streaks in his otherwise golden hair might suggest otherwise. He glanced up at Hannah with the same tawny eyes her sister had inherited and smiled.

"Is this a new recipe?" he asked, his face lighting up in a way she didn't see very often anymore.

Hannah nodded as she reached for the chicken and rice casserole recipe. "I thought it would be a good one for Quinn to start with." She took the plastic sheet from her father's hands and gave it to Quinn.

He looked over the recipe. "This is a bit complex, don't you think?"

Hannah laughed and shook her head. "It's easier than you think."

Her father chuckled as he walked around Quinn and patted him on the back. "Good luck." He flashed a quick look at Hannah. "You may need it."

"Hey," Hannah giggled. "What's that supposed to mean?"

"Don't you understand English?" Kailee strolled into the kitchen, opened the refrigerator door, and grabbed a bottle of water. She glared at Hannah. "What's he doing here?"

"Your sister is going to teach Quinn how to cook," their father answered, humor still lacing his voice.

Kailee rolled her eyes. "Then you'll definitely need luck. Hannah's a horrible teacher."

"I'm sure that's not true," Quinn argued gently.

"Be nice to your sister." Joseph's stare hardened on his younger daughter. "Hannah is a wonderful teacher."

"Not in the kitchen." Kailee took a sip from the bottle and looked at Quinn. "Weren't you at her place last week?"

"Oh?" her father said. "Really?"

Hannah glared at Kailee, who simply smirked around the mouth of her bottle, then looked at their dad.

"I wasn't feeling well, and he brought me dinner," Hannah said.

The curiosity in the depths of his eyes quickly turned to concern. Hannah waved him off. "It was nothing, Dad. Just a little headache," she said with as much of a smile as she could muster. She'd suffered headaches off and on throughout her childhood, but they'd only gotten worse as she grew older. The first migraine to incapacitate her had struck the first time Carter had come home after basic training.

"Now, out of my kitchen." She shooed her father away with her hands and giggled. "I have work to do, and you need to go sit and relax."

Her father scowled momentarily, his eyes dancing with amusement, then shuffled off into the living room. She watched as he leaned over her mother and adjusted the blanket, then kissed her forehead. He sat in his recliner and picked up the TV remote, then leaned the chair back and changed the channel.

"What makes you think Hannah's not a good teacher in the kitchen?" Quinn's question brought Hannah's focus back to her sister, who was now sitting on the counter next to the fridge.

"Because she's such a perfectionist." Kailee shrugged. "She probably won't let you get past the second step before she takes over."

Quinn laughed, and Hannah couldn't really argue. She did like to do things a certain way, especially in the kitchen, and Kailee had a tendency to not follow the directions she was given. Most likely on purpose. Nevertheless, it drove Hannah crazy to watch her sister chop incorrectly, take too long to measure something, leave out ingredients, or skip around the steps of the recipe whenever possible for convenience.

"Is that why you won't let me teach you to cook?" Hannah leaned her hips against the island.

"No. I don't let you teach me because I don't want to learn."

Hannah straightened her spine. "You have to learn sometime. You can't live with Mom and Dad forever."

Kailee shrugged and studied her fingernails. "Then I'll find a man who can cook." She flashed an arrogant glare at Hannah, then craned her neck to focus on Quinn. "Guess you're out."

"Poor me," Quinn murmured dryly.

Hannah stopped herself from laughing as Kailee's scowl darkened, and she hopped down from the counter and stood in front of Quinn.

"At least Carter could cook," Kailee hissed.

"Kailee!" Hannah warned.

"Whatever." Kailee rolled her eyes. "Just let me know when dinner is ready." She turned and went upstairs to her bedroom.

Hannah stared after her sister, breathing deeply and steadily through her nose. Kailee was constantly bringing Carter up.

"Hannah?" Quinn's voice pulled her back to the present. "You okay?"

She lifted her eyes to his blue gaze and felt the urge to rub the crease away from his forehead.

"Yeah," she answered with a small smile. "I'm good." She stepped around him to the stack of recipes on the kitchen counter and picked up the top one. "We have a lot of work to do. We should get started."

Hannah picked the last of the dinner plates off the table and took them to the kitchen. As she set them on the counter beside the sink, her father smiled at her.

"Dinner was great, as usual," he said as he washed a plate.

"Thanks." She gave him a quick kiss on the cheek then turned toward the dining room. Quinn met her in the doorway between the rooms with the casserole. "I'll take that." She reached for the dish, but he pulled it away from her.

"I've got it. Why don't you take a break." He leaned forward until their foreheads almost touched. "I think you've earned it."

Her stare traveled from the dish in his hands to the table behind him, then back again. She couldn't recall a time when Carter had helped clean up after a meal. He would always retreat to the living room with her sister while she and her parents cleaned up the dining room and kitchen.

"Thank you," she said with a smile. "I think I'm going to my room. Come upstairs when you're done. There's something I want to show you." She waited for his agreement, then walked through the dining room and straight up the stairs. Behind her, she heard her father ordering her sister to help clean up and her sister whining in protest.

Hannah strolled through her room and into the closet where the stairs to the attic were. She climbed the steps to her safe haven and went straight to her window seat, tucked into the gable. She pulled her knees to her chest and pressed her back to the wall. This room had been her haven since she was a little girl, and even now she found comfort in the confined space, away from everyone else, yet able to look out at the world.

Dinner had gone as well as could be expected, with most of the conversation happening between Quinn and her father. Hannah's mother had eaten very little, which was not unusual. Hannah's hunger had been replaced with a growing snowball of concern for her mother's well-being and embarrassment over her sister's behavior.

Kailee's attitude had only gotten worse as the day wore on. She hadn't been openly hostile toward Quinn, but she hadn't been friendly either. She'd made constant digs at Hannah's ability to teach and cook, and had taken every opportunity to compare Quinn to Carter in a way that had made Carter seem superior.

When Hannah and Carter came home for breaks from college, they'd spent most of their time together with his family or friends. His mother had always been cold toward her, but his father's company had kept her from getting frostbite during her visits with them. His friends usually tolerated her presence, which hadn't bothered her since she never enjoyed their company anyway.

They would only hang out with her family for special occasions or at her mother's request. It wasn't often, but it was often enough for Kailee to have formed a bond with Carter, no matter how one-sided. Only after his death did Hannah start to see how deeply Kailee cared for him.

Maybe her sister was right. Maybe Hannah shouldn't be moving on. Not because she should mourn Carter for the rest of her life, but because she hadn't mourned him enough. But Carter had never seemed to take her feelings into consideration. The thing that bothered her the most was when he'd joined the Navy. She'd tried to get over it, but it upset her deeply that he'd made such a big decision without asking her.

It was a rainy day in their senior year of college. He'd strolled into the dining room of their apartment with a grin on his face and a bouquet of flowers in his hand.

"You'll never guess what I did today," Carter had said.

"Went to class?" Hannah looked up from her textbooks.

He held out the flowers to her. "I joined the Navy." His eyes sparkled with excitement.

Her heart sank as she looked down at the engagement ring on her finger. Since his proposal a year ago, he'd put her off on setting a date. The only thing she'd been able to commit him to was "after graduation."

"I thought you'd be excited," he said, his tone heavy with disappointment.

The weight of his words settled over her. "Why would you think that?" She heard the whine in her voice.

"Because I thought you supported our military."

"I do," she answered calmly as tears stung the backs of her eyes. Her heart and mind raced for the words she wanted to say. She could simply smile and go along with his plans, but everything in her wanted to scream at him. It was one thing for him to plan a date night without asking what she wanted to do, even though she always went along with his plans. But this was different. This was their future he'd arranged. Being a Navy wife meant traveling from place to place, but she wanted to settled down in Rocky Creek.

"Then why aren't you happy?" He gave her arm a gentle rub.

"Why did you join the Navy?" Her brow furrowed. "In the last three years, you've never expressed an interest in the military before."

He shrugged. "I've been thinking about it for a while. When I saw the recruiter at the student union today, I just bit the bullet."

"Did you even think about me?" Hannah pushed away from the table.

"Of course I did. I thought you'd be proud. I thought you'd be happy. I thought you'd think it was an adventure." He held his arms out to her.

She stared at him. His behavior wasn't new, but she felt like she was seeing him in a new light. "Did you think about our future? We are supposed to be planning a wedding." She fought the urge to walk toward him.

He waved her words away with the flick of a wrist. "We haven't even set a date yet."

"Because you haven't agreed to any of my suggestions," she said, her volume rising. "The only thing I could get you to agree to was getting married after graduation, and that was after months of discussion. And now you've gone and joined the Navy, which means eight weeks of boot camp. And then what?"

"I don't know," Carter had said. "We'll just have to take it as it comes. It will be an adventure."

That was his answer to everything. She'd been pining for home, for her family and the community she grew up with. At the end of her freshman year, she had been on the verge of transferring to the college in her hometown when she'd run into Carter on campus. His had been the first familiar face she'd seen at the university the entire year. When she'd seen him bowling at the student union, she'd nearly cried tears of joy.

Even though they'd gone to the prom together, it wasn't as if they'd actually known each other. But in college, they'd bonded over their hometown: the people, the places, even some of the rumors they'd both heard since leaving home. As their acquaintance turned more into a friendship, he started to push her boundaries. "Think of it as an adventure," he'd often said, and she'd give whatever he was suggesting a try. Sometimes, it was something as simple as a new food. Sometimes it was a college party or a ropes course, both uncomfortable for her in different ways. She'd always wanted to be more confident. Trying to venture outside of her comfort zone. It was one of the best things about being with him.

"Aren't you proud of me?" His question drew her out of her trance. He was gliding toward her, his hands reaching out to her, his eyes glinting with amusement. "I just want you to be happy." He grabbed her hands and laid his forehead against hers. "Do you really want to fight about this?"

Yes, she really did, but she was also aware that it was a losing battle. He'd already agreed to this, and he never went back on his word.

"I'm starting to think you don't really want to marry me," she said with a pout.

His mouth fell open. "How can you say that? Of course I want to marry you. I just wanted something bigger for both of us." The look in his eyes shifted to confusion, and she blinked back her tears. "This will be a good thing for both of us. Trust me."

"Of course," she agreed, because that was what she did. It didn't matter what she really wanted. This decision made him happy, so she would simply have to go along with it.

A creak on the steps pulled Hannah from her memory.

"There you are." Quinn was standing just inside the door, his head swiveling as he took in the entirety of the room.

"What do you think?" Hannah asked. He was the first person she'd ever invited to enter this domain. She held her breath, desperate for Quinn's approval, unsure why she wanted it so badly.

His eyes finished their perusal of the room. "It's . . . pink."

Hannah looked at her surroundings with a fresh set of eyes. The curtains were pale pink with a darker floral pattern, and the cushion she was sitting on was the same fabric. The wall was a faded pastel pink, and the light fixture in the middle of the ceiling had a frosted glass globe that had been painted with flowers in varying shades of pink. The wooden desk that sat against the wall near the window, and the chair in front of it, had been painted white with faded strawberries that adorned the side. The oval woven throw rug in the center of the room was an assortment of pinks and whites. The only thing in the room that had remained untouched by paint was the hardwood floor, which had been freshly installed when her father had built the room sixteen years ago.

"Yes, I suppose it is." She looked up at him as he came to a stop in front of her. He leaned his shoulder against the angled wall, opposite the desk just outside of the gable. "I was eight when my father decorated this room for me," she said shyly. She tugged at the edge of the seat cushion. "But it is an improvement over the piles of old clothes and boxes that were scattered around the room the first time I came up here to hide."

Quinn sat beside her on the window seat. There was enough room for the two of them, but just barely. His thigh pressed against hers, and it became hard for her to catch a breath.

"Why did you need to hide?" he asked.

She sighed. "I had a colicky baby sister who screamed for three hours every night, and I needed sleep. This was the quietest place in the house."

He laughed. "I'm sorry to hear that." He took her hand in his, and she rubbed her thumb over his knuckles.

"Not as sorry as my father was," she said. "I snuck up here in the middle of the night, and he had a slight panic attack the next morning when he couldn't find me."

"Slight?"

"No. It was a rather large one," she confessed with a chuckle. "When he found me up here the next morning, he decided he should do something about it." She pointed to the wall opposite the window. "Instead of forbidding me from ever going into the attic again, he put up a wall, moved everything in storage into that space, and gave me this little sanctuary."

"And pink was your favorite color?"

She shook her head. "Not at all."

He chuckled.

"But I didn't have the heart to tell my dad after he'd gone through all this trouble," Hannah said. "He looked so proud of himself. I didn't want to disappoint him."

"I doubt you could ever be a disappointment to him."

Hannah's smile faltered and she lowered her gaze to their clasped hands. She wasn't as sure about that. She was disappointed in herself for not realizing how mismatched she and Carter had been. Disappointed that she'd never had the courage to break up with him before he died, freeing them both up for a better life. Would Carter have felt the need to go to OCS a second time if she'd ended their relationship sooner? Would her father be disappointed to learn that she wasn't as saddened by her fiance's death as others thought she should be?

Hannah suddenly felt stifled on the window bench and got up. She pushed away thoughts of Carter as she pulled out the desk chair and sat down. "I'm so sorry for Kailee's behavior. She and I have always had a strained relationship, but it just seems to have gotten worse over the last year."

"She seems to be going through a lot," Quinn said.

"I've always tried to be there for her and look after her. There's such a huge age gap, so it's been difficult to connect on anything. We're just two very different people. I avoided anything sport related, and she's a cheerleader.

Her extracurricular activities include shopping and cruising around town. She's more outgoing, carefree, seize the day, and I'm . . . not." The corner of her mouth turned up. "You and Rachel seem to get along pretty well. Sometimes I'm jealous of the way you two get along, and I wish Kailee and I had the same kind of relationship."

Quinn looked around the room. "Rachel and I don't always see eye to eye on things, and we've had our fair share of fights and arguments."

She laughed. "So I've heard."

"But she's still my sister, and I appreciate and love her. Has Kailee always been so disrespectful to you?"

"Not always." Hannah swallowed the sudden lump in her throat. Kailee's attitude and actions had been awful since she started high school. What little friendship they'd formed had all but disappeared when Carter entered the picture. She was sweet and friendly when he was around, but when he wasn't, Hannah sometimes saw his arrogance and condescension in her sister's behavior. Hannah simply let it roll off her back.

"She idolized Carter," Hannah said. She rarely talked about him and felt a tug in her chest. "He was so charismatic, and Kailee was drawn to him almost immediately. She wants people to see her and talk about her the way they still talk about him. His death really hit her hard, and I'm pretty sure she's not quite over it yet."

Hannah could still see her fifteen-year-old sister, dressed in all black, standing next to the empty grave as tears streamed down her face. Hannah hadn't cried on the day of the funeral—the tears came later—and she often wondered if it might have hit her as hard as it did Kailee if they had put more than an empty box in that grave.

"And our mother's cancer diagnosis is affecting her as well."

"It's affecting you too." He rose to his feet and strolled toward her.

"True." She stood to meet him. "But I get to go home. She's here every day and sees Mom's bad days more than I do. Some of her behavior is grief and stress, and I can't fault her for that."

"We all have things going on in our lives, Hannah. That doesn't give us an excuse to behave badly." His gentle tone softened the harshness of his words.

"She's still a teenager." Hannah sighed. "Right now, this is just who she is."

"And defending her is just who you are," he murmured, dragging his fingers along the edge of the desk. "Who you've always been."

"Wouldn't you do the same for Rachel?"

"Depends on the day," he said with a wink. "I can almost see you sitting at this desk studying for the Quiz Bowl."

"Yes, I definitely did that."

He reached for her hand, and she slipped her fingers into his.

She held his stare, and the silence between them became uncomfortable. "You know, you're the first friend I've had in this room."

"Really? You never brought Carter up here?"

"Nope." She tugged him closer. "The only other people who have been up here are my mom and dad, and Kailee when she's been sent up here to get me."

He smiled. "Only family, huh?" The twinkle in his eye turned mischievous. "So then." He closed the rest of the distance between them. "There are things you haven't done in this room?"

"Maybe a few." She touched his chest.

Quinn's eyes closed and his breathing became heavy.

Hannah slid her hand up and over his shoulder. He looked so content, so calm, so enthralled by her touch. As her hand came to rest on the nape of his neck, his eyelids slowly opened. Their usual sapphire color had darkened to the rich navy of a starless night sky. Without a word, his lips lowered to hers as he let go of her hand and his arms wound around her back. As their lips met, he pulled her body closer, and she melted in his arms.

The memory of the heat in their first kiss dwarfed in comparison to this one. His lips firmed and relaxed against hers, sending flames coursing through her body as she pressed herself against him. She met the shifting pressure of his mouth with a vigor she couldn't control. She threaded her fingers through his hair. One of his hands slid along the long planes of her back, trailing heat in its wake as she shifted closer to him and darted her tongue out to his lips.

He pulled back, breaking the kiss to look deeply into her eyes.

"You haven't done that in this room before?"

She fought a smile. "No," she said, pulling his head toward hers again. She wanted more, and she wouldn't be denied.

Their lips collided again, and the tip of his tongue touched the crease of her mouth. She opened for him, whimpering when the hand at the small of her back drifted to her rear and pulled her against his hard length. While this kiss was satisfying in more ways than she could have imagined, it wouldn't be enough. Fire skipped across every nerve ending in her body, her toes curled as their tongues wrestled, and she went where his hands directed, pressing her core against the part of him she shouldn't want as much as she suddenly did.

She slowly pulled away as she cupped his cheeks with her hands. She stared at him, waiting for him to do the same. When his gaze finally met hers, she smiled.

"I can definitely cross kissing off my list of things to do here," she joked, and he slid his hands to the center of her back.

"If there's anything else you want to cross off that list, let me know." He placed a firm kiss on her forehead, and she leaned into it, savoring the touch.

"You'll be the first person I call." She laid her head on his shoulder as she lowered her hands to his chest. "We should probably go."

"Mm-hm." His chest rumbled with his assent, but he made no effort to move.

She was okay with that. She liked having his arms around her. She felt sheltered in the circle of his body. She felt like she belonged there.

His arms eased down her back until she was able to step out of that safety net. Without a word, she took his hand and turned toward the door. She had always hated leaving the solace of her attic sanctuary to face the real world and all its expectations of her. This time, though, she pulled her shoulders back and turned off the light as she left the attic. She felt Quinn's fingers wrapped firmly around hers and no longer felt alone.

Fourteen

Hannah closed her eyes at the voice calling her name from the doorway of her classroom. It was Wednesday afternoon, the last bus had just left, and she was counting down the minutes until she could leave and head to her father's store.

"Mr. Keller," she replied, opening her eyes and pasting on a smile. As he approached her desk, she rose to her feet and met him halfway. He held a small stack of papers in his hand.

"How many times do I need to ask you to call me Anthony?" He grinned widely, his eyes bright with excitement and something else she couldn't quite place.

"It doesn't matter. I won't call you by your name."

"Why not?" He chuckled.

"It's a show of respect, Mr. Keller."

"The students aren't around." He waved his free hand toward the empty desks in her room.

"It doesn't matter. If I get in the habit of calling you by your name, I might slip in front of the students," she repeated. He opened his mouth to argue, but she held up her hand. "I know you think it's old-fashioned, but if we expect students to grow up respecting authority, we need to lead by example. This is one way I choose to do that." She'd lost track of how many times they'd had this conversation, and she cringed every time she heard another teacher use his first name.

The look in his eyes dulled and he fell back a step.

"Did you need something?" she asked sweetly as she glanced again at the stack of papers.

He studied her in silence. She tipped her head toward the papers. His eyes followed her nod, and his head jerked as if he'd just remembered what he was holding.

"Oh, yes." He held the stack toward her. "These are the OM applications and permission forms."

She took the papers from him and counted as she flipped through them. Ten, so far. It was enough for one team, with a few extras. Only two more would make a second team, but the students still had another week to turn in their forms. She'd hoped for more this year but was happy with the results so far.

"Do you need to go through them and decide on the teams? Or who won't be participating?" Mr. Keller asked.

Hannah looked up to find him a few paces closer, staring intently at her.

"I can help you with that, if you'd like," he continued as he took another step toward her.

She clutched the papers to her chest. She had the feeling there was more he wanted to ask, and she wasn't sure she wanted to hear what it was.

"There's no need," she said slowly. "They were all on the team last year or have at least expressed an interest before. I can't make any decisions until I have all the applications, but I probably won't reject any of them anyway."

She slipped around him toward the door to try to put some distance between them. He was still moving toward her, so she held up her hand and he stopped. Maybe Mr. Keller *was* interested in dating her, but he'd never been so blatant in his attentions toward her. Her skin almost crawled at his closeness.

"Well, if you change your mind, I'm always available." He gave her a half smile that she was sure other women fell for.

"I think I'll be fine," she said firmly.

"Oh," he said, then strolled toward the open door. He paused in the doorway and looked at her, his eyes filled with confusion and disappointment. "I'll get the other forms to you as they come in. I'm sure you can handle the rest."

"Thank you," she said with a slight nod, and he disappeared. She went to push the door closed as Dani appeared in the empty frame.

"What did he want this time?" Dani slipped around Hannah and sat down on the first student desk.

Hannah closed the door and returned to her desk. "He was just bringing me the OM applications." She held up the papers. "I think he was trying to ask me out."

"You're kidding," Dani said.

"His tone suggested he wanted to, but thankfully he never got the words out." There had been a brief flash of hurt in Mr. Keller's eyes. Not that it changed anything. She wasn't interested in dating her principal. Even if Quinn wasn't in the picture, dating Anthony Keller wasn't even an option for her.

But she'd never liked confrontation, and she hated hurting other people's feelings even more. "I think I hurt Keller's feelings," she said slowly. "I don't want things to get awkward. We have to work together."

Dani shook her head. "It's unprofessional of him to ask you out. Especially while you are at work." She leaned back on her palms and pinned Hannah with a stare that said she would not permit argument. "You have boundaries—I've heard you setting them. If he can't respect that, then maybe we need a new principal."

"It's not that bad," Hannah mumbled. She wasn't offended, and she didn't want to cost anyone their job. "I can deal with it. It's just a minor annoyance."

"Especially since you have a boyfriend," Dani teased with a wink. "I'll bet Quinn would put a stop to Keller's flirting quick, fast, and in a hurry."

Hannah laughed. "There's no need for that."

"Could be fun to watch." Dani's eyes sparkled with mischief.

"What's going on in that head of yours?" Hannah said.

"Just that you didn't deny he's your boyfriend."

"We haven't even had our first official date," Hannah replied as warmth crawled up her neck, still thinking about the kiss in her attic room.

"He's gone to your parents' house for a meal. You're practically going steady," Dani teased, and they both laughed.

"Just stop." Hannah began packing her papers to go home. "But seriously, he's invited me to a wedding in two weeks."

"Jackson and Kerri?" Dani asked.

"That's the one," Hannah responded.

"Are you going?"

Hannah took a deep breath. "I want to."

"But?" Dani picked up on the word Hannah had wanted to say but didn't.

"But that's a lot of people. A lot of sympathy I don't want."

"And it's a wedding." Dani pressed her lips together. "Have you talked to Quinn about that?"

Hannah shook her head. "What am I supposed to tell him?" If she told Quinn why she was hesitant to say yes, she'd be opening up to a conversation she wasn't sure she was ready to have with him. Gossip in this small town spread like wildfire, and if she showed up to a wedding with Quinn Taylor, everyone would be talking. But the idea of being the talk of the town bothered her less than the sympathy everyone had given her in the last year.

"What are the pros to going?" Dani leaned her hip against Hannah's desk.

"It's time spent with Quinn. I like Kerri and Jackson, and I especially like Nancy." Jackson's mother was one of the only women who checked in on her mother regularly. "It could be fun. I haven't been to a wedding in a long time."

Dani walked toward the door and Hannah followed, turning off the light as they stepped into the hall. "Cons?"

"So many people." Hannah matched her friend's stride as they moved toward Dani's classroom. "So many who will want to talk about Carter. Or will want to sympathize with me over his death, or feel bad for me because my wedding never happened."

"Tell them they're a bunch of busybodies." Dani laughed. "You don't owe anyone an explanation or a conversation."

"You make it sound so simple." Hannah sighed.

"Because it is." Dani strolled into her classroom toward her desk as Hannah waited in the doorway. "I know you hate hurting people's feelings, but you have boundaries, and people need to respect them." Dani picked up her bag of school supplies. "So the real question is, what do you want to do?"

As they left the room together, Hannah's thoughts drifted to the kiss in her attic. That kiss had rocked her to the core, and she wasn't sure what it meant for her. Or for them. She couldn't shake the feeling that her relationship with Quinn had already changed irrevocably.

And instead of feeling the dread she'd expected when she started dating again after Carter's death, she felt nothing but a calm excitement and a surety that nothing would be the same.

Fifteen

Quinn leaned against the large door at the end of the barn, looking out at the fields where the horses grazed in the bright October sunshine. It had been two weeks since his first cooking lesson and was the first Sunday he'd been there to help Hannah and Dani. He was in utter awe at the amount of work the two of them did in such a short amount of time. He would be the first to admit he'd been slower, but he'd been distracted most of the day. After a date with Hannah last week, and another cooking lesson at her parents' house the night before, Rachel's warning to tell Hannah about his plans to move away kept haunting him.

Five weeks ago, when moving away from Rocky Creek was wishful thinking and things with Hannah were just getting started, it hadn't seemed necessary. He still wasn't sure it was. Now, after three interviews, and one more to come, in large cities in other states, he was starting to wonder when he should tell her. He was also starting to worry about how she would react. He held on to the hope that she'd be okay with it. She had, after all, been engaged to a man who'd been enlisted in the Navy, and since Rocky Creek was nowhere close to a beach or open water, a move for Hannah had been inevitable. He and Hannah were nowhere close to being ready to move in together, let alone move to a new city together. Yet Rachel's constant nagging that he tell Hannah about the move at all made him uneasy. A vision of a future with Hannah was starting to take shape, and he didn't want to do anything to mess that up.

A warm hand touched his arm as Hannah stood next to him. He sighed with a contentment that he hadn't felt in a very long time.

"You've been awfully quiet today," she murmured.

He turned his head and pressed a kiss to her temple, the heat of her hand

and the softness of her skin instilling a sense of longing deep inside of him. A yearning that grew stronger daily.

"Sorry," he said. "Had a lot on my mind, I guess."

She looked up at him. "Everything okay?"

He nodded as he brushed a strand of blonde hair out of her face.

"Quinn," she started, "if you don't want to be here, it's okay. You can tell me."

He pulled her against his chest. Her arms slid around his back as his did the same to hers, and he smiled.

"If I didn't want to be here, I wouldn't be," he teased, then raised an eyebrow at the scowl that flitted across her face. "You really like it here, don't you?"

Her eyes sparkled as she looked out at the horses. "I've always loved horses," she said. "But I rarely got to be around them growing up. Only at 4-H camp, which was only one week every summer."

"Is that where you learned to ride?" He studied her profile as he waited for her answer. He thought he'd known her growing up, but he had learned so much about her over the past few weeks, things he'd never even heard a hint of during their childhood. It still wasn't enough. He wanted to know everything. But he always felt there was something she was holding back, so he grasped every little detail she gave him like a squirrel with a nut, hoarding it away for winter.

"I was always the first in line to sign up for the horseback riding class every year. I purposely sat in front of the table the minute I walked into the auditorium so no one could beat me to it." Her smile faded. "You were never there, were you?"

Quinn shook his head.

"Why?" She slid her hands from his shoulders to his waist.

"We couldn't afford it," he answered.

Her mouth formed a perfect circle. "Oh. I'm sorry."

"Don't be." He'd accepted a long time ago that his family couldn't afford for him to do a lot of things other kids his age did. He'd never gone without anything he needed, but money was tight, and he rarely got to do things like summer camps or field trips. "I didn't know what I was missing out on, so it really didn't make a difference."

Her features relaxed as she held his gaze.

"Besides, it made me learn to appreciate what I have." He pulled her closer. "And to work hard for what I want."

The corner of her mouth turned upward as her gaze dropped to his lips. "And what is it you want?"

"Right now?" He lowered his head toward hers. "You," he breathed across her lips and felt her shudder.

Her tongue darted out to wet her lower lip. Their eyes met again, and he felt suddenly off-balance. Something had changed in that moment, and he recognized his words were deeper than he'd meant them to be. He swallowed the thought, hoping she didn't see his wariness.

"And in the long run," he continued, hoping to ease his tension, "financial security for my kids." A vision of a blonde-haired girl with dazzling blue eyes flitted through his mind and he shook the image away. "I want them to do the things I didn't get to do growing up."

Her smile softened. "I don't know if I can help you in the long run." She stood on her tiptoes, lightly touching her lips to his. "But I can help with the right-now."

He lowered his mouth the rest of the way, pressed his hand against her lower back, and slid the other up to the nape of her neck. Her lips were soft but firm under his, meeting him in his need, returning all the desire he offered her with an equal ferocity. Her crisp pear and sweet magnolia scent mixed with the earthy scent of straw filled his sinuses as her soft touch slithered up his chest. Her fingers splayed over the back of his head, and a little mewl of pleasure escaped her throat.

"Ahem."

Slowly, Hannah pulled her lips from his, and they turned their heads toward the voice. Dani stood there with her arms crossed and an amused smirk. "Are we still going riding?" She held up a pair of riding helmets, and Hannah slowly backed out of his grasp, dragging her hand down his arm until their fingers met.

"Yeah," Hannah answered, then looked at Quinn. Her shoulders rose and fell with fast breaths, and her cheeks were still flushed. "You sure you don't want to come with us? Dani's a great teacher. And I'll try to be a good cheerleader."

He chuckled lightly as he gave her fingers a squeeze. "No, you go on without me."

Hannah's smile faded. "You'll be here when we get back?"

Quinn pushed away from the doorframe and pressed his forehead against hers. Dani cleared her throat, and he fought a smile.

He met Hannah's wide-eyed stare. "I'm not going anywhere," he murmured, kissed her forehead lightly, then released her.

Quinn watched them stroll toward the two saddled horses at the other end of the barn. He stepped into the closest stall where he could watch them ride off into the distance, then disappear over a hill. When they were completely out of sight, Quinn's heart rate had finally slowed from their kiss.

What was happening to him? He hadn't had such an acute reaction to any woman since Alexa, and that had come after several months, and after they'd slept together multiple times. While he had known Hannah for almost twenty years, they had only just reconnected and had only been dating for a couple of weeks. They hadn't even been intimate yet, and she already tied him up in knots. He couldn't decide if that was a good thing or not.

Quinn stepped out of the stall and grabbed the push broom from the office. He'd promised Dani he would sweep and clean the aisle before they got back, and now it was a welcome diversion. He didn't want to think about what was going on, why he was drawn to Hannah more than he'd been drawn to any other woman. He'd wanted to marry Alexa, and not once had an image of their child come to his mind.

He leaned against the handle of the broom. He couldn't picture Hannah living in a big city, or even just outside of one. Sure, she was great in the classroom, and he imagined classrooms were the same across the country— big city or rural countryside, it probably wouldn't matter. But here on the farm, she seemed to thrive. She was most at ease, her shoulders were less tense, her expressions more open and inviting, and she laughed more. Could he ask her to leave this behind for him?

Quinn shook the thought away and resumed sweeping the concrete aisle of the barn.

He was getting ahead of himself. He didn't have a job offer yet. The jobs in Philadelphia and Charlotte were most likely both noes. He hadn't heard from Boston and couldn't even guess how that would go. His interview in Atlanta was this coming Tuesday and was probably the only possibility if he was going to get out of Rocky Creek. And now, more than ever, he wanted to go. It was a good-paying job with a large architecture firm. He'd have upward potential, steady work, and, most importantly, a steady paycheck.

Maybe he hadn't been able to envision his and Alexa's children, but wanting to marry her had fueled something in him that hadn't been there before she'd come into his life: the need to provide for a family. He'd started to plan for his future. When Alexa broke his heart, that need to provide had shifted to a need to prove himself. The man she'd chosen over him had the income to give Alexa every luxury she could possibly want. Quinn knew he never could have competed with that kind of wealth, and it would have been a matter of time before she moved on anyway. So, along with the broken heart, his pride had taken a brutal hit. He'd taken a hard look at his life and realized something had to change.

Now, with Hannah, his insecurities were starting to rear their ugly head again. Carter had been wealthy, popular, and charismatic. All the things Quinn hadn't been. All the things Quinn still wasn't.

The worst thing was that Quinn wasn't sure how much Carter still haunted Hannah. Was she over him yet? Was she sorry they hadn't married sooner? She rarely spoke about him and always changed the subject whenever Quinn brought him up. He felt certain he could win if he were competing with something, or someone, tangible.

He had no idea how he could compete with a ghost.

Hannah climbed the steps to the hayloft, tightly grasping the handrail along the wall with each step. She and Dani had returned from their ride fifteen minutes ago, and after removing the saddle and blanket from her horse, she started looking for Quinn. He hadn't answered when she called for him, and she was beginning to worry that he'd called a friend and gotten another ride home. It was something Carter would have done.

If he'd come to the farm to begin with.

She had to stop doing that. Quinn had proven many times, in word and action, that he was nothing like her dead fiancé. It wasn't fair to Quinn to compare the two, or to maintain expectations of his actions based on her past experiences.

Her foot landed on the solid floor of the hayloft and she saw Quinn standing at the other end of the loft, his hand resting on the frame of the opening, his back to her. She smiled at the sight of his broad shoulders, narrow hips, and long, lean legs silhouetted against the midafternoon sun.

"There you are," she said, strolling toward him.

He turned and gave her an impish smile.

"You didn't answer when I called you." She wanted to scream at him for all the worry she'd felt, but that hadn't been his fault.

"If I had, would you have come up here to look for me?" He moved toward her, his pace matching hers in speed.

She shrugged. "If you had asked. What's so important up here?"

Quinn took her hands, pulled her close for a light kiss to her cheek, then turned and led her toward the window. As they got closer, she noticed the perfectly stacked hay bales had been rearranged. Part of her cringed as she wondered what Dani would think of this reorganization. The other part of her laughed outwardly at the large chair that had been created out of the repositioned hay bales.

"You did this while we were gone?"

He moved her to the seat. "I was thinking it might be like the window seat in your attic room." He waved to the view outside the window. "I thought you might like to come up and look out."

Her heart swelled at his thoughtfulness. Still staring out at the landscape of rolling green hills, bright blue sky, and fiery trees, she lowered herself to sit. A gentle breeze brushed her cheeks, and she closed her eyes to enjoy the wind on her face, slowly breathing in the crisp air that had a slight tang from the farm. She opened her eyes to find Quinn kneeling in front of her.

"I owe you an apology," he said.

"For what?" she asked.

"A few weeks ago, I made an assumption that you did everything you do out of a sense of obligation, not because you enjoy any of it." He took her fingers and laid the back of his hands on her knees. "After watching you work here, and in the kitchen at your parents' house, I see how relaxed you are, how much you laugh, and just how much fun you have, and I want to say I'm sorry for my assumption."

"Oh." She slowly looked around the hayloft again. "You did this as an apology?" He shrugged his shoulders, and she chuckled. "I can't help but wonder what you'll do when you apologize for a serious offense."

He turned his gaze to the window. "Sorry to disappoint you. I did this because I was bored."

They laughed, and she brushed her lips against his cheek, then laid her forehead against his temple.

"Regardless," she said into his ear, "I'll forgive you on one condition."

"What's that?" His voice cracked, and his smile widened at his obvious distress.

"You buy me dinner tonight."

"Whatever you want," he whispered.

The sincerity in the depths of his eyes made Hannah's heart rate speed up, causing her to feel a little dizzy. She couldn't remember the last time anyone had said those words to her and actually meant them.

For the first time in a long time, she felt like things were finally looking up for her. As she stared at Quinn, she realized how easy it would be to love this man. Loving Carter hadn't been hard, but she hadn't been fast to fall for him either. But Carter was charming, persuasive, and persistent. She grew to love him, despite how different they were. He was the only man she'd ever been with, and the only man who'd captured her heart. When he died, she had been certain she wouldn't want to date again for a long time.

Now she wanted it more than anything else.

"Thank you," she said softly.

He leaned closer, his lips slowly moving toward hers.

"I've got the hose ready. Don't make me come up there and use it on the two of you!" Dani's voice floated up through the window.

Hannah laughed as she backed away and saw the scowl on Quinn's face. "I have no doubt she'd do it."

"Me either," he grumbled, causing her to chuckle harder.

"We should go down and help her brush the horses we rode." Hannah rose to her feet. "And we need to feed and water them all before we leave."

Quinn mumbled an agreement, but the glower on his face eased when she pressed her palm against his cheek. He slipped his hand around her back and pulled her closer.

"Don't worry," she whispered. "We have plenty of time."

His warm kiss held the promise of more. When Dani started counting down, they separated and quickly moved to the steps of the hayloft, laughing as they descended.

Sixteen

Hannah sat at her desk, flipping through the OM permission slips. It was only Tuesday, but they'd managed to get four additional slips, a total of fourteen, enough for two full teams. She couldn't complain because that was three more than the previous year. She was excited to get started and couldn't wait to tell Quinn.

Suddenly, she heard a shrill, unwelcome voice in the hallway.

"This is the room?" Tori was speaking to someone Hannah couldn't hear. "Thank you so much."

Hannah stood and walked toward the door of her classroom as Tori sailed through.

"Oh my goodness, such a cute classroom," Tori said as she walked past Hannah, her gaze bouncing around the room.

Tori had never visited Hannah at school before. She was dressed in a gray pencil skirt and dark-blue blouse with lacy see-through sleeves. The handle of a small gray plaid handbag sat in the crook of her elbow. Her blonde hair was in a messy bun at the back of her head, and long tendrils hung loose around her face.

"Oh, and that principal is gorgeous." Tori stopped and turned to face Hannah. "Is he single? I wouldn't mind hooking up with that handsome piece of meat."

Hannah rolled her eyes. "What are you doing here?"

Tori set her tiny purse on a desk and held her palm to her chest. "Do I need a reason to visit you, my dearest friend?"

"No." A knot formed in Hannah's stomach. She couldn't help but feel like Tori was up to something.

Tori's tinkling laugh rang throughout the room. "You're so funny," she said. "I was just in the neighborhood, you know, between showings, and I thought I might stop in for a visit."

Hannah didn't believe her. Tori was a realtor, but she liked to sell larger homes closer to town or the lake. There weren't very many homes in Tori's desired price range in this more rural part of the county.

"It's been weeks since I saw you. I wanted to catch up." Tori elegantly lowered herself into the desk seat.

"You could have just called," Hannah said.

"What fun is that? Face-to-face conversations are always so much better," Tori beamed. "Besides, I hear you've been a little busy during your hours off. I wasn't sure I'd be able to reach you."

Hannah tipped her head. "What have you heard?"

Tori's blue eyes sparkled with mischief. "You have a boyfriend."

"I thought that's what you wanted." Hannah leaned back in her chair and folded her arms over her chest.

"So, it's true?" Tori laughed. "Of course it's what I wanted. I'm just a little surprised, that's all."

Hannah narrowed her eyes. There was something in Tori's tone that said there was a little disappointment mixed in with that surprise.

"I mean, I did try to fix you up with some of Carter's friends at the party, but Quinn Taylor? Really, Hannah." Tori's smile slowly faded. "You can do better than that."

"Excuse me?" Hannah's shoulders tensed. "What is that supposed to mean?"

"That's a great question," Rachel said as she walked into the room. Dani was right behind her, scowling.

Tori's eyes rounded, and she grabbed the handle of her purse and rose to her feet. "It's . . . I mean . . . he's . . ." she stammered. "He's just not the same class as Carter, that's all I meant."

Rachel's scowl took a menacing turn.

"No," Dani snapped, her glare shooting daggers at Tori. "You meant he's not good enough for Hannah, which is an insult to both Quinn and his sister." She thumbed over her shoulder. "I think you owe them both an apology."

Tori lifted her chin. There was a shakiness to her inhale. "Sorry," she muttered, her stare somewhere over Rachel's head.

Hannah looked at Rachel and wondered if that was enough of an apology. She didn't think Tori was being sincere.

"Carter wasn't good enough for my brother's friendship," Rachel said, daring Tori to argue.

Tori smoothed her skirt and slipped the strap of her purse over her arm. She looked at Hannah, her eyes wide and desperate.

Hannah shrugged. "You should go now."

Anger flashed in Tori's eyes just before she averted her gaze. "If you think that, then you clearly didn't know Carter that well." She tossed her head back and walked toward the door. Dani didn't budge. "Excuse me."

Dani held Tori's stare, her lip curling in disgust. "Stay out of our lives and I'll consider it."

Tori's nostrils flared. "I told you, I didn't know you and Chas were still married."

Rachel gasped, and Hannah gritted her teeth. Dani hadn't told anyone else about seeing her then-husband and Tori having dinner on the night he'd asked for a divorce. She'd been so ashamed of the situation that she hadn't wanted to fuel any gossip if she could avoid it. Hannah felt certain Tori knew that.

Dani's jaw tightened. "You seem to know everything else that goes on in town."

"Clearly not that." Tori stepped around Dani. "And I won't apologize again."

"You never apologized the first time," Dani snapped.

Tori paused in the doorway and flashed Hannah a smile. "Call me sometime so we can catch up." She wiggled her fingers in her signature wave and glided out of the room, ignoring the other women.

Hannah, Dani, and Rachel stared at the open doorway before releasing a simultaneous sigh. Hannah couldn't shake the chill of foreboding that slithered down her spine and settled in the pit of her stomach.

Seventeen

Round tables covered in snowy-white cloths dotted the edges of the room. The centerpiece of each table was an overflowing floral arrangement in blues and purples, matching the colors of the bridesmaid dresses. Guests sat at a few of the tables, some watching the dancing, some lost in conversations with others. Most guests stood on the outskirts of the room doing the same.

In the center of the room was a pine-colored dance floor where a few of the guests were dancing in couples or groups. Hannah and Quinn hadn't taken their turn on the dance floor yet, but she wasn't complaining. Dancing would just bring more unwanted attention, and at the moment, all she wanted to do was fade into the wallpaper behind her.

She'd enjoyed the wedding. It had been a beautiful ceremony, and she was glad Quinn had invited her. But she was tired of the curious looks and the concern she saw in his eyes every time he looked at her. Sure, it was the first wedding she'd been to since Carter died. She wasn't avoiding weddings; she just hadn't received any invitations. As far as she knew, none of her friends had gotten married in the past year, so there really wasn't anything for her to miss.

Quinn wasn't the only person who gave her that curious, concerned look. And while she didn't really mind his interest, the obvious curiosity from the other guests had rubbed her nerves like a medium-grit sandpaper. She was currently doing her best to avoid eye contact with anyone except those she knew well, which meant she was avoiding eye contact with almost everyone.

"Hannah, darling," a feminine voice sang from over Hannah's shoulder.

Hannah glanced to her left and saw a woman about her mother's age, with a smooth complexion except for the few wrinkles that stretched from the corners of her eyes and lips, and dark-brown hair falling to her shoulders.

Her face was faintly familiar, and Hannah struggled to figure out how she knew the woman.

"It is so good to see you out and about," the woman said. "And looking so beautiful, I must add."

Hannah remained silent as she looked down at her dress. She hadn't bought anything new for herself in a long time—she hadn't needed to—so she'd splurged on a new dress. It was knee-length and royal blue, with a flared skirt that sashayed with her hips, and a lacy three-quarter sleeve. The deep V in the front of the dress was hidden by the crocheted overlay that gave the impression of being see-through. It was nicer than anything she'd ever owned, and she hoped she'd have a chance to wear it again.

"I'm sorry, I just realized we've never officially met. I'm Edith Michaels. I'm in your mom's book club." The woman shook Hannah's hand.

"It's nice to meet you, Ms. Michaels."

"You too, my dear. I was just telling Jaclyn over there . . ." She waved to another woman Hannah didn't know, but who waved and smiled as if they were old friends. "Anyway, I was just telling Jaclyn how good it is to see you out and about. You poor thing. You've had such a rough year. First with your dear fiancé, and now with your mother's cancer. I just can't imagine."

Hannah couldn't believe the words that came out of Edith's mouth. Luckily, it seemed all she needed to do was bob her head along to satisfy the woman.

"How is your mother, by the way? I haven't seen her in so long." Edith smiled brightly.

Hannah sighed with relief. At the word *fiancé*, she'd feared the conversation would drift to him. She was much more comfortable talking about her mother.

"She's okay," Hannah answered with a genuine smile. "She has one more chemo treatment."

Edith laid her hand on Hannah's again. "Already? That's great news."

"Yes, for now. Her last one is in two weeks, and she'll have a few weeks off before starting radiation."

Edith lifted a hand to her heart. "I am so happy to hear that. Jaclyn and I were just wondering how she was handling things."

"Oh." Hannah's mouth fell open, a feeling of dismay settling in the pit of her stomach. "You could always pay her a visit."

The sparkle in Edith's green eyes faded. "Well, you know," she began, sliding her foot backward in a clear preparation to leave. "I am just so afraid of accidentally bringing some sort of illness to her."

Hannah's dismay became an ice cube of irritation. "She wears a mask around visitors. She'd love the company."

Edith waved Hannah's comment away. "Still," she said with a shrug. "I've just been so busy. Let her know we're thinking about her, if you could. It was so nice to meet you." The woman quickly rushed toward another table.

"I'm sure you were busy," Hannah muttered. She walked back to her table and picked up the goblet of water at her seat and took a long sip. When she looked up, she made eye contact with another older woman who was heading in her direction. Hannah put on another wooden smile.

"Hannah, it's so good to see you."

"Hi, Mrs. Gardner. It's good to see you too," Hannah said to her family's neighbor as she gave her a brief hug.

"You're so brave to come to this wedding." A large smile was plastered on Mrs. Gardner's face. Her graying hair sat in a bun at the nape of her neck, hiding what was left of the light brown she'd had for most of Hannah's youth. "It must have been hard, given your circumstances. It's such a shame too. Carter was such a nice boy."

Hannah glanced over her shoulder toward the bar where she thought Quinn should be. Hopefully, he was on his way back to her side. She looked back at Mrs. Gardner. "Oh, uh," she stammered, trying to recall what had just been said. "Yes . . . yes, he was a nice boy."

Mrs. Gardner nodded. "And your poor mother. How is she?"

Hannah narrowed an eye on the woman who lived three doors from her parents, on the same street, and had been there for nearly fifteen years.

After swallowing around the lump of growing frustration, Hannah said, "She has one more chemo treatment."

"Oh my," Mrs. Gardner said, her surprise sounding genuine. "I saw her just after her surgery. It feels like that was yesterday. I didn't realize she'd gotten that far into treatment already. If she needs anything, you be sure to let me know."

"You could always call her," Hannah answered, "or stop by for a visit." As much as she wanted to suggest it, she thought it might be too much to let the neighbor know that a meal or two would be appreciated. A visitor or two, however, would help relieve her father of some of the pressures he felt. He hated leaving Hannah's mom alone for so long, which had led him to leave work early almost every day, sometimes taking the work with him, sometimes leaving it at the store for Hannah.

"Oh . . . well . . ." Mrs. Gardner's eyes jumped from Hannah's face to something in the distance. "Oh, my husband is waving me over." She turned to Hannah. "I'll do what I can."

Hannah watched the older woman walk away. "Unbelievable." She scanned the room again, looking for Quinn, first at the bar, then in the sparse crowd. She finally found him in a corner talking to several men, including the groom and the bride's brother. She was ready to leave. It was exhausting having to put on a happy smile and pretend to not be offended by these women who were clearly more concerned about appearing to care than actually caring about her or her mother. Inwardly, she cringed, wishing she had the courage to tell them all exactly what she thought of their false interest.

With a huff, she gave in to her restless urge to ask Quinn to take her home instead of waiting for him to come rescue her from these phony dragons.

On her way toward him, she was approached by two more women who were delighted to see Hannah out and about, and "at a wedding no less," and expressing their concern and curiosity for her mother and the cancer treatment. They both conveyed their desire for Hannah to pass along their well wishes to her mother and to let them know if they could do anything. Hannah swallowed her disgust at she watched these women, who declared they were her mother's "dear friends," scurrying away at the mere mention that they could pay her mother a visit.

She made eye contact with Quinn and realized she was still scowling when he frowned at her. Forcing her features to relax, she waved his concern away. He nodded and returned to his conversation as Hannah strolled in his direction. He looked dashing in a dark gray suit that fitted his broad shoulders perfectly. His shirt was white, but his tie, coincidentally, was a royal blue that matched her dress.

Several feet away from Quinn, she was stopped short by another matron. She sighed, almost audibly, with relief at the laughing eyes of Nancy Harris, the groom's mother.

"I'm so happy you're here," Nancy said as she wrapped Hannah in a warm, floral hug. "How's your mother? Wasn't her last chemo treatment this week?"

Hannah's eyes stung with happy tears. Nancy visited her mother on a regular basis. Hannah's father would call her to come sit with Faith if he couldn't get out of work. The genuine concern in Nancy's voice warmed Hannah's heart.

"She has one more treatment left," she answered.

"I'm so sorry I wasn't able to see her this week. We've been getting everything ready for the wedding, and I was so busy." She gave Hannah's hand a squeeze. "But I will make up for it next week. Is there anything I can bring?"

Hannah giggled. "She's always raving about your chicken pot pie. I'm sure she'd like one of those."

Nancy tipped her head back with a laugh. "It has been a while since I took one of those to her," she replied. "But then, her freezer is always so full when I get there. You don't have to do that, you know. Other people might like to help."

Hannah opened her mouth to argue, but as she considered Nancy's words, she was no longer certain what was the truth. She'd never asked anyone else to help. Hannah had simply cooked for her family out of her own concern for their well-being. It had never occurred to her that preparing the food and filling their freezer herself had prevented others from helping because they thought her family was already taken care of. She suddenly felt bad for judging the other women for not lending her family a hand.

"I don't mind doing it," Hannah said slowly.

"I'm sure you don't," Nancy said. "But I'm sure you could use a break every now and then too."

Hannah didn't know what to say.

"Tell you what. I'll bring a few extra meals for her next week," Nancy started, then tapped her finger to her lips. "I think I'll bring my daughters-in-law as well. I'm sure they'd love to visit with your mother and can help out however they're needed."

Hannah frowned. "I thought Kerri and Jackson were going on a honeymoon."

"Oh, goodness." Nancy chuckled. "Of course *they* are. I meant Janelle and Charlotte, my other two daughters-in-law. Although, I'm sure your mother would love to meet Kerri as soon as they get back." She waved her words away. "But we don't need to worry about that yet, do we. I should let you go find that handsome date of yours." She winked. "And I need to go mingle with some of the other guests. Have a good evening." Nancy bussed a kiss on Hannah's cheek and hurried off.

Laughing lightly, Hannah watched Nancy hurry off. Quinn was walking toward her, and a strand of his dark hair hung loose alongside his temple. Her stomach fluttered at the concern she saw in the depths of his blue eyes.

When he was close enough, Quinn took her hands and gently pulled her closer, giving her a light kiss on her forehead.

"Everything okay?"

"It is now." She slid her arms around his waist. "I want to leave."

He frowned. "So soon? We haven't even danced yet."

She really wanted to get out of here before another person pretended to be concerned for her or her mother's well-being. Although, it would be nice to dance with him.

"Fine," she agreed, still somewhat reluctant. "One dance."

He narrowed his eyes. "Five dances. And cake."

Hannah looked at the cake table and was surprised to see they hadn't cut it yet. It felt as if they'd been at the reception for hours already.

"Two dances," she negotiated, raising an eyebrow at his smirk.

"Three dances . . . and cake," he added.

She tried not to laugh. "You really want that cake."

Quinn's smile widened until a dimple appeared in his cheek. "It's the best part of a wedding. And it's chocolate."

Hannah laughed as a slow song began to play. "Fine," she agreed. "Two dances and we'll stay for cake."

Quinn took her hand in his. "Deal," he said, and placed a kiss on her knuckles. "It sounds like they're playing our song."

"We don't have a song," she said as he led her to the dance floor.

"Not yet."

He swung her against him and slid an arm around her waist as he took her hand in his. As they swayed to the slow, soulful music, he stared into her eyes, and something deep inside of her stirred. Something she hadn't felt in a long time. Something that had almost frightened her the first time she'd felt it, but she now welcomed it.

She wanted him. In all ways imaginable, she wanted to be with him. He made her feel safe and desired. He made her feel confident and secure in her own skin. The thoughts of what he might do to her body caused a shiver of anticipation to run through her, and she saw the same need in the blue depths of his gaze.

"How dare you."

The icy voice stole the warmth from Hannah's body, and she froze. She turned in Quinn's arms to face the one person in the world who'd never liked her.

Sylvia Elliot's narrowed eyes shot daggers, and her mouth puckered like she'd been sucking on a lemon. "How dare you," she repeated as she took a step closer.

Hannah held her ground. "I heard you the first time." Her words may have been bold, but her heart was racing, and her voice was low and on edge. "How dare I what?"

"How dare you show up here with . . . him," Sylvia spat and glanced at Quinn. "My son gave you three years of his life, and you can barely spare a year to grieve him?" She stumbled further into Hannah's space. "And with one of his friends too."

"Hardly," Quinn scoffed.

Hannah's shoulders tensed as her spine became ramrod straight. "I have a feeling it wouldn't have mattered who the next man was."

Sylvia lifted her chin a little higher and swayed on her feet. "You were never good enough for my son. I always told him he could do better than a social-climbing harlot like you."

There were a few gasps in the crowd behind her, and Hannah's cheeks flamed to life.

"From my understanding, you're not much better," Hannah hissed.

"I have . . . I can't . . . how dare you," Sylvia sputtered. Hannah could smell the fruity tang of wine on her breath.

Hannah took a step back. "How long would be long enough for you? Should I mourn him for the rest of my life? Never date? Never marry? Or would that not even be enough for you?" She glared at Sylvia. "Your son left me first," she hissed.

"You drove him away," Sylvia slurred.

Tears stung the back of Hannah's eyes. She wouldn't give Sylvia even a hint of weakness.

"He left to prove himself to you. You—" Sylvia continued.

"I never asked him to do that," Hannah barked, her volume rising. Quinn tried to ease her closer to him, but she pushed him away and took a step toward Sylvia.

Sylvia glowered at her, and a lone tear trickled down her cheek. "You made him leave. He'd still be alive if it weren't for you. It's your fault he's dead."

"Sylvia! That's enough," a terse male voice said. The crowd parted, and Darren Elliot came storming toward his wife with Nancy Harris hot on his heels.

Darren grabbed Sylvia's arm and pulled her away. Hannah's eyes darted around the room. How many of these people thought the same thing? She'd never told anyone the truth about Carter's decision to join the Navy, that he'd made the choice without her input. Would these people pity her more, or would they agree with Sylvia if they knew that?

"We've talked about this," Darren hissed close to his wife's ear. "It is not *her* fault Carter is gone, and I warned you about confronting her." He looked at Hannah and gave her a soft smile. "It's good to see you again, Hannah. I'm so sorry for my wife's outburst."

Hannah's head bobbed once. She didn't trust herself to speak.

"I think it's time you left, Sylvia. I will not allow you to cause problems at my son's wedding reception," Nancy said. Her tone made it clear she would brook no argument.

"I completely agree, Nancy," Darren said as he tugged his wife further away.

"It's all your fault, you little bitch," Sylvia sobbed, clearly bent on getting the last word in. "You killed my son."

Darren dragged his spiteful wife away, his displeasure clear on his face even though his words weren't loud enough for anyone to hear.

Hannah turned to Quinn. "Can we please leave now?" she whispered, her stomach twisted in knots.

Quinn draped his arm around her shoulders and pulled her against his side. All eyes were on the Elliots as they left the room—women talking quietly behind their hands as they nodded toward Sylvia, men shaking their heads in sympathy, and probably, at least in Hannah's imagination, relief that their wives had never done such a thing.

Nancy gently touched Hannah's shoulder. "Sweetheart, I'm so sorry," she said, her voice soothing and sympathetic. "You have to know that no one blames you for what happened to Carter."

Hannah wished she could believe that.

Nancy stepped closer. "And no one judges you for moving on." She glanced at Quinn and winked. "You deserve to be happy. Don't let anyone take that away from you." After a quick pat on Hannah's back, Nancy moved toward some of the other guests with a smile on her face.

Most people had resumed chatting openly with the people around them, but some were still casting surreptitious looks toward her.

"Quinn," Hannah said in a small voice. "We need to leave."

Quinn grabbed her hand. "Let's get your things."

"I hate being put on the spot like that," she said as they walked over to the table, and she grabbed her purse.

"I know you do." He pulled her closer and rested his cheek against her head. "And I'm willing to bet she knew that too."

"I'm sure she did," Hannah said. "If you take me home right now, I'll buy you cake on the way home."

He snorted with laughter, and she tried not to smile. "Chocolate cake?"

Hannah nodded. "Chocolate makes everything better."

He turned her toward the door. "In cake or on ice cream sundaes."

Eighteen

Hannah set two plates of cake on the dining table and sat down. Quinn followed with two glasses of milk and the forks. This private party of two was much nicer than a crowded reception anyway.

When they'd danced at the wedding, holding her in his arms had filled him with a sense of peace and maybe something a little more urgent. He'd known since that first kiss outside of the pub that he wanted her, but this was more. He longed for that physical connection, but this feeling went deeper. Having her physically would never be enough. Their dance had been interrupted, but if Quinn were lucky, he'd find a way to have her in his arms again before he went home.

His only concern now was that she'd have to relax enough to let him. She'd stayed by his side as they'd said their farewells to the bride and groom and some of the other guests, but she'd only responded when asked a direct question. Otherwise, she'd been completely silent.

"You're awfully quiet over there," Quinn murmured, casting a quick look at her. She looked beautiful.

Hannah gave him a small smile. "Just thinking."

"Good thoughts, I hope." He slid his hand toward her. Without hesitation, she slid her fingers into his and he gave them a slight squeeze.

"Of course." She lifted a forkful to their eye level, as a sort of salute, then slid it into her mouth. As her lips closed around the fork, he swallowed around the lump of surprise in his throat. He never thought eating cake could look so erotic.

Quinn shook his thoughts away as he stabbed a bite of cake with his fork and put it into his mouth.

"Thank you for leaving early," she said. "I didn't realize she was even at the wedding, and she caught me off guard."

Quinn lowered their hands to the table. "She doesn't like you?" He wasn't sure why that surprised him. In his limited experience with Sylvia Elliot, he'd learned that she rarely liked anyone she deemed beneath her social status. The irony was that Sylvia had grown up in a lower social circle. She'd married up when she married Mr. Elliot, but then turned her back on her humble roots.

"She never liked me, but wasn't blatant about it until after Carter proposed. Before we were engaged, her insults were veiled and less obvious. Sometimes I wasn't even certain she was insulting me. After he proposed, though, she didn't even try to be subtle anymore."

Quinn got lost in the honey depths of her eyes. He was looking for hurt, or maybe even anger. The only thing he found was a calm resignation that made his blood simmer unpleasantly.

"Hey, mothers-in-law get a bad reputation for a reason. It happens." Hannah shrugged. "It certainly would have made married life difficult, but I probably would have avoided her as much as possible. Which I did anyway."

They silently ate cake as he processed her words. He suddenly disliked Sylvia more than he'd ever thought possible. If what he'd seen at the reception was a fraction of how badly Hannah had been treated by that woman, he didn't want to think of what she'd suffered on a regular basis.

"How did you manage that?" Quinn asked, needing to know more even if he wanted to end the conversation. "I can't see her letting Carter get away with not visiting her. Or vice versa, really."

"Oh, she didn't," Hannah replied. "She asked him to come home every weekend and every break while we were in college."

"Did he?"

"At first, yes," Hannah said. "Before we started dating, he went home about every other weekend, unless there was something he wanted to do on or around campus. Once we started dating, however, he came home less often, which she blamed me for, of course." She rolled her eyes. "But when we did come home, his parents' house was always the first stop before he brought me to my parents' house. I always spent the weekend or holiday there."

Quinn wanted to ask what Carter thought of his mother's treatment of Hannah, but he knew all the parties involved well enough to know that Carter would have gone along with whatever his mother did. He wanted to believe that Carter wouldn't participate in any condescension toward Hannah, but he doubted Carter would speak up against it. If what Quinn had experienced firsthand during their acquaintance was any indication, Carter would pretend his mother hadn't said anything rude or patronizing and never bothered to offer an apology. Still, it was almost too much for Quinn to fathom that Carter could really allow his mother to get away with insulting the woman he'd chosen to spend his life with.

"Enough about that woman," Hannah said, her tone relaxed and airy. She pushed away from the table and stood. Her smile widened, and an impish twinkle danced in her eyes as she held out her hand to him.

He took her outstretched hand, then followed as she pulled him toward the living room. She stopped in front of her stereo and bent to fiddle with the knobs.

"What are you doing?" he asked.

"I'm looking for some music," she said. He noticed her bent back, the swell of her rear end, and the hem of the skirt that exposed more of her legs in that position. She finally settled on a song.

"Since I didn't let you have as many dances as I'd promised," she said.

He smirked as he eased one hand around her waist, and with the other, took hers and held it between their chests.

"I thought you said we didn't have a song," he teased as the same song they were dancing to at the reception now filled the room.

She laughed lightly, and a weight lifted from him to see her so cheery again. "We don't . . . yet. I'm still testing a few to see how they fit."

He pulled her closer, pressing her breasts against his chest as he lowered his lips to her ear. "I think this one fits quite well." He kissed the spot on her neck just below her ear and heard her sigh as he felt a shiver run through her.

"Why do I get the feeling you're not talking about the song?" she said breathlessly, and he chuckled. She tipped her head to the side as he trailed kisses down her neck.

"I have no idea," he whispered against the skin of her collarbone.

As they swayed, he pressed a few more kisses along her collar and shoulder. Her face was relaxed and her eyes were closed, her lips curving faintly upward. She opened her eyes and met his gaze. After a few beats, she pulled him in for a kiss, and he held back his smile as he lowered his head toward her eager mouth.

As their lips collided, he was swept up in a conflagration of lust and need he'd never known before. Her lips moved hungrily against his, and her hand slid up his shoulder to the back of his head, leaving a trail of fire in its wake. He slid his hand down her back until he cupped her cheek and pulled her against him. She moaned through the kiss and released his other hand to splay hers on his chest, branding him with her touch. He brushed his tongue against the crease of her mouth and it parted for him. His now free hand wrapped around her waist to cup her other cheek, and he started to back her toward the couch.

She pushed against his chest, breaking the kiss, her eyes dancing with desire. She inhaled deeply as she held his gaze.

"Upstairs," she said and started moving them both toward the steps.

"You're sure?" He lifted her so her feet barely touched the ground as he moved in the direction she'd set off in.

She nodded and slammed her lips against his again as she lifted her knees to his hips, and he carried her up the steps, taking only a hand away from her body to hold on to the railing. When they reached the landing, she lowered her feet to the floor and backed toward her bedroom, pulling him along with her.

Hannah had never felt so bold and impulsive in her life, but the moment he kissed her body, she knew she needed this and everything that would come next. The movement of their lips against each other had become second nature to her, so she was able to focus on what his hands were doing, aside from heating her blood everywhere they touched her. His left hand was now spread across her back, caressing with an almost frantic pace. It took her a moment to realize he was looking for something.

"Under my arm," she said, breaking the kiss only long enough to speak, then nipped his bottom lip before she pressed hers to his again.

His hand slid to the zipper, brushing the side of her breast as he lowered the tab along the chain. She pulled her mouth away, gasping at his touch, at the sudden fullness in her breasts, and he moved to her jawline, peppering light kisses along her jaw and neck.

Once her zipper was loosened, he slid the lacy material over one shoulder, kissing the exposed skin. As she reveled in the tickling sensation of his kisses, she started unbuttoning his shirt, slipping the plastic circles through the holes, making sure to drag her knuckles along the flimsy fabric of his undershirt as she did.

She tugged his shirt out of his waistband and looked into his eyes. His midnight-blue gaze burned with a passion that matched her own. Almost of one mind, they quickly set to work on taking off their own clothes. In one fluid motion, she pulled her dress over her head, then sat on the bed to strip the hose off her legs. Her eyes never left his body, and his eyes never left hers.

He stripped off his undershirt and her mouth went dry. Now clad only in her bra and panties, she stood and moved toward him, reaching for his broad, hard chest with one hand. He closed his eyes and groaned when her fingers touched his skin, and she held back a smile that she could have this effect on him. The more he responded, the more emboldened she felt. She couldn't remember ever feeling this daring with Carter.

She dragged her fingertips along the hard planes of Quinn's chest, marveling at the smoothness of the skin and firmness of the muscle. Stepping forward, she placed her hand on his pectoral muscle and slid it lower, along the dusting of hair between his pecs, as her other hand unzipped his pants. Their lips met again as he wrapped his arms around her body, and his hands fumbled to unclip her bra. She sighed with relief when the fabric loosened and fell from her body. His hands immediately took the place of the bra, cupping her breasts, lifting their fullness as he gently kneaded, stoking the flames of her desire higher.

As quickly as her fumbling fingers would allow, she slipped the button at his waistband free, lowered the zipper, and forced his pants down his legs. She stepped backward, her legs brushing the mattress, as he stepped forward, out of his pants. In the next breath, she was lying flat on her back, and he was hovering over her, both breathless, as she stared deeply into his eyes. Her hands roamed his chest and abdomen, teasing the waistband of his boxer briefs, his erection pressing against her lower stomach.

Hannah's palm itched to wrap around him, her body pulsing to have him inside of her. Her head urged her to slow down, but her heart soared. There was no doubt to her that this was just the beginning for her and Quinn. And the road ahead was long. Her breath hitched, and her eyes widened at the realization.

He frowned at her changed expression. "Hannah, are you sure you want this?"

She smiled as she hooked one arm around his neck and pulled him toward her. She slipped her other hand under the waistband of his underwear and wrapped her hand around his length. His eyes rolled into his head as his lids lowered and he groaned. She pressed a kiss to the corner of his mouth.

"I've never been more certain," she whispered.

He took her lips with his, hard and desperate, as he freed his erection, slid his underwear off, then crawled onto the bed. She was light-headed, giddy, as she moved with him toward the pillow, her hand still wrapped around him, lightly squeezing and stroking. He pulled her panties off her hips and down her legs as she settled her head on the pillow.

Quinn broke the kiss and lifted his head so he could stare at her. As his eyes traveled over her body, her skin warmed where his gaze touched. She fought the urge to cover herself; she hadn't felt this vulnerable in a very long time. At the same time, the heat in his eyes, the knowledge that he desired her as much as she did him, was a comfort that eased her sense of exposure.

"So beautiful," he whispered, as he lowered his head and pressed his lips to her cheek. He pushed her knees apart with his hips and anticipation coursed through her body. Reluctantly, she released him and spread her hands over his back. He deepened the kiss, pressing her into the pillow, and glided a hand lightly up her leg.

Her hips came off the bed when he brushed his finger against the apex of her thighs. She gasped when he finally touched her, skin to sensitive skin, and tears of joy threatened to overflow when he probed her with his finger. He took her lips again as one hand worked sensual magic on her most intimate area, his other hand returned to her breasts, fondling one and then the other, gliding across her nipples, driving her mad with need.

She slid her hands over his back, trying her best to pull him as close as she could, but he refused to budge. His sole focus seemed to be the erotic torture he was inflicting on her. For a brief moment, she wondered when she'd lost control of the situation, but he tweaked her nipple at the same time the fingers on his other hand grazed the nubbin at her opening and all thought stopped.

"Quinn!" Her entire body convulsed around his fingers, flames shot through her, and she gasped for air. Her hips shot off the bed, and she reached for his hard length again. She needed him in her body, needed him to feel this with her. "Now!"

His fingers left her body and were replaced by the gentle nudge of his erection. She opened her thighs further to accommodate him. Her eyes widened on his face, holding his lusty gaze as they joined. She sighed with relief as he filled her. He closed his eyes and groaned. He remained motionless while her fingers explored the expanse of his chest, now exposed to her wandering hands as he held himself over her. She dragged a fingertip over his nipple and his eyes flew open. She marveled at their color, so dark they were almost black.

Quinn lowered to one elbow, and with his other hand, flattened her palm against his chest as he slowly began to thrust into her body. His heartbeat rushed beneath her palm. The raw hunger in his eyes left her breathless, and she held his stare as she learned his movements. In a few thrusts, she was moving with him, lifting her legs to draw him further in.

They moved together, the sensations drawing them close to the edge before one of them would change the pace and pull back. They worked together, silently reaching for that peak, that ultimate release they both craved. When the wave finally crashed over her again, she cried out his name and lifted her hips, pulling him with her. She felt him spasm inside of her and fell to the mattress with a smile as her eyes closed. Quinn collapsed on top of her, and she relished his weight.

Once their heart rates had slowed, he rolled to his side, pulling her with him. Hannah tucked her head against his chest and curled into him, feeling safer, and more loved, than she had in a very long time.

Nineteen

Quinn sat across the small dining table from his sister and niece. His brother-in-law was beside him, and his parents sat at either end. Conversation throughout most of dinner had been fairly benign. Rachel had talked about some of her students, Seth had given the dates of the weekends he was scheduled to be with the Naval Reserves, and Quinn had talked about his classes and his few new jobs. Lily, in typical four-year-old fashion, had talked about whatever popped into her little head, providing a lively distraction from more serious topics, for which Quinn was very grateful.

He had yet to tell his parents about Hannah's new role in his life, not from fear of their disapproval, but because he wasn't ready to get the dirty looks from his sister. Every time they saw each other, Rachel asked if he'd told Hannah about his potential move. He was tiring of her persistence in butting into his life. The longer he could put off bringing up Hannah, the longer he could put off Rachel's demands.

"How's the job search going?" his father said from the far end of the table.

Quinn met his father's questioning stare. "The interview in Atlanta went well. I'm still waiting to hear back from them."

"When will you know something?" his mother questioned.

"Probably in another week or two." He shrugged. "Definitely by Thanksgiving."

"That's a month away." Rachel had a mischievous look in her eyes. "Why haven't you been at church lately?" she asked sweetly.

It was Quinn's turn to glare at his sister. She knew very well where he'd been.

"Oh, that's right. Thank you for the reminder, Rachel." His mother turned to him. "Where have you been?"

Quinn's glance bounced between his mother and sister. Rachel's lips slowly turned up.

"I've been helping Dani and Hannah." He focused on his mother.

"Oh, I didn't realize Hannah was seeing someone." His mother tucked a strand of graying brown hair behind her ear. "What are you helping them with?"

"No, Dani . . . Danielle Prescott. She was in our class," Quinn clarified.

His mother turned to Rachel. "Is she the teacher you work with?" she asked, and Rachel nodded. "I thought her last name was something different."

"It's Johnson," Rachel said. "But probably not for much longer."

Sadness filled his mother's eyes. "Poor dear," she muttered. She turned back to Quinn. "What are you helping them with that requires you to miss church every week?"

"Dani owns a horse farm," Quinn answered, happy that his mother had chosen to focus on Dani instead of Hannah. "They take care of everything that needs to be done and prepare for the week."

"Can't she hire someone for that?" his father asked.

"On a teacher's salary?" Rachel scoffed. "Maybe if her rat of a husband hadn't left her, she could afford to."

His mother gasped.

"Surely they can't do everything in one day." A wrinkle marred his father's brow. His face was an older mirror of Quinn's, his hair, once a pale milk-chocolate color, was now silvery gray, clipped short on the sides and longer on top.

Rachel shot Quinn a dirty look. Quinn chuckled as he sat back in his chair and folded his arms across his chest. He knew the story, but since Rachel had brought it up, he was more than happy to let her explain the situation.

Rachel sighed. "Dani pays people two days a week to take care of things while she's at school. The FFA students from the high school come to the farm two days a week after school, and she teaches them the things that need to be done on the farm, and some of them are learning how to ride. And on Saturdays, a 4-H club comes in and helps out."

"Dani does all of it the rest of the time, so Hannah's been helping her out every Sunday," Quinn chimed in.

"Is that why Hannah hasn't been at church?" his mother asked.

Quinn shrugged. He wasn't going to tell his mother why Hannah had stopped going to church just in case she'd been one of the people who constantly gave her pity. Besides, it was Hannah's story to tell, not his.

"I would think she'd want to be with her mother more than her friend." His mother's tone was disapproving. "Her mother could use the support."

Quinn wasn't sure he'd ever heard his mother express any concern for Faith Murphy before now.

"She supports her mother," Quinn said, hoping his voice didn't sound as defensive as he felt. "She cooks several meals for her family every other Saturday, and she takes her dad's place at the store twice a week after school so he can be with his wife."

He peeked at Rachel, who now had a cat-in-the-cream smile on her face. Quinn groaned inwardly. She'd set a trap, and he walked right into it. After all these years, he should have learned not to let her guide him into waters he didn't want to be in.

"Really?" his mother said slowly. "Is there any special reason you know so much about Hannah's comings and goings all of a sudden?"

Quinn's cheeks felt warm, and he glanced around the table. Seth was smirking, and Lily was completely oblivious to the conversation as she pushed a green pea around her plate with her fork. His parents both wore curious expressions on their faces, and Rachel was barely holding in her mirth.

"We're dating," Quinn answered. "Have been for a few weeks now."

His mother beamed widely at him. "Is that so?" She pressed her palms together in front of her chest and clapped her hands. "Oh, how wonderful," she added.

"She's a nice girl," his father said.

"She really is," Rachel agreed. "And a great teacher and friend. And so helpful." She gave Quinn a pointed look. "Everyone who knows her loves her."

Quinn stared at his sister. "I know they do."

"Do you?" Rachel's tone dripped with a sweetness that contradicted the steely look in her eyes. "I, personally, would hate to see her hurt again. She deserves to be happy."

Quinn's jaw pulsed as he clenched his teeth against the things he wanted to say.

"Who's ready for dessert?" Rachel asked brightly as she pushed away from the table.

"Me!" Lily screamed. "Ice cream?"

His mother chuckled. "I made a cake, but I'm sure there's ice cream in the freezer." She began to rise as Rachel moved around her and placed a hand on her shoulder.

"You stay right there, Mom. Quinn can help me," Rachel said.

"Of course," he replied as she grabbed his arm, subtly yanked him from his seat, and pulled him along beside her. He was happy to go.

There were a few things he wanted to say to his sister, but he started to fight her high-handedness when she bypassed the counter where the cake sat and dragged him into the living room. He shook her off and she spun to face him. "Do you abuse your husband like this?" Quinn scowled at her.

Rachel folded her arms across her chest. "Of course not. I chose to be with him," she answered. "I'm genetically stuck with you."

Quinn rolled his eyes. "What is your problem, anyway?"

"Have you told her?"

"Told her what?" Quinn sighed as he looked at the collage of family photos on the living room wall. His gaze landed on the picture of his parents, smiling widely at the altar in their wedding finery. He suddenly pictured himself in his father's place with Hannah in his mother's. He shook the image from his mind and hoped his surprise didn't show on his face.

"That you're moving?" Rachel ground out, drawing his focus back to her face.

"Nothing's been decided yet. I don't even have a job offer. Why should I tell her something that may not even happen?"

Rachel tipped her chin upward. "Whether or not you get an offer, don't you think she should know there's a possibility that you'll be leaving town?"

"No," Quinn snapped. He'd thought about it, mostly because of Rachel's nagging, but Hannah had enough on her plate, and he didn't see the point in worrying her until he knew something definitive.

While he had no doubts they would reach that level of commitment, they weren't at that point in their relationship yet. And if he were being honest, Rachel constantly bringing it up made him less confident that his relationship with Hannah would progress the way he wanted it to if he told her of his possible move to a city. He wanted to make sure Hannah felt as strongly for him as he did for her before he brought it up . . . if he had to bring it up at all.

Rachel threw her hands out to her side. "Fine," she said. "Just know that the longer you wait, the less I think you'll like her response." She strolled past him. "But I guess you know what you're doing."

"I do." He looked at his parents' wedding photo again. "Stop worrying about me."

Rachel turned to look at him. "It's not you I'm worried about."

He held his sister's stare, watching her gaze shift from irritation to pity, before he looked away. Quinn had the sudden need to be away from his family. He needed to clear his head. He needed to think about his future, the possibilities, and which ones he wanted to pursue. Without a word, he started toward the front door, grabbing his keys out of the glass bowl on the table, and yanked his coat off the rack.

He'd thought to drive home. Had started out heading that way. He had told Hannah earlier that he would probably end up there, sleeping in his own lonely bed that night.

Yet he wasn't surprised when he found himself pulling into the parking lot of her complex and stopping in front of her townhouse.

He threw his truck into park, turned it off, then hopped out without even stopping to think if he should be there. Yes, he'd stayed with her every night since the wedding, but he didn't want her to feel like they were moving too fast if he stayed over too often.

Quinn bounced up the steps, opened the screen door, then turned the knob as he rapped on the door. It was unlocked, so he let himself in, calling to Hannah to let her know it was just him.

She appeared in the doorway between the living room and kitchen, dressed in a pair of loose yoga pants and an old T-shirt.

"What are you doing here?" she asked. "Is something wrong?"

He cupped her face in his hands and kissed her thoroughly. He realized then why he was here. He needed her reassurance. He needed to know that she was truly with him. As her lips softened and held to his, it was a balm to his soul. With the pressure of her mouth against his came the memories of the last three nights, their limbs entwined in passionate embraces and calm aftermaths. It was enough to calm him and reaffirm his path, his trust in her.

He pulled back and looked into her eyes. "I just needed to see you," he confessed.

She laid her hands on top of his. "I appreciate that." She turned and led him into the living room, where he saw her grade book open on the coffee table and two stacks of papers on the couch. "I'm still grading papers. Shouldn't take me much longer if you want to stick around."

"Anything I can do to help?" He lowered himself into the glider seat.

She sat in the spot between the stacks, then sank further to the floor. She grabbed a paper as she extended her legs out under the coffee table. Then she picked up her red pen and scribbled a note on the page. "No, it's just this one assignment, so there's not much you can do."

They sat in comfortable silence for a few minutes, but when she finished grading the paper, she looked at him and frowned.

"Are you sure nothing's bothering you? You're not usually this quiet."

He shook his head. "Everything's fine. I just wanted to see you."

She held his stare for a few seconds, then sighed as her expression relaxed. "If you want to watch something, feel free. The remote is on the end table."

"It won't bother you?" He picked up the television remote as she resumed her work. He turned on her streaming account and found the series they'd been watching together.

For the most part, she worked, but he spent more time watching her than the TV. He noticed her attention drifting to the screen every now and then before she'd return to her work.

"We started OM today," she said, her head bent over her papers. "Each team picked their problem today."

"That's great," he said. He'd been on a few OM teams with Hannah in middle school. "Which ones did they pick?"

"I'm glad you asked." Her slow speech trailed off, his first warning that she was up to something. "One team wants to do the balsa-wood challenge . . . and I was wondering, since you've been on teams in the past, would you be willing to help coach them. They could use your help with architectural questions. Of course, you can't do the work for them, but I thought they might appreciate your expertise." She smiled. "I would appreciate it."

He lowered himself to the floor and scooted next to her. When he squeezed through the space between the coffee table and sofa and was finally in front of her, he leaned closer and gave her a quick kiss on the lips.

"I'd be happy to help," he answered. The building challenge had always been his favorite.

She sighed deeply. "Thank you."

He rested his back against the couch and stretched his legs out in front of him, mimicking her position. Without a word, he picked up a paper from the stack she was grading and held out his hand. She placed her red pen in his hand, and he began grading the paper as she searched her bag for another pen.

Several hours later, Hannah rolled over and flopped her arm across an empty pillow. She pushed herself up to her elbow and looked at the spot in the bed beside her where Quinn should be. Pushing up further, she looked around the room and out into the hall. She saw a faint light coming from the spare bedroom across the hall.

She slipped her legs over the edge of the bed and grabbed her pale-blue satin robe from the back of her vanity chair. Sliding her arms into the sleeves and loosely tying the belt, she crept into the hall and slowly turned the knob of the spare bedroom door.

Quinn stood at the foot of the bed, his back to her, staring up at the photography she'd hung on the far wall. She took a moment to admire his naked backside. The long planes of his back and the firm roundness of his butt made her skin tingle with warmth. She tiptoed toward him and glided her hands around his waist and up his chest. Pressing her chest against his back, she lightly kissed his shoulder as he covered her hands with his. She set her chin on his shoulder and followed his gaze with her eyes. He was staring at one of her pictures, a morning landscape with a pond in the midground and silhouetted mountains in the background, mist rising off the pond, which reflected the sky just over the mountaintop that was pink with the early morning sun.

Dani had convinced the farm's previous owner, whom she'd worked for since she was fourteen, to allow the two of them to take horses out one morning so Hannah could practice taking landscapes. This had been the best of the bunch that she'd taken that morning. She wasn't sure what it was about the picture that she loved so much, but it was easily one of her best and one of her favorites.

"It looks so peaceful," he murmured. "It's a reminder that every day is a fresh start."

She looked at the picture as if she were seeing it through his eyes. The light shining through the dip in the mountain, the sky pink and bright, the mist over the water—all of it looked fresh and new. She could almost smell the clean dew of the morning air and hear the birds waking with the sun.

"Where did you get it?" he asked, his eyes still focused on the picture.

"I took it," she whispered in his ear.

He turned to look at her with a surprised look on his face.

"With a camera," she added with a laugh.

She waved her hands to both walls that she'd filled with her photography. "I took all of them." She tried to keep the pride from her voice, but it was rare for her to show off her work. This little gallery she'd created had been solely for herself. To show that she could do something artistic and because she'd enjoyed doing it.

"When?" He turned to look at the walls again.

She moved to the foot of the bed behind him and lowered herself to the mattress. "About two years ago," she answered. Not many people knew she'd taken a photography class. "When Carter finished boot camp and was still as serious about the Navy as he'd been when he started, I thought I needed to prepare for a career other than teaching."

Quinn lowered his gaze from the pictures, and she could see his attention was on her even if he wasn't looking at her.

"I couldn't think of anything I could do that could travel with me," she motioned to her photos, "except, maybe, photography."

Quinn turned to her. "Why didn't you think you could teach?"

She lifted a shoulder and her robe slid over it. His eyes darted to her bare skin, and she fought her smile. "Because I didn't think I would be in any one place long enough to establish myself. Sure, I could probably teach the kids on whatever base we ended up on, but for how long?"

Quinn sat down next to her on the bed and continued looking at the photos.

"I always wanted to stay in Rocky Creek, where I could teach in the same school and establish relationships with the students, parents, and teachers I worked with. I didn't think my life as a Navy wife would allow for that," she said.

She examined the photos, remembering where she was when she took them. "I'd always had an interest in photography and thought I could be a wedding or family photographer. I took some classes at the rec center, and here we are." She ended with a flourish of her hand.

They remained silent as Quinn studied each picture. She wondered if he was seeing them in a different light knowing now that she had been the artist behind all of them.

"You definitely have a hidden talent. They're all beautiful."

She smiled meekly as her cheeks warmed.

"I guess this is how you ended up in charge of the yearbooks?" Laughter laced his words.

She chuckled. "Pretty much."

He nodded, but she noticed his gaze had dropped to her bare shoulder again, then lower to the belt of her robe. One glance at him below the waist showed her where his mind had gone, and she warmed at the idea. Within a heartbeat, he had his hands on her belt, and she was on her back under him, laughing as he stripped off her robe and showered her with kisses.

Twenty

It was the day of her mother's last chemotherapy treatment and Hannah felt lighter than air. Everything with her mother's treatments was running as smoothly as could be. She would still feel the effects for a few months, but the cancer was nowhere to be found in her body, and she'd survived the worst of the treatments. The doctors were going to give her a few weeks to recover before they started the radiation therapy, but even they were optimistic at this point.

Hannah was in the office at the store running the inventory lists so her dad could be at home with her mother. If she finished early enough, she was tempted to join them for dinner tonight to celebrate. She'd done the meal prep on Saturday, so it shouldn't be a huge inconvenience if she dropped in.

As she prepared the order from the lists her father had left with her, she glanced at the security monitors and smiled. Quinn was walking through the store, and from every indication, headed her way.

She'd never imagined that their intimacy would bring such a joy to her life. But maybe she had it backward and the joy came from their relationship, and the intimacy only heightened it. Even in the first weeks after she and Carter had started having sex, she worried that his interest in her was too good to be true. In spite of his professed commitment, she'd always been waiting for the shoe to drop, so to speak.

The delight when she saw Quinn, on the other hand, was pure and laced with security and comfort.

She turned to face the door and rose to her feet as he walked into the small office. He reached her in two steps, grabbed her hips, and planted a kiss on her mouth. When he released her, she retreated to the seat at the metal desk, and he sat on the small love seat beside the desk.

"What are you working on?" he asked, looking at the paperwork in front of her.

Over the past few weeks, he'd learned her routine and knew he could find her at the store on Monday and Wednesday afternoons. He'd started joining her and helping when he could, learning the computer programs and their recording process, and keeping her company when he couldn't help. Today would be one of those couldn't-help days.

"Preparing the order," she said, turning to the computer and setting to work. She was determined to get everything done as quickly as possible.

He watched her work for a few minutes. "How did your mom's last treatment go?"

Hannah gave him a large smile. "It went well. Dad's home with her, and I'm thinking of joining them for dinner."

Her smile was contagious, and Quinn couldn't fight his grin. How could he not share her joy? He could feel her relief. Even when she cooked for her family, he'd always detected an underlying tension infusing her body.

He could definitely sense a difference today.

"Would you want to come with me?" she asked without looking away from the computer screen.

"I can do that," he said offhandedly. He was game for going wherever she went, he just wanted to spend time with her. The real question was, if he told her what he came here to tell her, would she still want him to?

He'd spent the last week wrestling with the fact that he would very likely, and probably very soon, be moving. He'd gotten a job offer from the firm in Atlanta two days ago. It was a large architecture firm, headquartered on the outskirts of the city, that specialized in family homes of all sizes, as well as high-rise condos and offices. The variety of work was the reason he'd applied to them in the first place, and the money would be more for one project than he might make in six projects in Rocky Creek. He hadn't yet had the courage to bring it up to Hannah.

Her photography collection had been eye-opening. He'd heard the resignation in her tone when she talked about needing to find a new career. As good as her photographs were, he couldn't imagine her doing anything but teaching. For two years, she'd been building relationships with her students and establishing her life and career here. He heard often enough from Rachel, with maybe a hint of jealousy, just how much Hannah's students loved her.

But if he moved, and she moved with him, as he hoped she would eventually, she could still teach. He wouldn't be asking her to give up her profession the way she'd felt she would have had to with Carter. He hoped that was a point in his favor.

The only hangup was her obvious desire to stay in Rocky Creek. She'd spent a lifetime establishing herself in the community. How could a big city possibly compete with that? How could he ask her to walk away from all the relationships she'd built over the years?

It didn't help that Rachel still asked him every chance she got if he'd told Hannah about his potential, now probable, move. The more she asked, the more he wondered if she knew something she refused to tell him. So far, having a sister who worked with his girlfriend was not as beneficial to him as he'd hoped it might be.

"How was your day?" Hannah asked, pulling him out of his silent debate.

"Not bad." He told her about his new project. He'd taken on a kitchen remodel in a 1920s-style Prohibition-era house. The homeowners had asked that the remodel be as close to the style of the era as possible, and he was looking forward to stretching his creativity to accommodate that. The project should be finished just before he graduated in December, so he'd be done with it before any move would take place.

He left that last part out.

They continued to make small talk, about her students, about the OM teams they were coaching and how practice had gone the day before, about anything and everything, except what he'd come there to say.

As she finished up her work, he accepted the fact that he was a coward. He would tell her he was moving, but only when he'd made a decision. Things had changed for him so much since he started interviewing that he was no longer sure exactly what he wanted to do.

Twenty-One

For the first time in three and a half months, Hannah didn't have to go her parents' house to prepare meals for them. Thanks to her preparations, with a few additional meals made by Nancy Harris and her daughters-in-law, the Murphy family's freezer was well stocked. They would be set for meals at least until her mother began radiation therapy in three weeks.

This morning, she'd woken up in Quinn's arms, in his bed. He'd been asking her for the past week if she wanted to see his home. She'd actually been excited to see his house, but what she saw was more than she'd expected. As he showered and got ready for their day out, she roamed freely through the house.

Quinn lived in a two-story colonial that had been built in the mid-1970s. By the looks of some parts of the house, she guessed it hadn't been touched since. The only room he'd completed renovations on upstairs was the master bedroom suite. He'd started renovations on several of the rooms downstairs, but the only one completed so far was the living room, to the right of the entry. It was the first thing she'd noticed the night before, so the rest of the house had come as a surprise.

She wandered into the kitchen, which was located in the back of the house. There was a beautiful view of the mountains and a small pond at the bottom of a shallow hill. No wonder he hadn't learned to cook. He had nothing to cook on. All of the appliances were missing, and the dark wooden cabinets that remained were shells with no doors and missing shelves. The yellow counter remained but was old, stained, and broken in several places. From what she could tell, even the layout wasn't the greatest. There was no island, and the work triangle between the sink, stove, and refrigerator, was more of an L. The original, unfaded yellow-and-brown-striped wallpaper was on display in the hole in the wall where the refrigerator had been along with the sink. The empty hole for the stove sat on the shorter wall near the sink.

For a man who remodeled kitchens for a living, this was surprising. But, with his classwork and his job, she guessed he didn't have much time to address his own home. To the left was the dining room. Again, nothing extraordinary. The overall style could be termed "late 1980s," and nothing about it said "Quinn." The dining table was small and old, but he was the only person living here, so she guessed it met his needs.

Through the dining room, a door was tucked away in the corner that led to an office space. There were large windows that looked out onto the driveway and front yard. A large desk sat in front of the window, and it was probably the only thing she'd seen so far that had any personal touches.

On the surface of the desk were several pictures of his family. There was a framed photo of his parents and a photo of Rachel's family. The school picture of Lily brought a smile to Hannah's face. She picked up the picture and studied it. She hadn't realized Lily's eyes were an exact match to her uncle's.

A large calendar on the desk caught her eye. Notably, the words "job interview" and "Atlanta" were written in red ink. She put Lily's picture down and reached for the calendar. She picked up a small stack of papers, feeling nervous that she was snooping, and flipped through them. October? She checked the date. This interview had been three and a half weeks ago. And he hadn't said anything?

She glanced at the papers. The top sheet was a handwritten itinerary, but not for Atlanta. It was for Charlotte, North Carolina. The word "interview" was written halfway down the page. She flipped through the other papers and saw they were all itineraries, all for different cities, all with "interview" written on them.

Was he leaving her?

She dropped the papers, only to spot a pile of business cards on the lower corner of the calendar. A quick glance confirmed what she'd suspected. They were cards for the architecture firms in the cities he'd interviewed in.

She sank into the desk chair and looked out the window, her heart too sluggish to process what her mind already knew. Quinn was planning to leave. From the looks of things, his first interview had come just before he'd asked her on a date, yet he hadn't said anything to her about it.

"Hannah?"

She heard him call her from the kitchen, but she didn't have the voice to respond. She was too busy holding back the tears of anger or hurt, she wasn't really sure which. It was Carter all over again. He'd simply made the decision to join the Navy, then told her after the fact.

At least she and Quinn weren't engaged, so it wasn't like he was making this decision for her the same way Carter had. But she still would have liked to know the possibility that he might leave was there before they'd started dating. He could have saved her this heartache.

"There you are." His words slowed as he spoke. "Oh no," he muttered. She heard his tentative footsteps grow closer. "Hannah, I can explain."

"Explain what?" Her voice sounded as cold as she suddenly felt.

"I was going to tell you. I just wanted to wait until I had something definite to tell you."

"Something definite to tell me," she repeated monotonously. "Like a move? How was that supposed to go? 'Hannah, darling, it's been fun, but I'm taking a job in'"—she picked up the handwritten schedules—"'Boston. Hope you don't mind. Maybe I'll see you when I come home for a visit.'" Her voice had grown in volume as her heart raced. She popped out of the seat and paced the room. "Is that when you were going to tell me?" She glared at him.

"It wouldn't be Boston," he responded meekly. "I've actually been offered a job in Atlanta."

"Oh, that's so much better." Her tone dripped with sarcasm. She was impressed she could put so much into such a short sentence, but she was too furious to focus on that. Anger was much easier to deal with than the pain. "And I'm supposed to . . . what, exactly? Move with you? Have a long-distance relationship while I wait for you to come home? Or is this over?"

Quinn averted his gaze. "It doesn't have to be like that."

"No, Quinn," she snapped. "That's exactly how it has to be. I love my life here. I'm not moving, and I won't have a long-distance relationship. So, there's really only one option for me." She'd never wanted to leave Rocky Creek, and she always planned to come back after she graduated from college. It was the main reason she'd been so mad at Carter for joining the Navy. The distance had only strained their relationship further. She wouldn't go through that again.

Quinn's eyes were wide and full of fear. "Hannah, I haven't accepted the job yet. I may not . . . I haven't really decided. But this is a great opportunity for me. I can't get that kind of upward mobility anywhere around here." He took a step toward her. "We can talk about this when I decide what to do." He held out his hands to her.

"When *you* decide?" she scoffed as she looked toward the door. She blinked furiously against the tears. "I'm sorry, I guess I thought things between us were a little more serious than that." Her voice started to fail her, so she paused. "I thought we were a *we*, but I guess I was wrong." Pulling her shoulders back, she pinned him with a gaze. "Fine. You decide what to do for you, and I'll decide what's good for me."

His shoulders dropped on his exhale.

"Take me home." She turned and walked out the door.

They rode in silence all the way to her townhouse. She did anyway, as Quinn continued to try to plead his case for a little while. When she refused to answer, he'd fallen silent as well. She was okay with that. It gave her time to think.

Maybe she'd been a little hasty. He'd told her, numerous times now, that he hadn't decided to move yet. However, in the next breath, he'd told her how great the opportunity was and all the things he'd have if he took it.

Except, he wouldn't have her if he moved. She didn't want to move. Her family and friends were here. She had a job, students, and coworkers she loved. And she couldn't imagine herself living in a city. Even the consideration of living on a military base had been a struggle for her. She was a country girl through and through. Nothing else appealed to her.

And right now, she wasn't sure she wanted to stay with him if he was planning a move. It would do nothing but set her up for more heartache, and unlike with Carter, she wasn't sure she would recover from this one. It was bad enough that her heart tightened every time she considered not being with Quinn.

Was she really being unreasonable? Would it be better to end things now and put an end to her suffering? Would she be happy if she stayed with him now, knowing he'd be leaving her in the future? And what if they did break up and then he opted not to move?

Would things between them ever be the same?

"Hannah, can I come in so we can talk about this?" Quinn begged.

She was surprised to find they were parked in front of her townhouse. She opened her door, then looked at him and nodded once. He gave her a fleeting smile as he threw his door open, then reached into the back seat and grabbed her bag before she could. Hannah fumbled through her purse, looking for her keys, as she made her way up the porch. Quinn grabbed the screen door and opened it for her so she could unlock the door.

Inside, she deposited her purse on the bench in front of the window and hung her keys by the door. Quinn closed the door behind them and dropped her bag on the floor. Hannah took two steps into the room and froze. Her senses were buzzing.

Something wasn't right.

She turned and looked at the window bench, studying it. Everything was in order there. Slowly, she turned in a circle, studying every surface until she saw something on the dining table. Stepping closer, she stared at the ball chain and metal tags that hadn't been there the night before. With a shaking hand, she picked them up, her eyes rounding and her mouth dry.

"Hannah?" Quinn's voice drifted to her through a tunnel as she stared at the tags in her shaking hand.

There was only one person in her life who had ever worn dog tags. And as far as she knew, they were still on his body at the bottom of the ocean. Her hand shook as she tried to read the embossed writing when she heard a movement on the stairs. She lifted her head and saw Carter step off the last step and enter the living room, his black hair wet and mussed, a smile on his face.

"Hi, sweetheart," Carter said as he strolled toward her. "I'm home."

Hannah's knees weakened, her arm dropped, and the dog tags fell to the floor. Everything went black.

Twenty-Two

Quinn scooped Hannah into his arms as she slumped to the floor. His eyes never left Carter's face, who'd watched her fall with a smug smile on his lips. With her secured in his arms, Quinn wanted to turn and leave, to take her back to his house, to never let her out of his sight.

Quinn elbowed Carter out of the way as he carried Hannah to the living room and laid her down on the couch. He sat on the edge of the couch at her knees, his stomach churning, his chest tight as he focused on her. He was faintly aware of the anger bubbling through his blood as Carter moved toward them and stopped on the other side of the coffee table.

"What are you doing here?" Quinn growled.

It *would* be like Carter, the golden boy, to come back from the dead. He'd triumphed in almost everything he set his mind to, whether on the athletic field or with the girls. Carter had only ever lacked in his academics, but he'd had Quinn there to help him through that. The only question now was *how*.

How had he managed to beat death?

"It's my house," Carter answered, his tone as arrogant as always.

"It's Hannah's house." Quinn narrowed his eyes on Carter's face.

The corners of Carter's mouth slowly lifted into a superior smile. "It's our house. We signed the lease together before I left for basic training." He turned his gaze back to Hannah. "And when I checked yesterday, my name is still there."

Quinn clenched his jaw and looked toward the stairs. She'd never taken his name off the lease. Had that been on purpose? Had she not been ready to accept his death so she hadn't taken him off the lease? Or had she simply forgotten?

"You're supposed to be dead." Quinn's voice sounded surprisingly calm considering the turmoil and confusion boiling through him.

"Am I?" Carter chuckled.

Quinn scowled at him.

"Clearly, I'm not." Carter folded his arms across his chest. "And what are you doing here, Quinn Taylor? You're the last person I expected to see in my house."

Hannah groaned and, while her eyelids remained closed and still, the corners of her eyes crinkled. Quinn had seen that look before. He got up and strolled toward the bathroom to retrieve the ibuprofen for her. He'd already caused her a great deal of stress, and he couldn't imagine what Carter's return might do to her.

"Why are you *here*? How are you here?" Quinn asked again. What did Carter want? What was he hoping to achieve?

"Isn't it obvious?" Carter pointed a finger at Hannah. "I'm home now, and Hannah and I are going to start our life together."

Quinn bit back a growl as he set the bottle of pills on the table and lowered himself back to the couch. "What if that's not what she wants?"

The corners of Carter's mouth lifted slowly. "Of course it's what she wants." He laughed. "It's what I want, and you know how she is."

Quinn fought not to react as the words stung him in the chest. He did know how Hannah was, which was one reason he'd been so careful not to guide her. She was a people pleaser. For almost as long as he'd known her, she'd done whatever was asked of her. She'd always been respectful of the adults in her life and done whatever they'd expected of her, whatever would make them happy.

She stirred again, and Quinn watched as her eyelids fluttered, then opened to reveal clear, honey-colored pools. Hannah looked at him and blinked several times, then turned her head. Her brow furrowed as she stared at Carter.

"You're alive?" she whispered, her voice soft and raspy. She slowly pushed herself up to her elbows, then further into a sitting position.

It had just been her legs beside his hip, but the disappearance of her warmth chilled Quinn to the core.

"You're alive," she repeated, her voice still soft and full of confusion.

Maybe he should take her away so they could both process what was going on before Carter reinserted himself in her life.

"Hannah, we should go," Quinn murmured as he slid closer to her.

She didn't move. Her eyes were still glued to Carter's face.

"You should go, Quinn," Carter said quietly. There was a hard glint in his eyes.

Quinn inwardly snarled but kept his reaction from making an outward appearance. It wouldn't do him any good to give Carter the response he was hoping for.

"How? You're alive?" Hannah's voice grew stronger.

"Hannah, let's get out of here." Quinn took her hand, surprised by how limp and unresponsive it was. He tugged anyway, hoping to jerk her attention back to him.

Slowly, her eyes met his. "No," she said, and his heart stopped.

"Hannah and I have a lot to catch up on. You need to leave, Quinn," Carter said in a firm tone.

Quinn's jaw clenched as he stared at Hannah. Aside from the brief glance she'd given him when she'd woken up, she'd only acknowledged his presence to reject his request. He was losing her. First, she found his itineraries. Now this.

He squeezed her fingers. "Hannah, please."

Even as her stare met his for a moment, Quinn heard the desperation in his own voice and was suddenly in a different place, at another time, begging Alexa to choose him over another man. Promising her the world if she'd stay with him. He'd sworn to himself then that he would never be in this situation again.

Yet here he was.

The wrinkle in her forehead deepened. "I can't." She almost sounded like she was pleading. She focused on Carter. "How?" Hannah said, her voice the strongest it had been since her eyes opened.

Quinn laid her hand in her lap. He wouldn't beg. Not again.

Hannah looked at Quinn. There was clarity in her eyes, but it seemed as if she was looking through him. "You should go," she said.

Ignoring Carter—he really didn't want to see the smug look on his face—Quinn stormed through the living room. He wrenched the front door open, stomped through it, and took his frustrations out on the door as he jerked it hard behind him.

Twenty-Three

The slamming of the door snapped Hannah out of her daze. Her eyes refocused on Carter's face, which until now had been a blur.

His hair was as dark as always, jet-black, and longer now than the last time she'd seen him. Still not as long as it had been in college, but messier than usual. His eyes sparkled like brown jasper, even across the room. His tanned skin was dark against his white T-shirt. The muscles in his arms and broad shoulders were larger than she remembered. He looked as if he'd just come back from an island vacation, not the dead.

She must be dreaming. There was no other explanation for it. She could still picture the empty flag-draped casket at the funeral. The smiling pictures from his high school and college days spread across the front of the chapel. The detachment that had haunted her for months.

Hannah took him in again as she searched her heart and soul. She combed through her feelings, trying to find the love that had prompted her to accept his proposal. The frustration she'd felt when he left her for a third time, putting their future on hold again. The anger she'd briefly felt when he'd died.

She found nothing.

She was happy he was alive; she'd never wished him dead in the first place. But as far as her feelings went, she was completely indifferent to the man who was now standing in front of her.

"How?" She planted her feet flat on the floor and clasped her hands at her knees. "What?" She didn't even know how to finish any of her questions. Her shock was wearing off but was quickly being replaced by a growing twinge in her temple.

"Hannah?"

"Carter," she replied. His eyes widened at her stiff tone. "What are you doing here? We buried you. I was at your funeral. You're supposed to be dead."

He held her stare for a moment before his eyes relaxed. "Sounds almost as if you would prefer that," he chuckled.

Hannah tried to feel ashamed for her tone. She couldn't muster any embarrassment, but habit still prompted her to add, "No, I wouldn't prefer that. I don't understand. How . . . why are you here?"

"Where else would I be?" Carter moved around the coffee table and sat on the edge closest to her. He took her hands in his. "You're my fiancée. My place is by your side."

She looked at their clasped hands and inwardly examined her feelings. There had been a time, early in their relationship, when his touch would make her heart race and her stomach flutter. But now she felt nothing but a slight throb in her head.

She pulled her hands away.

"I was thinking we could start planning our wedding," Carter continued, clearly oblivious to her inner turmoil. "I know it would be short notice, but how about a Christmas wedding?"

Hannah inhaled deeply. As she exhaled, she lifted her eyes to his. "No."

Carter's arrogant smile fell a fraction and he blinked. "No?" he repeated, then he smiled. "No, you're right. Six weeks probably isn't long enough. Although, I thought you'd already have plans for almost everything, so I didn't think it would be a problem." He reached for her again.

She tucked her hands between her thighs.

Annoyance flashed through his eyes before he relaxed and leaned forward.

"How about Valentine's Day?" His expression turned seductive, his signature look when trying to get his way. "You've always loved that holiday. We could get married then and have even more reason to celebrate it for the rest of our lives."

Hannah tipped her head and stared at him, seeing him again for the first time. Did he know her at all? She'd never been fond of Valentine's Day, and his level of overkill on flowers, chocolates, and the useless stuffed animals, which had been the first things she'd thrown out after his death.

Unlike most women she knew, she never kept a book full of magazine clippings for her ideal wedding. After becoming engaged, she'd collected bridal magazines, more for the informative articles than the pages and pages of perfect dresses, floral arrangements, and locations she knew she'd never be able to afford.

They'd never been her style anyway.

She closed her eyes and shook her increasingly aching head. She couldn't let her mind drift to wedding plans now.

"No, there won't be a wedding," Hannah firmly stated.

Carter's mouth fell open. She held his wide stare, relaxed and confident in her words.

After a few more silent seconds, he said, "I don't understand."

"What's not to understand?" She folded her arms across her chest. She stood and moved toward the doorway into the kitchen. Then she turned to face Carter.

His eyes dropped to her naked ring finger and his frown deepened. Sympathy tightened around her heart at the lost expression on his face. Knowing him the way she did, he'd come back from wherever he'd been for the past fourteen months, fully expecting her to fall in line with his plans. As she always had.

Anger and confusion overwhelmed her senses. She didn't understand what was going on or how Carter could be standing here in her living room. "Where *have* you been for the past year?" She narrowed her eyes at him.

"That's not important right now. Why aren't you wearing your ring, and why don't you want to get married?"

Hannah scoffed, as any remaining sympathy she had changed to wariness. Carter never shied away from talking about himself. Unless he was hiding something. She looked around the room, searching for the right words. Her gaze fell on the bottle of ibuprofen sitting on the coffee table. She didn't remember how the bottle got there. A wave of dizziness washed over her and she gripped the doorframe. *Quinn. The slammed door.* She glanced at the door.

"Hannah," Carter snapped. "Why don't you want to get married?"

She slowly turned to him, recognizing for the second time that he hadn't said "to me." She guessed it was easier for him to think she'd turned her back on marriage completely, not just marriage to him.

"How are you back from the dead?" she asked again, using her stern teacher voice.

He waved off her question as he sauntered toward her. "I was never dead. They made a mistake."

"You've been gone for over a year," she snapped. His pace slowed, and he looked at her as if she were a stranger. "Even if it had been a mistake, someone would have figured it out in the last fourteen months."

Carter held his hands up, palms facing her. "I know you would think that, but it's not always the case." He took another cautious step toward her. "It was just a minor oversight."

"A minor oversight?" Hannah scoffed. "You, not being dead, is not a minor oversight. Where have you been?"

"I can explain everything," his tone was placating, which only made it worse. "Let's just sit down, and talk calmly—"

"Start talking now," Hannah demanded as she stomped into the kitchen to get herself a glass of water. As she filled her glass, she heard him shuffle into the room.

"You still haven't answered my question about why you don't want to get married." Carter rubbed her shoulder lightly, and she smacked his hand away.

"Don't touch me." She stormed back into the living room, grabbed the bottle of ibuprofen, and took two pills. She felt Carter's eyes on her.

"Since you aren't going to answer my question, I'll answer yours first," she said. Her voice was shaking from the adrenaline. "We're not right for each other, Carter. I think you know that. We were always so different. It's a wonder we made it as long as we did. I don't want to marry you. We don't like the same things, we don't like the same people, and we rarely saw eye to eye on anything." She sighed. "As much as I didn't like it when you joined the Navy, I'm glad you did. It gave me a chance to learn who I am and what I like. It gave me the confidence to be myself."

She watched the slow rise and fall of his chest as he regarded her. Her muscles tensed as she fought not to react to his silence. The longer he was quiet, the less likely he was to agree with her.

"I never saw our differences as a problem," he began slowly, his voice deceptively gentle. "As a matter of fact, I enjoyed them." He shrugged. "I thought you did too."

"Carter," she began, but he held up his hand.

"You had your chance to explain your reasons." He lowered his hand. "It's my turn."

She tightened her fist around the bottle of ibuprofen.

"I hear what you're saying," he said, inching closer to her. "You think we're different, but I think we balance each other. As for not liking the same things, you never brought that up before. And you say you've discovered yourself, but I wonder if it's more that you've gotten used to being alone and you think you enjoy it."

Her mouth fell open a fraction.

"I think your apprehension comes from that. You've gotten used to being alone. You've gotten used to doing your own thing, and so you think you'd rather continue that way." He reached for her arm, and she pulled away. He flashed a smoldering grin. "Honey, we just need some time to get used to each other again. And once we do, you'll remember how well we actually do fit together."

"Carter—"

"Just wait . . . please." Carter gently touched her arm, and this time she didn't pull away. "I love you, Hannah. Thoughts of marrying you, loving you, and a life with you is what has kept me alive for the last year. I know that my being here is probably a huge shock to you, and I'm sorry for that. But nothing has changed for me. And I think if you give it time, you'll see that it hasn't really changed for you either. You'll realize that you just got used to living without me and doing things without me, and you made yourself enjoy it."

"But—"

"Sweetheart." He ignored her protests and grabbed her other arm.

She jerked away from his hold and bit back a growl of frustration. The nerves in her temple were pulsating with increased strength.

"Give it time," he cooed. "You'll see that we really do fit. We were good together and we can be that way again."

"You're out of your mind," she said. "How can you even think we would just fall back into life as if nothing happened after you'd been dead for a year? You won't even tell me where you've been." She moved toward the stairs, putting as much distance between them as she could.

This was all too much. The pounding in her head had a fuzzy edge, the dizziness was building, but it didn't feel like her usual vertigo. Even her muscles were heavy, as if she were still asleep, like this was all a dream she could wake up from. But Carter was standing there, staring at her.

"No, Carter," she said forcefully. "I don't need time to know how I feel. I don't want to marry you, and nothing you do will make me change my mind about that."

She refused to look at him but heard his muffled groan.

"Is this about Quinn?" he snapped.

She pressed her teeth together and remained silent.

He crossed his arms over his chest. "Well?"

"No," she said tightly. "It's about us. You and me. No one else."

Even if she and Quinn had still been on more steady ground, he wasn't the reason she no longer wanted to marry Carter. Nevertheless, she now needed to convince Carter it was over, which would be easier said than done.

Carter was used to always getting his way. She hated to admit it, but for the longest time she'd allowed him to have whatever he wanted. It was who she'd been through high school with her peers, and even after college, it was who she was for the longest time. Only after he died did her attitude start to change.

Once Carter was out of her life, she could think about Quinn and whether they had a future.

"Then I still don't understand, Hannah." He shrugged.

She studied his face, the lost look in his eyes, and could see he wasn't just being stubborn. He really didn't understand. For a fraction of a second, pity squeezed her chest, but was quickly replaced with anger and betrayal.

"You don't understand? Really?" she asked, her voice rising an octave. "You have been gone for two and a half years. For the last year, you were dead. I don't know where you've been. I don't even know how you're here now. But I do know that I've changed, Carter. It's really that simple. I don't want to be that person I was when I was with you."

She saw the pain in his eyes and hated herself for causing that. But when she was with him, she was a people pleaser, always worried about how to make other people happy. That was who she was at her core.

"I know you're angry and confused, and you have every right to be. But please give me some time so I can explain everything." He took a step toward her. "So, what if we don't talk about a wedding right now and just be together for a while and see what happens?"

Hannah fought the urge to scream. "What?" she began but hesitated when his eyes lit with victory. Inhaling deeply, she thought about what he was asking. With a slight shake of her head, she held his gaze. "Absolutely not."

"Come on, Hannah." He moved toward her. "If, as you say, you have changed, then we can get to know each other again. We can take the time to reconnect, and you'll see that we belong together."

Hannah closed her eyes against the expanding pain in her head and folded her arms across her midsection.

"Why don't we give it until the end of the year?"

He gripped her forearm, and she pulled away. It didn't matter if it was one week or one day: she was not getting back together with Carter. And nothing was going to change her mind.

"No, I don't need that long."

"What about Christmas?"

"Carter," she blew out in frustration.

He grabbed her arms and gave them a gentle squeeze. "You have to work with me here, Hannah. I'm trying to give us the future we were planning before I left."

She began to argue as a sharp pain shot from her temple to the back of her eye. He wasn't going to relent; she knew that from experience. Arguing with him was futile, but she couldn't give him even an inch.

"You're not going to give up on this, are you." She sighed. It wasn't a question. She knew the answer. "I'm not going to change my mind."

"And I'm not going to give up on us," he replied, his firm tone growing in volume.

Hannah spun on her heel and glared at him.

He fell back a step. "Five weeks."

Gritting her teeth, she declared, "No."

"Four weeks?"

"I said no," she snapped, and the throbbing in her head grew stronger. She winced and lowered her gaze to the floor, breathing deeply until it passed. With a calming sigh, she lifted her eyes to his again. "I can't legally make you leave since your name is on the lease, but I will give you one week to find another place to live. If you don't like my offer, you can go now." She pulled her shoulders back, daring him to argue. "But just know, if you stay, I will not cater to your every whim and desire."

She watched the telltale sign of frustration in the pulsing of his jaw.

"I'll agree to that, if you promise to keep an open mind about us," he said.

She shook her head. "I'm not promising anything. You don't play fair."

"Hannah, I always play fair." He tried to laugh, but she glared him to silence, and he sighed. "Fine, I promise to play fair," he muttered petulantly.

They stared at each other for a few taut breaths. When Hannah recognized the battle of wills was over, she felt the tension in her shoulders lessen.

"If you'll excuse me, you've given me a migraine," she began, then added, for emphasis, "I'm going upstairs to lie down."

Carter frowned as she turned toward the stairs. "Can I do anything to help?"

Hannah paused on the small landing and gazed down at him.

"Just leave me alone."

Twenty-Four

Quinn parked his truck in front of Dani's barn and turned off the engine. He wasn't sure this was a good idea. He didn't know if Hannah would show up this morning. He wasn't sure what he would do if she did. He still couldn't get her words out of his head: *You should go*. He replayed the moment over and over, trying to figure out why she would want him to leave.

She'd been angry at him for the job interviews—he understood that—but would she really give up on them that easily? Maybe she wasn't giving up; things were just too confusing with Carter's return. She never talked about her feelings for Carter, so maybe she wasn't over him. Then again, Quinn couldn't help but wonder now if her reaction to Carter would have been different if he and she hadn't just had an argument about his potential move. Rachel's warnings had haunted him all day. Would things have turned out differently if he'd kept Hannah up to date about his plans? Quinn had wondered how he could compare to a ghost.

Now he knew.

His mind raced. How did Carter come back from the dead? Almost everyone who was close to him thought he was perfect, but even this defied reality. He knew a little about the ins and outs of the Navy because his brother-in-law was a Navy recruiter. He knew at least enough to know that they didn't go around telling family members their loved ones were dead if they didn't have enough evidence to do so. He couldn't believe Carter's "death" was a mistake. So the real question was where had he been for the past fourteen months?

He had one booted foot on the ground when Dani stepped through the open barn door.

"I was wondering when—" She looked past him, then met his blank stare. "Where's Hannah?"

Quinn eased his other foot to the gravel, then stepped away and closed the door. When he turned to look at her, he shrugged a shoulder.

Dani placed a hand on his forearm as he strolled around her, and he froze. "Quinn, where is she?" she asked.

"Not here," he ground out.

Dani's grip on his arm slackened enough for him to shake free. He continued toward the barn and was almost at the open door when he heard the determined crunch of gravel behind him.

"Quinn, stop."

He came to a halt just inside the door and turned to face her.

"I see she's not here." Dani stopped directly in front of him. "Why is she not here?"

Quinn couldn't answer her. He shoved his hands into the pocket of his hooded sweatshirt and shrugged.

"Where is she then?" she shouted. "Don't even try to tell me you don't know, Quinn Taylor. What's going on with the two of you?"

Quinn turned and strolled into the barn, collecting his thoughts and temper with each step. He didn't want to think about where Hannah was or, worse, who she was with. He still didn't understand what was going on. He heard Dani's quick steps behind him, and she hurried forward and stood in front of him.

He held up his hand. "We had an argument."

She remained silent but crossed her arms and lifted an eyebrow, a sure sign that she wanted more information. The stare-down continued for a few seconds before Dani relented.

"What did you fight about?" She relaxed her stance.

"Hannah found out I've been interviewing for a new job."

"That shouldn't have upset her." Dani took a step closer. "What are you not telling me?"

"The interviews were all out of state."

Dani tipped her head. "Out of state like North Carolina? Or like Oregon?"

"Atlanta," he said. "Boston, Philadelphia, and Charlotte."

"Yikes," she whispered.

She seemed to understand better than he did why that would be a problem for Hannah . . . or would have been. He doubted it mattered now.

"Okay," Dani said, drawing him back to the moment. "How long have you been interviewing?"

"For a while now, right around the time when we first started dating," he answered.

"Okay," she said slowly. "And after you told her that, she was still mad at you?"

Quinn walked farther into the barn, stopping at the door of the tack room before he faced her again. She'd followed on his heels and had closed the distance between them.

"I didn't get the chance to tell her that." He stepped into the tack room and grabbed a corded rope lead.

"Just so I get this right," Dani began, "y'all were at your house, she found out you were interviewing for jobs, and . . . ?" She waved her hand in a circular motion.

"She insisted I take her home, and she gave me the silent treatment the entire way," Quinn finished.

With a nod, Dani continued, "And y'all didn't talk about this at her house because . . ." Another flourish of her hand.

"Because she had company," he said through a tight jaw.

Dani opened her mouth to say something, but her phone rang, interrupting their conversation.

"It's Hannah." She answered the phone, putting the call on speaker so he could hear it too. "Good morning," Dani said brightly, as if she hadn't just been giving Quinn the third degree.

"Hey," Hannah said softly, almost a whisper.

Quinn swallowed the lump in his throat. Just hearing her voice hurt.

"Everything okay?" Dani frowned at the phone.

"No," Hannah said, even quieter. "Give me a second."

Her side of the line went mostly quiet. Quinn stepped closer to Dani and could hear the muffled voices over the open line. He could almost distinguish between Hannah's tone and a masculine voice. After a brief back-and-forth between them, Hannah came back on the line.

"I'm back," she said sharply. "Sorry about that."

Quinn schooled his features, hoping to hide his frustration and anger.

"What's going on?" Dani asked.

"I can't make it to the farm today," Hannah answered. "I'm so sorry to leave you in the lurch on such short notice."

"No worries. Quinn's here to help." Dani looked up at him, scowling.

There was a breath of silence on the other end.

"Quinn's there?" Hannah stuttered. "Can you take me off speaker?"

Quinn felt a stab to his chest at her clear wish to distance herself from him.

"Yeah." Dani pushed the button on her phone and held it up to her ear. "So, what's going on?" Dani's eyes widened as she listened. "You're kidding me," she said. She narrowed her eyes on him as she nodded to Hannah's words.

With a shrug, Quinn walked further into the barn. He knew the routine. They'd have to take all the horses out of their stalls and into the fenced pen before they could start mucking stalls. Dani had already taken two out, so Quinn went to the next full stall closest to the other side of the barn.

After clipping the lead onto the horse's halter, he stepped back into the aisle and began to lead the horse toward the open doors, away from Dani.

"Well, would you look at that," Dani said with a snide tone. Quinn slowed his steps. "It's not often I see two horses' asses walking through my barn at the same time."

Quinn stopped and met her eyes.

"Why didn't you tell me her guest was Carter?" She stepped around him, and he lowered his gaze to her. "Why did you leave her there with Carter?"

"She told me to leave," Quinn scoffed.

"Yes, Quinn." Dani's steely eyes shot daggers at him. "She told you to leave. But you could have stayed. We all thought Carter was dead, but none of us were as affected by it as much as Hannah was." She waved her hands in the air. "Lose whatever male ego trip you're on. You're not the victim here."

"She's not a victim either," he muttered as he strolled past her, leading the docile horse out of the barn.

"Excuse me?" Dani snapped.

Quinn opened the gate, led the horse into the pasture, then unhooked the lead. He stepped out of the pen and closed the gate behind him. Dani stood a foot away with her arms folded over her chest, her toe tapping, and a glare that held him hostage to her anger.

"What was I supposed to do? She was mad at me and didn't want me around. She told me to leave, so I did." He threw his arms out in a resigned shrug.

The look in her eyes softened. "Being mad at you isn't the same as not wanting you around. Trust me, there were plenty of times I was mad at my husband, but that didn't mean I didn't want him by my side."

Quinn looked at his feet. He knew coming here was a mistake. Regardless of what she said, Dani would always side with Hannah. He never would have gotten much sympathy, because in order for that to happen, Quinn would have to tell Dani everything. Not just what had happened the day before with Hannah, but everything that had happened with Alexa.

That wasn't going to happen.

He stood prepared to take whatever vitriol she decided to throw at him, regardless of whether he thought he deserved it or not. He shouldn't have left Hannah with Carter, but he couldn't change that now.

"What were you thinking?" Dani sighed, defeated.

Quinn's breath hitched when he saw the sympathy in her eyes.

"Well?"

"I asked her to come with me. She looked directly at me and told me to leave. I thought I was giving her what she wanted," Quinn said slowly.

Dani cocked her head to the side. "What she needed was a friend. Imagine what she's going through right now. She's finally living her life again and her dead fiancé just shows up on her doorstep."

Quinn tried to keep the guilt at bay. Hannah had been in shock, so maybe she hadn't known what she was saying. He walked toward the fence and rested his forearms on the top rail as he looked over the horses. He felt a small hand on his shoulder and fought the urge to shake it off.

"Quinn?" Dani said softly.

"He was her fiancé," Quinn said. "I thought she would know how to handle him." *Once the shock wore off.* "She never talked about him. She almost always changed the subject when someone brought him up or simply didn't respond at all." He hated the monotony in his voice. He didn't like feeling so down.

"Handle him? A man who came back from the dead?" Dani dropped her hand from his shoulder. "You were friends with him—how many people did you know who could *handle* him?"

Quinn shrugged. "Nobody handled Carter Elliot." He commanded everyone.

"Exactly." Dani leaned her hip against the fence post. "What makes you think Hannah was any different?"

"They were engaged."

Dani shook her head. "That doesn't mean the manipulation stopped."

"He manipulated her?" Quinn asked, though he wasn't surprised.

"He manipulated everyone," Dani scoffed. "How else do you think he convinced Hannah—the only person I ever knew who didn't want to leave Rocky Creek—that being a Navy wife and traveling the world would be an adventure? He knew what to say to get what he wanted out of her. By the way, did you ever talk to her about your exes?" Dani asked.

"No," he said.

"Are you not over them?"

He turned his face toward her. "Of course I'm over them."

"Then what makes you think it's any different for Hannah?"

Words failed him as he looked out toward the landscape again. Why did he think it was any different for her? He hadn't once mentioned Alexa or any of the other women he'd previously dated, not because he wasn't over them, but because they didn't matter in his relationship with Hannah.

Had he been wrong? Dani was giving him the distinct impression that he had been, but how could he be certain?

"That's what I thought," Dani muttered. "Think carefully about what

I'm about to ask you, Quinn." She remained silent until he met her stare. "Did she ever actually choose him over you? With words?"

Quinn fought not to think about everything that had happened the day before, but as the memory came to him, he understood what Dani was asking. Hannah had barely said a word. Sure, she'd stared at Carter and hadn't really acknowledged Quinn's presence. She was in shock. And who wouldn't be? Her fiancé had come back from the dead.

He swallowed around the new lump in his throat. He'd walked out on her. Even if she could get past him possibly moving to Atlanta, could she forgive him for that?

"You understand what I'm asking," Dani said. "Quinn, she deserves better than Carter, and if she means as much to you as I think she does, you need to fix this."

"I don't know that I can." To his own ears, he sounded defeated. Given the look of pity in her eyes, he guessed she'd heard it too.

"It won't hurt to try," Dani said, pushing away from the fence. "But first, we muck stalls." She took a step toward the barn, holding her arm forward as if leading a charge on the battlefield.

He smirked as he followed her into the barn.

Twenty-Five

"My baby's back," Sylvia cried as she threw her arms around Carter. Darren pulled his son and wife in his arms, and the three of them huddled together on the front porch, sobbing and hugging.

Hannah stood near the edge of the porch and wondered how she'd ended up here. She'd told Carter that she wouldn't cater to his every whim, and she'd held firm. But he'd convinced her to take him to see his parents, since that was where his car had been sent. The only reason she'd agreed was so he wouldn't use his lack of transportation as an excuse to spend time with her. Last night, she'd locked herself in the spare room, and had spent as much time as she could in there today, until it was time to go to his parents' home so they could arrive just after the Elliots returned from church.

Being at his parents' house was somewhat of a relief because she knew she wouldn't have to say much of anything. Sylvia would prefer it that way.

Hannah let the family have their moment. She leaned against the porch post and studied the house. Vinyl gray boards stretched the length and height of the two-story home. The porch stretched the length of the house and wrapped around halfway to the back. On the other side of the door, the porch was open with three stone steps that led to a small patio in front of the large bay window. It had been over a year since she'd been here, immediately following the funeral.

Sylvia patted Carter's cheeks, coddling and fretting over him. Hannah lifted her gaze to the ceiling and smirked at the small nest tucked into a corner over the door. She was surprised Sylvia would let something so imperfect mar her pristine porch.

"Why didn't you tell us you were home?" Sylvia cooed. "And why is *she* here?"

If Hannah had her way, Carter would have been home with his mother the night before instead of tapping on the door to the spare bedroom at regular intervals, looking for something or wanting to talk about something, as she tried to sleep off her migraine. It had quickly progressed to a full headache, nausea, and vertigo as soon as she'd reached the top of the stairs. His constant interruptions had only delayed her recovery. She was still feeling the effects and wanted to crawl back into bed as soon as she could.

"She's my fiancée, Mom," Carter answered with a dismissive chuckle.

"Oh really?" Sylvia snapped, narrowing her eyes at Hannah.

"That's enough." Darren stepped back and directed the party into the house. With his son and wife inside, he smiled sympathetically at Hannah and motioned for her to follow. "How long has he been home?"

"He came home yesterday," Hannah said.

"Are you happy he's home?" Darren draped his arm over her shoulder and led her inside.

"Of course." She smiled softly at him as he closed the door behind them. They paused in the foyer, and he studied her face.

She could probably be honest with him. Over the years, she'd developed a sort of camaraderie with the man who might have been her father-in-law. But she decided against it. His son had come back from the dead, and she didn't want to burden him with her problems.

"I'm just tired," she answered gently. "I didn't sleep well."

"That's understandable." He gave her arm a squeeze, then strolled into the living room and settled on the end of the plush white leather sofa close to his son. Hannah followed at a slower pace.

Carter sat in his father's leather armchair and his mother sat on the edge of the sofa, leaning as close to him as she could. Hannah sat in the armchair near the white brick fireplace.

"Where have you been?" Sylvia patted Carter's leg. "I just can't believe you're home. I hoped and prayed for this." She cast Hannah a quick scowl. "At least I never gave up on you."

Hannah forced her features to remain neutral. She refused to let Sylvia's words anger her.

"I knew you wouldn't give up." Carter beamed at his mother. "As for where I've been," he said. "I was in Afghanistan."

"Afghanistan?" Sylvia gasped. "Oh my."

"We were on patrol when we were ambushed and captured."

Sylvia's lower lip trembled.

"I thought you were at OCS," Hannah said.

"Hush," Sylvia hissed, her words directed at Hannah, her gaze remained on Carter. "No one asked for your input." Hannah held up a hand in surrender.

"Sylvia, be nice," Darren ordered.

"It was a top-secret mission," Carter whispered. "They made me use OCS as a cover story."

"Oh, I knew you wouldn't have flunked out." Sylvia's voice dripped with pride.

Hannah was confused. Carter had told everyone he was going through Officer Candidate School a second time because he'd flunked out the first time. Given he'd always needed a tutor in order to pass his classes, it wasn't out of the realm of possibility that he might fail.

"Where in Afghanistan were you?" Darren leaned forward, his elbows on his knees as he looked at his son.

"Kandahar," Carter said.

"Were you in a helicopter?" Hannah rose and moved toward the white marble mantle and watched him.

"No, it was a caravan of Humvees," he answered. "They took out the first one and the last one, and the rest of us were stuck."

"Oh," Sylvia gasped. "That sounds horrible." She gave his knee a squeeze. "You're so lucky to have survived."

"How many others were captured?" Hannah asked.

"Uh . . ." Carter hesitated. "At least eight." His voice lifted a little at the end of his statement, as if he weren't sure of his answer.

Hannah glanced at the photos on the mantle. They were all of Carter at various stages of his life. There was even one of him at the prom with her, except Hannah had either been cut out completely or Sylvia had just folded the photo in half.

"How many Humvees were there?" Darren asked.

"What does it matter? Such minor details," Sylvia tutted. "The important thing is that Carter is alive and well. And home where he belongs." She leaned forward. "You could always move back home if you want," she whispered.

Hannah ignored the pointed look from Sylvia. "So, how many Humvees?" Hannah repeated Darren's question.

Carter scoffed as he shrugged his shoulders. "I don't really remember. Maybe five total."

Hannah was confused. So many lives lost, yet she couldn't remember hearing anything about it on the news.

"Are you hungry, my love?" Sylvia asked.

"How did you get away from your captors?" Hannah asked. Carter's eyes twitched, and he clenched his jaw.

"That's a great question," Darren added.

"No, it's not," Sylvia snapped at her husband. "All that matters is that he's home. That's it, end of story."

Carter held Hannah's glare. "We dug a hole in the wall and escaped during one of their shift changes. It took us over a year, but we managed to do it."

"Where did—"

"That's enough," Sylvia exclaimed as she jumped to her feet. "No more questions. He's home, and that's all I care about." She flashed a bright smile and turned to her son. "Now, would you like to eat?"

"Yes." Carter pushed himself up from his chair. "I'm starving, and there wasn't much choice for breakfast."

Fighting the urge to roll her eyes, Hannah said, "There were sausage biscuits in the freezer."

"I've never liked those." His voice was light, but Hannah heard the challenge in his tone. He wanted her to argue with him in front of his mother. He knew he had at least one ally in the room and that Sylvia would take his side and make Hannah feel small in the process.

"That doesn't surprise me," Sylvia said as they passed Hannah. "But don't worry, I have plenty of your favorites here. And if I don't, your father can run out and get it." Her voice faded as she and Carter walked into the kitchen.

Hannah glanced at the photos on the mantle. She'd never seen the photo in the center before. Two men in uniform presented Sylvia with the flag that had draped over the empty casket. They were the same men who had delivered the news of Carter's death. But there was something else about them that niggled at her mind. Something else about them was familiar. She took her phone out of her pocket and snapped a picture of the photo. She'd have plenty of time later to study it.

Darren rose to his feet. "Are you sure you're only tired?" he asked. "Carter's return is a rather dramatic event."

Hannah smiled. He had no idea how much his son's return had turned her life upside down. "It is unbelievable," she said, "but I'll be fine."

"I know you will." He gave her upper arm a squeeze.

"Sweetheart, would you like to join your son and I for some lunch?" Sylvia sang from the kitchen.

Darren looked at Hannah with a question in his eyes.

"I'm not hungry. Go eat with them."

Darren disappeared into the kitchen. Hannah took a deep, cleansing breath. She would have liked having him as a father-in-law. She cast a quick glance at the photos on the mantle again, then headed for the front door with every intention of sitting on the little patio. It may be cold outside, but it was still warmer than Sylvia's company.

Hannah stood on the porch of her parents' house and reached for the doorknob as Carter parked his car behind hers on the street.

"You know the plan, right?" Carter hopped out of his car and rushed toward her lest she open the door and ruin his fun.

She'd agreed to take him to his parents' house because that was where his car was . . . or so they thought. His parents had put it in storage so it wouldn't take up space in their driveway. Darren had wanted to sell the car, but Sylvia wanted to keep it to preserve her son's memory, so the storage facility was their compromise. After lunch, Hannah had driven Carter to the storage unit to pick up his car, then she headed home.

She'd considered going to the farm, but Quinn might be there, and she wasn't quite ready to see him. So Hannah had spent the afternoon resting and packing. She didn't believe for a minute that Carter would actively look for a place to live, let alone find one by the end of the week. So she started to plan for her own escape. As dinnertime neared, she got ready to go to her parents' house, hoping to get out of the house before Carter returned. But as her luck would have it, he was walking up the sidewalk just as she closed the door behind her.

Carter was persistent about going with her to visit her family. "After all, they are my family too," he'd said. After much arguing, and a headache starting to throb behind her right eye, Hannah finally relented.

"Hannah? The plan?" Carter whispered, and she turned to face him.

"Sure," she absentmindedly replied. He wanted her to go in and talk up the surprise of his arrival as much as she could. He wanted her family to fawn over him and his return with delight and, he hoped, tears of joy. Hannah was disgusted by his need for the hoopla and fuss, but her headache was getting worse, so going along with him was easier than trying to fight the idea.

"Let's do this then." Carter stepped into the shadow of the house cast by the porch light. Hannah watched him hide and rolled her eyes.

She opened the front door to find her father standing in the hallway. She closed the door behind her and greeted her father with a quick hug.

"Hey sweetie," he said, and tears pricked her eyes. Her father had always been a source of security for her, but knowing that, right now at least, he was probably the only man she could count on, made the hug that much more special.

"Hey, Dad," she whispered and looked up to see her mother walking toward them. She pulled away from her father. "Mom, you're up and moving." It was so good to see her mom feeling well enough to greet her at the door. That hadn't been the case for several months.

"Hi, darling," her mother said, wrapping Hannah in a weak hug. When they separated, her father slid his arm around his wife's back, and Hannah realized she wasn't as strong as she appeared. "You said you have a surprise for us?" Her mother glanced down at Hannah's hand. Was she looking for a ring?

Her heart fell at the obvious expectations. Sadly, an engagement wasn't in the cards for her.

"Oh yeah," Hannah muttered. "He's on the porch." She waved toward the door with the back of her hand as she turned toward the dining room on her way to the kitchen. "Go ahead and open the door."

Kailee bounced down the stairs. "Ugh, you're here."

"There's a surprise for you on the porch, you brat." Hannah ignored the open-mouthed look Kailee gave her and turned toward the kitchen.

"Surprise!" Carter exclaimed as he burst through the front door.

Hannah cast a glance at her parents and sister, long enough to register the look of shock on their faces. *Mission accomplished*, she thought wryly, then turned to the freezer and tried to tune out the exclamations and conversation by the door.

"OMG! Carter! You're alive!" Kailee squealed as Hannah buried her face in the freezer and examined the frozen meals.

"Carter?" Her mother sounded confused.

"Carter?" Her father's tone was apprehensive, which didn't really surprise Hannah. Her father had always questioned Hannah's relationship with Carter, but once they were engaged, she had convinced her dad that she truly was happy with him.

"Murphy family!" Carter exclaimed. "It's so good to see you all!"

Hannah pulled out a chicken pot pie. While she liked the things she prepared for her family, nothing could beat Nancy Harris's chicken pot pie for comfort food.

"I . . . I don't know what to say," her mother said.

"What? How?" her father exclaimed. Then he said, "Let's go to the living room and sit."

Hannah pushed the freezer door closed with her thigh. Her father walked past, his arms tightly around her mom, who looked utterly bewildered. Carter followed her parents into the living room, Kailee hanging off his arm, her eyes alight with joy.

Hannah shook her head in disgust; her sister had never been half that excited to see her. A small wave of sadness washed over her. She tried to listen to the conversation in the other room as she dropped the foil dish on the stove. As expected, Carter was wallowing in her sister's enthusiasm to see him again. Her father appeared at her side, his eyes clouded with concern.

"Do you think Mom will mind a chicken pot pie tonight?" Hannah spoke before he had a chance to question the current situation. "I know it's her favorite, but I saw another in the freezer. I can always call Mrs. Harris to ask her to fix more, if you'd like."

"Hannah," her father said softly. "What's going on?"

"It's a miracle. Carter has returned from the dead."

He pressed his lips together. "I mean with you."

"Nothing, Dad. Nothing is going on with me," Hannah said. "Look, he showed up yesterday, and I still can't wrap my head around it. I hadn't planned on bringing him tonight. After lunch today with his mother, I've spent the day trying to avoid him. I'm really not in the mood to talk about him or what's going on with him."

Her father's frown deepened.

"I just want him to say his hellos and goodbyes and leave. As much as I love all of you, I want to get dinner over with as quickly as possible so I can go home and put an end to this miserable weekend." Hannah turned away from him, blinking back tears, as she preheated the oven. She'd been stressed and on the cusp of tears most of the day. She'd taken three doses of ibuprofen already, with little success, and was trying very hard to avoid taking another before she got home.

While Carter's return, and everything that came with it, had been at the forefront of her stressors, the one causing the most pain was the situation with Quinn. Trying not to let her mind wander to Quinn as she moved clothes from the master bedroom to the spare had been harder than she'd prepared herself for. Especially after a sleepless night, punctuated by Carter knocking on the door until he went to bed himself.

"I can take care of this if you want to take a break." Her father laid his hand on her shoulder, and she turned toward him. With a slow nod, she stepped into his arms and let herself relax into his embrace. She drew strength from him, then stepped back and gave an unsteady smile.

"Thanks, Dad."

He kissed her forehead, and she walked out of the kitchen and started up the steps. When she heard her sister ask where he'd been, Hannah paused and turned back toward the living room.

"I was being held hostage in Kabul," Carter answered.

Hannah scrunched her face in confusion. That wasn't what he'd told his parents.

"How did you get captured?" her father asked. Hannah took another step closer, leaning her shoulder against the wall so she could see into the room. Carter sat in an armchair, while Kailee sat on the end of the couch, hanging on every word.

"I was in a caravan of Humvees that was ambushed."

"That sounds scary." Kailee scooted closer. "Were you scared?"

Carter met Hannah's stare and smiled. "Not for a minute," he answered. "We fought back as much as we could, but in the end, we were all captured."

"How many were taken?" her mother asked.

"Twelve of us were captured, three were killed," Carter answered. "They tortured us, questioned us, and tried to trade us for their own people. But we managed to escape six months ago and have been trying to get home ever since."

Hannah turned on her heels and went up the stairs toward her safe haven.

Twenty-Six

Hannah sat on her window seat, looking out at the graying skies. She'd hoped to escape her problems up here but only half succeeded. She could avoid Carter, which had been part of her reason for wanting to come to her family home in the first place. But she'd had more time to spend with herself, and her thoughts, which had been bad. She hadn't been able to stop feeling sorry for herself.

Now that Carter was home, she felt like her life was in a holding pattern. Until she could convince him that their relationship was over, he was going to make moving on as difficult as he could. He didn't like to lose, and he rarely heard the word "no." He was never going to convince her to work it out. She was never going to persuade him it was over.

She felt ashamed that she was still not strong enough to say what she wanted in a firm enough way to be believed the first time. Before going to his parents, she'd argued with Carter, telling him exactly how she felt about him. Or what she didn't feel for him. He'd laughed her off, then promptly changed the subject. She'd known then that they were destined to repeat the same discussion, with the same results, at some point in the very near future.

She was sorry that she'd gotten her hopes up so quickly with Quinn, only to have them dashed so hard. She hated the way things had ended with him. She still wanted to have one last conversation with him. She still hoped that, just maybe, they could make things work.

And that small hope was probably what she was most sorry for.

"Hannah, could you come down here please?" Her mother's soft tone drifted up the attic stairs.

Slowly, she rose and walked to the open door of her attic sanctuary. She stuck her head through only to find her mother standing at the bottom, leaning against the doorframe and looking up at her.

"Dinner ready?" Hannah started down the steps.

"Not yet," her mother said. "I just thought we could talk for a bit."

Hannah heard the breathlessness in her tone and hurried down the last few steps. She reached for her mother's arms, and her mother shook her hands away.

"I'm fine," she said lightly. "I just forget how tiring the steps are. Your dad usually helps me." She sat on the edge of Hannah's bed and patted the mattress beside her.

Hannah dutifully sat next to her mother. "What do you want to talk about?" she hesitantly asked.

Her mother held her stare. "I want to know how you're doing." She waved toward the closed bedroom door. "With everything."

Hannah slumped and looked toward her window.

"And don't tell me you're fine."

Hannah bit back tears. How did her mom always know? Where should she begin?

"How are things with Quinn?" She took Hannah's hand and held it on the mattress between them.

"Over." Hannah felt the sting of tears behind her eyes again. She blinked them away furiously.

"Because of Carter? That doesn't seem right."

"No, it was almost over just before Carter came back," Hannah said. "Carter was just the final nail in the coffin." She let the tears fall. She'd been fighting them all day and was tired.

"What happened?" Her mother's soft hazel eyes filled with pity.

"He's moving, Mom."

Her mother chuckled. "So?"

"So?" Hannah scoffed lightly. "So, I don't want to move."

"Did he ask you to?"

A new wave of tears flowed freely down Hannah's cheeks. Would he have asked? She'd refused to talk to him, so she had no idea if he even thought enough of her, of their relationship, to ask her to move with him. They hadn't been dating long enough to make such life-altering decisions.

Hannah swallowed the lump in her throat. "We didn't get the chance to talk about it."

"You want to tell me what happened?" Her mother cupped Hannah's cheek and thumbed a tear away.

Her mother listened in silence as Hannah talked about everything she'd thought and felt after finding the different itineraries. She confessed to giving Quinn the silent treatment all the way back to her house as he'd tried, in vain, to explain the situation to her. Then Hannah told her that Quinn had left her with Carter.

"He just left?" Her mother raised her brows. "That doesn't sound like him."

"I may have asked him to go. I was in shock. I honestly didn't know what was going on at the time. I was so confused and it's all fuzzy." Her tears eased to a stop. "Not that it matters. Our relationship would have ended when he moves anyway, so I guess it was inevitable."

"Why?" Her mother tipped her head to the side. "I've never understood your adamant refusal to leave Rocky Creek."

They'd had a similar discussion when Hannah had cried on her mother's shoulder when Carter had joined the Navy. Her mother had encouraged her to view a move as an adventure. She wanted her daughters to see more of the world.

"We'll still be here for you. And your friends—if they really are friends—will still be a part of your life too, Hannah." Her mother slid closer. "The people who love you will always be around for you, no matter where you live."

"But my students, and the store, and the farm." Hannah sighed. "Those aren't things I can replace."

"You would have new students to nurture, wherever you go." Mom smiled. "And I'm sure you would find other things to fill the extra time."

Hannah scoffed at the idea. None of it mattered at the moment. Quinn hadn't asked her to move. And if he'd ever meant to, it probably wouldn't happen now.

"So, then, what's going on with Carter? I know you're not happy." She gave Hannah's fingers a light squeeze.

"You know how I felt about him before he disappeared." Hannah waited for her mother to nod. "Well, I can't convince *him* of that. He thinks that my feelings are a result of him being away for so long and that if we spend every waking moment together, I'll change my mind." Hannah rolled her eyes. "I'm not going to change my mind. I don't want to be with him anymore, but I can't convince him of that."

Her mother clicked her tongue. "I'm so sorry, baby. I know this isn't easy. I'm confused, so I can't imagine what you must be feeling. He was in Afghanistan? I thought he was going through OCS."

Hannah heaved a heavy sigh. "Me too."

She didn't know what to think. Carter didn't look like someone who'd been in a POW camp six months ago. He looked as healthy as the day he'd left. Something didn't add up. The story he'd told her family was just a little more dramatic than what he'd told his parents. Maybe he wanted to impress her sister, but maybe he was just remembering things better. Either way, she had a hard time believing the Navy would claim he'd died if he'd been captured, or that they would have failed to inform his family once he'd been discovered alive. Since she wasn't getting any answers from Carter, she decided to have a conversation with Rachel's husband, Seth, to see if he could use his ties as a Navy recruiter to find out the truth. Hopefully, she could have that talk with him tomorrow.

"You don't believe that he was really captured, do you?" her mom asked quietly, as if she were trying to work it out in her own head. The concern and curiosity etched in the lines of her features.

"I don't know what to believe," Hannah said.

Her mother scooted closer and patted her hand. "We'll figure it out."

There was a rap on Hannah's door before it swung open to reveal Kailee on the other side. Hannah cast a quick glance at her sister before looking away. Knowing how excited Kailee was for Carter's return made it hard for Hannah to face her.

"Dinner's ready," Kailee sang as she spun and sped off down the stairs.

Mom squeezed Hannah's fingers. "If you need anything, don't hesitate to ask. I'll never be so ill that I can't help you."

Hannah smiled. "I will." She embraced her mother in a hug. "I love you."

Carter cruised through the door of the townhouse as soon as Hannah had the door unlocked.

"Today was a great day." Carter's voice reverberated through the house.

Hannah dropped her purse onto the table. She was emotionally drained. She had zoned out over dinner while Carter talked about basic training and the situation that had gotten him captured. Her parents were mostly silent, while Kailee had gushed over Carter's stories of heroism.

Carter's stories sounded too good to be true. His tales were almost too scripted, maybe in the way they happened, and certainly in the way he told them. As she'd listened to him kissing up to her parents, she'd texted Rachel to set up a meeting with Seth after school the next day. Not that anything Seth said would change Hannah's mind, but she needed to know the truth, and she wouldn't get that from Carter.

At least not willingly.

Wasn't today fun?" Carter asked. He was leaning against the doorframe between the kitchen and living room, beaming at her.

She took a deep, calming breath. "No," she said. "Not really."

He chuckled. "C'mon. We had lunch with my parents—"

"Your mom hates me," Hannah snapped.

He snorted. "My dad likes you," he continued. "And we had dinner with your family. At least that should have made you happy."

"Not because I asked you to."

He pushed away from the doorway and walked toward her. "I thought you would enjoy seeing your family."

"I was going to their house without you." She crossed her arms and strolled past him into the living room. "You only wanted to go today so you could make a big deal of your return from the dead." Hannah lowered herself onto the seat of the glider and leaned her head back. Her head was pulsing stronger than it had all day. She closed her eyes and rocked in the chair.

"I wasn't dead." Carter's voice was a low grumble as she heard him move through the room.

"Right," Hannah said slowly. "Where were you being held?"

"I told you already." He plopped onto the couch. "I was in Kirkuk."

That wasn't what he'd said at all. "And how were you captured?"

"Hannah, why are we discussing this again?" he snapped. "You heard what I told my parents. You heard what I told your family. You already have all the answers you need."

She turned her head toward him. He'd never physically hurt her, but the look in his eyes dared her to continue at her own peril. He hated being questioned, and he hated being doubted. She could only imagine what he thought about her right now, and she was sure it was nothing good. Hannah was pleased to realize she didn't really care that he was angry with her.

That was a new feeling.

She closed her eyes and focused on easing the tension in her head. She couldn't afford another migraine; she didn't want to be home with him. She was actually looking forward to going to work tomorrow, if only to get away from Carter.

She heard him slide across the sofa, closer to her. His hand wrapped around hers and she pulled away.

"Why don't we spend tomorrow doing what you want to do?"

She opened her eyes and stared at the ceiling, then lowered her gaze to his face. "I have to work."

"Take the day off." He beamed at her. "It will be fun."

"Like today?" she scoffed.

"More." He leaned closer. "We'll do your favorite things."

She lifted her head. "Really?"

He nodded.

"And what would those things be?" She felt confident that he had no idea what her favorite activities were, but she was willing to be surprised.

"We could have brunch," he started. "Then go bowling. Then maybe go to the lake and play some mini golf and rent a boat."

Hannah laughed. She couldn't help herself; his suggestions were ridiculous.

"What?" He chuckled with her. "Doesn't that sound nice?"

Hannah's laughter faded to a giggle. "It sounds awful."

The humor in his face died. "What?"

"First, no one offers brunch on a Monday."

The corners of his lips turned down and his shoulders fell. She almost pitied him.

"Second, it's November. You can't play mini golf or rent boats at the lake. It's too cold and the rental places are closed."

She waited for him to respond but he remained silent.

"I have school tomorrow." She rose to her feet and started toward the steps.

"Where are you going?" He stood up and grabbed her wrist as she reached the bottom step.

She stopped and stared at the hand that gripped her. "I'm going to bed." She gave her arm a shake.

He released his grasp. "But it's early. I thought we could watch TV or a movie."

"Carter, I'm tired, I have a headache, and I have to get up early in the morning." She climbed two steps.

"But—"

"Goodnight." She climbed the stairs, feeling lighter the closer she got to the top.

As she prepared for bed, she reviewed everything she had heard Carter say throughout the day and made a mental list of questions for Seth. After she washed up in the bathroom, she locked herself in the spare bedroom.

The cigar box that Sylvia had dropped off was sitting on top of the vanity. Hannah sat on the bed and slowly sifted through the pictures, studying each one. There were photos of her and Carter, and toward the bottom of the pile were photos from his days in basic. Finally, she found the photo she was looking for.

It was a photo of Carter with two men who didn't look like they belonged in the Navy. Their longer hair, brushing the tops of their shoulders, stood out in the crowd of high and tight haircuts, including Carter's. They all wore huge smiles on their faces. She finally realized why the photo on the Elliots' mantle was so familiar. Staring back at her were the men who had delivered the bad news to her. The men who'd shown up at her house to tell her that Carter had died. The men who had given Sylvia the flag. The men who clearly weren't who they'd led her to believe.

Her stomach clenched, and her head thumped with the beating of her heart. These men weren't in any branch of the military. Did they help Carter fake his death? And, more importantly, why? Had he wanted out of marriage so badly that he faked his own death? Her heart ached at the thought. Even if she had wanted to call off the engagement, part of her wondered if there was something wrong with her. Was the idea of marrying her so repulsive to him?

She shook that thought away. Why was he now so determined to pick up where they'd left off? None of it made sense anymore. Maybe it wasn't her that he was running from after all. Maybe he was in danger. Or maybe he was trying to hide something else entirely.

Suddenly, the three different cities Carter listed made sense. He likely hadn't been in any of them. Where he had been for the past year remained a question, but as she recalled everything Carter had said today, a quiet resolve settled over her. She had more questions than answers, but hopefully a conversation with Seth would fix that.

With a shaky hand, Hannah closed the lid to the box and set the picture on top. She'd be sure to take that to her meeting with Seth tomorrow. She rolled the stress from her neck and shoulders. Her eyes landed on the photo of the sunset that Quinn had admired so much. Her heart ached and tears stung the back of her eyes.

She missed him.

She had started, then deleted, several text messages to Quinn throughout the day. She missed seeing his smile, hearing his laugh, feeling his touch. She couldn't remember ever feeling this way about Carter. Even in the early days of their relationship, Carter hadn't caused this level of heartache with his absence.

Hannah heard movement on the stairs and popped up from the bed to turn off the overhead light. As her eyes adjusted to the darkness, she listened for movement outside. How had her life turned so upside down in such a short time? She was hiding from the man who still considered himself her fiancé, while the man she wanted to be with was probably packing to move away.

As she shuffled to the bed, she forced herself to remember that Quinn was leaving. He was moving to a big city so he could pursue his dreams. She couldn't stop him; she shouldn't stop him. If this move, and the career that came with it, was everything he wanted, she had to let him go. That was the only way she could protect her heart. After changing into her pajamas, she eased herself onto the mattress and under the covers, and sobbed herself to sleep.

Twenty-Seven

The knock on his front door pulled Quinn's attention away from the new kitchen plans on his desk. After leaving the barn the day before, he'd buried himself in work. He swiveled in his chair to look out the window and saw Tori smiling widely, waving her fingers at him. With a heavy sigh, he pushed away from his desk and walked through the house to greet his guest.

He opened the front door. "Hello, Tori."

She threw her arms around his neck. "Hi, Quinn, it's good to see you." She released him and pushed her way into the house. "What a cute home."

"Thanks." He closed the door with a grumble. "Why are you here?"

"Oh, I was just in the neighborhood."

She walked the perimeter of the living room, studying everything she came across.

Quinn watched her make her circle around the room as he strolled toward the kitchen. He stopped in the doorway between the rooms and leaned his shoulder against the doorframe.

"Did you remodel this room?" Tori stopped at the fireplace, bent over, and looked into the hearth.

"A little bit," Quinn said. "Why do you ask?"

Tori continued to peruse the room. "Are there any other rooms you modified?" She cast a quick glance at him before focusing on the hardwood floor.

"The master bedroom and bathroom," he said. "Why are you asking these questions?"

Again, she ignored him as she finished her loop around the room. Stopping in front of him, she beamed up at him. "Rumor has it you're moving out of state."

Quinn's mouth fell open. Who was talking about his possible move? He'd told Hannah, Rachel, and Dani, but felt certain none of them would have told anyone else, least of all Tori. He'd also told his parents, so maybe they were sharing that information around town. Regardless, he was fairly certain he now knew why Tori was here.

"You shouldn't believe rumors."

Tori laughed lightly. "So, you haven't been offered another job?"

Quinn started to answer her, then clamped his mouth shut. The last time he told Tori a secret, she'd used it against him. She was the only person he'd told about his wish to take Hannah to prom. First, Tori had tried to talk him out of it by attempting to convince him that Hannah wasn't good enough—she was too much of a nerd, she was so uncool, she wasn't that pretty. When that didn't work, she'd dared Carter to ask Hannah to prom, right in front of him. He'd stopped talking to her after that and had barely spoken to her more than once or twice in the past six years.

"That's really none of your concern," he said.

Tori's smile fell as she scanned the room behind him. "This kitchen could use some work." She glided around him.

Quinn pivoted to face the kitchen as she began her stroll around that room.

"I don't know why you haven't taken it. It sounds like a great opportunity for you." She stared at the empty hole where the refrigerator once stood. "Are you going to fix this room before you sell?"

Quinn clenched his jaw. "I haven't said anything about selling."

"You'll rent this place out then?" She tipped her head sideways as she slowly nodded. "That could work too."

"I didn't say that. You're not listening," Quinn snapped.

He wasn't really surprised. She rarely ever listened to anything she didn't want to hear. He walked to the dining table and lowered himself into a chair. "I may or may not have a job offer, and I haven't even hinted at selling my house. So, why are you here?"

"Oh, Quinn." She clicked her tongue as she strolled toward him. "You poor thing." She eased into the chair beside him. "Why?"

"Why what?" Quinn growled.

She leaned forward. "*If* you have a great opportunity for a lucrative career in a big city, you should take it. Why would you turn that down to stay here?"

Quinn forced a long, low breath out of his nose. "Are we friends?" He knew what she was hinting at, but he wanted her to say it.

"Of course," she said brightly as she reached for his hand again.

"Then be honest." He leaned away from her reach, crossed his arms, and glared at her. "You want to sell my house. Why?"

Tori withdrew her hand and pulled her shoulders back. "Fine. Yes, I want to sell your house. It's a nice little piece of property, and I have several buyers who would like it." She looked over her shoulder. "After you finish the kitchen, of course."

"What if I don't want to move?" Quinn's jaw was aching from being clenched.

"Why would you stay?" She gave him a sweet, placating smile. "More importantly, why would you stay in such a large house?" She hummed lightly.

His temper boiled in his chest. "Stop beating around the bush. Say what you're trying not to say."

The bright mask fell away, and Tori lifted her chin. "Fine. Since you insist." She popped up from her seat and walked toward the sliding glass door. "I don't know why you bought this house in the first place, but since you have no one to share it with, I thought you might be willing to give it up. I don't really care if you move out of town or not, but I don't think you need all this space." She waved her hands around the room. "It's selfish."

"You would know all about that," Quinn seethed. Tori stiffened, but he wouldn't regret his words. She had always been the most selfish person he knew. She never did anything unless she thought it would benefit her in some way.

She walked toward him. "I just thought since Hannah and Carter are back together . . ."

Quinn forced his face to remain impassive as he shifted his gaze toward the glass door.

"And since I've never really seen you dating anyone else, you might be up for a change of scenery." She placed her small hand on his shoulder. "You know it's for the best. It will be easier."

"For who?" He brushed her hand away and rose to his feet.

"For everyone involved." She sighed. "You could use a change, and Hannah doesn't need you around to distract her."

They were finally getting somewhere.

"Hannah and Carter need time, without distraction, to remind her why they are so perfect together." Tori beamed up at him. "Surely you can understand that."

Quinn walked toward the living room. "What I understand is you think I should be out of Carter's way. What I can't understand is why you think I would be a distraction if they are so perfect for each other."

Tori's eyes widened with surprise.

"Hannah is smart enough to know what, or who, is perfect for her, and if she thinks it is Carter, then my presence shouldn't be much of a problem." Quinn turned to the front door. "Now, since I'm not interested in selling my house, there isn't much reason for you to be here."

He opened the door and waited. Then he heard the clack of her heels on the wood floor. She stopped in front of him and opened her mouth to say something, but he held up a hand to stop her.

"And I don't think Hannah would appreciate your interference in her life." He waved toward her car. "If you want to keep that little secret between us, I suggest you leave without another word."

Tori remained silent as she stomped across his porch and down the steps. She threw her car door open, paused to glare at him, then huffed as she slid into her car.

Quinn stepped onto the porch as she sped away. He shoved his hands into his pockets and watched her spin out on the gravel as she pulled onto the main road. As her car faded in the distance, his shoulders released their tension.

Maybe Tori was right. Maybe he was a distraction to Hannah. But if that were true, then was she really happy? Could he abandon her if she wasn't? Yes, he still wanted to be with her, but it was more important to him that she was happy.

And if she were happy, could he stay around and watch?

A breeze blew through him, causing a chill to run down his spine.

Somehow, he thought watching Hannah's life from a distance would be far worse than anything he'd felt with Alexa.

When he stepped back inside, he shook the chill away. Before Tori had shown up, he'd almost had a plan. He had been settled on not moving and fighting for Hannah's affection. He'd been formulating a plan to try to gain her forgiveness. Even though Tori was trying to get a reaction out of him, he couldn't help but doubt everything. There was always the *what-if*. What if Tori wasn't just taunting him? What if Hannah really was happy—happier than Dani thought she might be—with Carter? What if staying to win her back was a fruitless endeavor? He leaned his back against the closed door and lifted his gaze to the ceiling. He was back to square one.

Quinn checked his watch, then grabbed his coat and checked the pockets for his keys. School was almost out, and if he wanted answers, he needed to go straight to the source.

"Thanks for meeting me on such short notice, Seth." Hannah closed the door to her classroom as Rachel's husband sat in the seat at her desk.

"When Rachel told me you had questions about the Navy, I thought I should come right over." He leaned his elbows on his knees. "She also told me you needed to get to the store, so we'll make this quick. What do you know, and what do you need to know?"

Hannah picked her bag up and pulled out the photo of Carter and the two men. "I assume she gave you a quick synopsis?"

"Very quick. She said it would be better for you to fill me in since the details were fuzzy for her."

"My ex-fiancé came back from the dead this weekend."

Seth said, "Rachel did mention that. What does that have to do with the Navy?"

"They—the Navy—told us he was dead fourteen months ago."

"Where was he really?" Seth asked.

Hannah shrugged. "That's the problem. I've heard his story, but it doesn't add up to me. And then there's this picture." She held it out to him.

Seth's eyes perused the picture. "Maybe you should start at the beginning."

"I am. It all started with the knock on my door, and those two men were in dress blues and delivered the news that Carter was dead. They also presented the flag at the funeral." Seth nodded as Hannah recalled everything she'd heard Carter tell everyone yesterday. "And when I questioned him again, he got angry."

Seth's jaw clenched. "Did he threaten you?"

"No, nothing like that. He never threatened me."

Seth's features slowly relaxed as he stared at the photo. "You're sure it was these two men?"

"The hair was shorter, not high and tight like Carter's is there, but certainly within regulation." Through Carter and Rachel, she'd learned a lot about the military and their requirements.

"Wait, there were only two?" he asked, and Hannah nodded. "Were either of them a chaplain?"

"Not that I could tell."

"Could you describe their uniforms?"

Hannah told him what each man was wearing, down to the buttons on each abdomen. He asked a few more questions about the day the news of Carter's death was delivered. When she finished retelling one of the worst days of her life, he hopped up from his seat and began to pace. Something was wrong and her knees felt weak.

"What is it?" she asked.

Seth paused in front of the whiteboard. "You've done nothing wrong, but I need to explain the process to you."

As he paced back and forth, he told her how the death notification should have happened. First and foremost, it should have happened within eight hours, but she hadn't been notified for over twenty-four hours. Second, the party making the notification should have included a military chaplain, and the uniforms were wrong for any rank that would have been appropriate for making the death notice.

"Write down what you know," Seth said. "Especially the contradictory things. I will need to know everything in order to investigate, and it needs to be documented."

Hannah pulled her legal pad out of her bottom desk drawer and recorded everything she'd just told Seth. When she was finished, she ripped the paper off the pad and handed it to him.

He folded the sheet and tucked it into his pocket. "Are you staying in the house with Carter or are you at Quinn's?"

"I'm at my house. With Carter. Quinn and I aren't really speaking right now."

"I'm sorry to hear that. Rachel hinted that things might not be good with Quinn," he said. "Are you safe in the house with Carter? We have a spare room we would gladly give you."

Hannah stood up and grabbed her bag. "I'm safe, but I have bags packed just in case."

"Good to know," he said as they strolled toward the door. "If you need anything, just say the word."

"Of course," she answered. "But you're already helping me out. I appreciate your assistance."

He tapped his first two fingers to his forehead in a mock salute. "Just doing my job, ma'am." She laughed as he wrenched the door open, and they found Rachel and Dani standing in the hall with their ears to the door.

"Well?" Rachel asked.

"I'll keep you all posted." Seth stepped into the hall and pulled his wife's arm through his own. "Right now, let's get out of here."

Hannah headed down the aisle of her father's store toward the cashier counter.

"Good afternoon, Donna." She strolled toward the cooler with the bottled water.

"He already has one for you in the office," Donna called after her.

Hannah stopped with her hand on the handle of the door. "He's still here?" she asked. Her meeting with Seth didn't take up too much time, but she was still late. It was odd for her father to stick around when he knew Hannah was coming in.

"Yes," Donna said.

"Thanks," Hannah said with a quick wave as she walked toward her dad's office.

When she reached the door, she froze. It wasn't her father sitting at the desk working on the payroll for the store.

She stared at Quinn's back, careful not to make a sound as she drank in the sight of him. She was still hurt and confused over their fight, but her heart still fluttered when she saw him.

She cleared her throat. Quinn slowly turned to face her.

"What are you doing here?" She tried to keep her emotions out of her voice.

"I'm working on the payroll." He rose to his feet.

"Why?" She took a few tentative steps into the office. "You know I do that on Mondays."

"I wanted to help."

She eased past him into the room. "After Saturday, I wasn't sure you wanted to see me again."

His blue eyes focused on her, and his jaw clenched. She lowered herself into the chair he'd just vacated and turned around to the desk.

"I was an ass on Saturday." He sat on the love seat near her. "I'm sorry. It's just . . . when Carter showed up, I was that fat kid he'd pushed around in school all over again."

She frowned at him, a fist squeezing her heart. "You weren't fat," she murmured. She hated hearing him talk about himself so negatively. Kids used to tease him about his weight, but she'd never thought he was overweight.

"Not really the point, but thank you," Quinn said as she swiveled to face him. "He had stupidly convinced me that you would resume your engagement, and once again I just let Carter have what he wanted. I didn't know what to do—whether I should have stayed or gone. I didn't think I had a chance, and I couldn't go through that kind of rejection again. I wasn't even home before I regretted leaving you with him. I'm so sorry."

As easy as it would be to forgive him, his actions still hurt a little. "You felt rejected? By me?"

"I asked you to leave with me." He lowered his gaze to the floor. "You barely acknowledged me, and then you told me to leave."

Had she really said that? She searched her memory but came up blank. "I don't remember that."

"You looked at me, then at him, and you told me to leave," he said and looked away.

"Quinn." She paused to wait for him to look at her. When he did, she placed a hand on his knee. "From the time I saw Carter until the door slammed behind you, I don't remember hearing, or really seeing, anything."

What did she say? Quinn couldn't believe his ears. She didn't remember telling him to leave?

"Did I make you feel rejected?" Hannah repeated.

"No, not you," Quinn said. "My ex-girlfriend."

"What happened?" she asked in a soft tone.

Quinn looked away again. If he wanted her to tell him everything regarding Carter, he had to do the same concerning Alexa. And he wanted to know where she stood with Carter; it was the main reason he was here. He had to know if he stood a chance with her, and this might be his only opportunity.

He rose to his feet and began to pace.

"Her name was Alexa," he said, waiting for the stabbing pain he always felt in his chest when he thought of her, but it didn't come. "We met at a bar in the city, almost two years ago. She wasn't having a good night, and I started chatting with her to try to make her feel better. By the end of the night, she was laughing again, and we'd exchanged numbers. Our first date was a few weeks later."

Hannah's eyes were following his movement and gave nothing away. He had no idea what she was thinking.

"We texted or emailed every day, dated every other weekend, but I thought it was enough," he said. Again, hindsight was always twenty-twenty. "After three months, I thought she was special. After six, I wanted to marry her."

Hannah listened intently.

"Around nine months, I bought the house, thinking we could remodel it together and make it our home. I started with the living room and master suite. For our one-year anniversary, just before Christmas last year, I finally took her to see the house for the first time. I'd finished renovating the master bedroom and had decorated the living room. I had a ring in my pocket and had planned to propose after I showed her the changes. Needless to say, things didn't go as planned." Quinn waited for her to say something, but after a few silent heartbeats, he continued his story. "She saw the house and wasn't impressed. She said it looked fitting for me but couldn't understand why I wanted her opinion of it. She said she could never live in such an old house."

"Oh no," Hannah said.

"Yep. I told her then that I wanted to make the house her home as well. That we could fix it up and modernize it together. That's when she gave me the most pitiful look you could imagine and told me she was already engaged."

Hannah gasped.

"She'd been with her fiancé for three years and had been engaged for five months." Quinn plopped down on the couch and put his head in his hands. "I felt so stupid. I hadn't seen the signs. Even after she told me about him, I still asked her to choose me." His words were bitter in his mouth. "I pointed out that there must be something wrong in their relationship for her to cheat on him with me. I begged her to dump him and marry me instead." The thought still turned his stomach. "Things went from bad to worse. She said she could never marry someone with a blue-collar job. Her fiancé made six figures, and I could never reach that level. She said I'd never be able to give her everything she wanted, and she was going to marry him regardless."

Hannah moved from her chair to beside him on the love seat. Her knees turned toward his without touching them. The pity in her eyes was misplaced, and he didn't feel worthy. What had happened with Alexa caused him to think the worst of Hannah on Saturday.

"The worst part was, she said we could still see each other. She'd only wanted me for the sex and company when he was out of town. She never loved me," Quinn said. "After I ended things with her, I swore I'd never beg a woman to pick me over another man again. So when Carter showed up and you told me to leave, I thought the worst, and it was Alexa all over again."

After a short pause, Hannah said, "I'm not her."

Those were the three hardest words for him to hear. The weight of his mistake sat heavy on his shoulders, and he realized there was no guarantee he would win her back, even if she no longer wanted to be with Carter.

"I know," Quinn said. "I know you're not her."

"Do you?" She tipped her head to the side. Her tone was quiet and considering. "I can see the similarities in the situations, I guess. But you made an assumption, and that's not fair. Why would you think I'd choose him?"

"I didn't know if you were over him or not." Quinn stood and began to pace again.

"How could you not know?" Her voice grew in strength. She stood up and faced him. Her cheeks were flushed. "Do you honestly think I would have slept with you if I wasn't over him?" Her calm tone contradicted the tension in her features. "It wouldn't be fair to either of us if I had." She took a step back. "If you had a question, why didn't you just ask?" Her face was a blank mask.

"Hannah, I'm sorry." Quinn closed the distance between them by two steps before the look of pain in her eyes stopped him. "I know the situation with Carter's return was confusing and jarring. Can you please forgive me?"

She'd told him what he needed to know. She was over Carter. She still wouldn't have chosen to be with Carter, and Quinn had been foolish enough to run away. Dani was right: he should have stayed to support her. Maybe the sadness in her eyes wouldn't be there if he had. But the ground under his feet was shifting sand, and he had no idea what direction they were going in now. All he knew was that he wasn't about to give up on them.

"Hannah, I lo—" He cleared his throat. He wasn't ready to finish that thought. "I care so much about you, and I was such an idiot. Can we just forget this ever happened?"

"It's not that simple, Quinn," she said softly.

He shuffled closer and took her hands in his. She remained stiff and kept her eyes down.

"You just admitted that you don't want to be with Carter," he whispered.

She pulled her hands away. "That may be true, but actions have consequences, Quinn."

"I know that."

"Would you like to know the consequences of you willingly walking out, even if I did ask you to?" She pressed her lips together in a flat smile.

"Okay." He shrugged. He'd thought they were past the consequences of his actions.

"Carter thinks he's won me again." She held out her arms. "I have told him repeatedly that it's over between us, but no matter what I tell him, he won't listen. When you left, he took that as a victory on his part."

The resignation deep in her stare wrapped around his heart like a vice. "What can I do to fix this?" Quinn asked.

She let out a small chuckle. "Nothing." She plopped down onto the sofa. She leaned her head onto the cushion and closed her eyes. Stress lined the creases of her eyes. "I have to take care of this myself. He barely believes my words. I doubt he'll believe anyone else, and he certainly won't listen to anything you have to say."

Quinn lowered himself to the couch beside her. "What happens to us in the meantime?"

Hannah snapped her eyes open and stared at him. "I can't think about that right now. I still don't know how I feel about you moving away. Or the fact you didn't even tell me it was a possibility."

"I'll apologize a thousand times for that. The first interview was set up before you kissed me, so I didn't even think about it." He took her hand in his and almost got on his knees in front of her.

The corner of her mouth lifted, and she looked away as her cheeks turned pale pink. The vice in his chest loosened a little.

"Just tell me when and I will make it up to you," Quinn said.

She laid her hand on top of his and gave it a pat.

"As for the move, I haven't decided anything . . . yet," he stated earnestly. "But can you tell me why a move bothers you so much?"

"I thought . . ." Her voice trailed off. "I don't want to leave Rocky Creek. I never have."

"But you went away to college, and you would have moved away with the Navy."

"That doesn't mean I wanted to," Hannah said quickly. "And we were engaged. I didn't have a choice."

"What do you mean?" he asked.

A wave of sadness washed over her eyes. After everything he'd confessed, he could only hope she'd be as honest with him.

"I mean that, as his wife I wouldn't have had a choice. I would have had to move with him," she answered. "And I never had a choice because he joined the Navy without even discussing it with me." Her shoulders lifted, as if a weight had been taken away. "One month before graduation, we were supposed to be planning a wedding, but he joined the Navy instead."

He replayed her words to see what he could find that might give him hope, but he kept getting hung up on what she hadn't said. "You didn't want him to join the Navy?"

She grimaced. "It's not that. It's just that he never showed any interest in the military, and he didn't talk to me about it first." She paused. "When we met on campus my freshman year, I was ready to come home for good. He helped me have fun in college, and he convinced me to stick it out just a little longer. When we started dating, he promised me that, if we were still together, we would move back to Rocky Creek after we graduated. But more than that, we were engaged, and we should have been making decisions like that—decisions that affected us both—together."

He looked at the floor. "You never told me that." It wasn't fair to be bothered by her secrets when he hadn't told her everything either. But he wouldn't have left her alone with Carter if he'd known all of this.

"I didn't tell a lot of people," she murmured.

"Why?"

She huffed. "I didn't want anyone to think I was disrespecting my fiancé. Not many people really know who Carter is, and they wouldn't have given me the chance to explain my position if I'd simply said I didn't want him to join the Navy."

He shrugged. That may or may not be true. It would have depended on who she'd said it to. He doubted anyone who knew Carter would have thought he was a good fit for the Navy, or any branch of the military for that matter. Carter was too used to getting his way and hated being told what to do. When Quinn first heard that Carter had joined the Navy, his first thought was how undisciplined Carter was and how that wouldn't work in the military.

"The worst part is, I've been so dishonest with people for the last year." Tears filled her eyes, and he moved to kneel in front of her.

"What?" he asked. "What have you been dishonest about?"

Her mouth opened as if to speak, then closed. She glanced at the set of security monitors and muttered something under her breath.

He looked over his shoulder and saw Carter on the monitors, headed their way. He gripped her fingers tighter as she tried to pull away.

"We can finish this later." She yanked her hands away and rose to her feet as Carter appeared in the doorway.

Quinn chuckled as he rose to his feet, finally feeling lighter than he had in days. There was still hope that she wanted to be with him. He also knew how much he'd hurt her with his actions. He'd have to make up for that.

Even the thunderclouds in Carter's eyes couldn't dampen Quinn's mood.

"There you are, my love," Carter said as he came into the office, his hands outstretched, reaching for Hannah. She eased her hands into her pockets.

"What do you want?" Hannah's tone was brusque and businesslike. Quinn hid a smile as he returned to the neglected payroll.

"Sweetheart, I was expecting you home hours ago." In the security monitor, Quinn could see Carter glaring at him. "What are you doing here, Quinn?"

"I help my father with the payroll on Mondays," Hannah answered. Quinn felt, more than saw, her slide closer to him. "I told you that yesterday."

"Oh." Carter laughed off her comment. "I guess I forgot. But what is he doing here? Does he work for your dad too?"

"Quinn's been helping for the last few weeks. He was just about to leave," she said smoothly. He looked up and met her pointed stare. "I can finish the rest," she added.

Quinn pressed his lips together.

Please, she mouthed.

"Yeah," he said without thinking. "I was just leaving." He retrieved his jacket from the rack beside the desk, then slid his arms into the sleeves.

Thank you, she mouthed, then turned back to Carter.

"So, dinner tonight?" Carter asked as Quinn walked past him.

"I'm eating at home," Hannah said abruptly.

"Why don't we go out instead," Carter said, his eyes meeting Quinn's. Then he closed the door in Quinn's face.

Despite the effort Carter was making to ruin his mood, Quinn walked out of the store feeling somewhat elated. He'd learned everything he'd needed to know. Well, almost everything. He wasn't sure why Hannah thought she was being dishonest, but in the grand scheme of things, he'd cleared up a lot of confusion, and things had gone well. As much as he hated to leave her to deal with Carter on her own, he understood he'd made a mess of things, and there really wasn't much he could help with. He'd give her the space she needed, and they'd talk about where they stood once Carter was out of her life for good.

With any luck, that would be sooner rather than later. In the meantime, he needed to come up with a new plan for his future. One that could give them both what they wanted.

Twenty-Eight

Hannah stared at the double doors of the pub, willing herself to relax. She didn't want to be here. The only reason she'd agreed to meet Carter for dinner was because, with the chaos of his return, she hadn't had the chance to go grocery shopping. Eating out meant a faster meal before she went home and locked herself in the spare bedroom for the third night. She had most of her things packed. She held onto the hope he would find a place and move out, but she already knew that wasn't likely.

With a deep breath, she pulled the door open and walked into the pub, pausing to let her eyes adjust to the dimly lit room.

"Hey, Hannah." A delightful feminine voice drifted toward her from the bar.

"Hey, Claire." Hannah smiled as she was wrapped in a warm hug by the younger woman. "How are you today?"

Claire pulled back and tipped her head from side to side. "Busy, but that's a good thing, right?"

Since the sudden death of her father at the beginning of the year, Claire was now running her family's pub. She still had her mother, but with four younger siblings, one of which was her sister's best friend, Hannah imagined Claire had her hands full at home as well.

"We're training a new bartender." Claire waved toward the bar, where a familiar-looking redheaded man was mixing a drink with the guidance of Jim, who had been working here for as long as Hannah could remember. Hannah was pretty sure the redhead had been a groomsman at Jackson and Kerri's wedding. "And he's Scottish." Claire clapped her hands and bounced on the balls of her feet.

Hannah laughed at her excitement. Given the pub had been the county's only taste of Scottish and Irish cuisine since Claire's grandfather built it in the early 1970s, having an actual Scotsman could only help make things more authentic.

"Are you waiting on Quinn?" Claire asked brightly.

Hannah fought to smile, to not let her aching heart show on her face.

"Hey, sweetheart." Carter strolled up to her and put his arm around her shoulder.

Claire's expression went blank, but not before Hannah saw the confusion in her eyes.

Hannah shook free of Carter's heavy arm.

"I have a table in the corner," Carter said as he took Hannah's hand.

"Talk to you later." Hannah pulled her hand free from his grip and waved to Claire with the other. Claire smiled, then headed back to the bar.

She followed Carter to the back booth. Carter slid into the booth, facing the door, and she slid into the other side. He handed her a menu and she perused it, even though she already knew what she wanted.

"Well, would you look at that," Carter said, waving to someone over Hannah's shoulder. Hannah turned and saw Tori and Phillip walking toward them.

"Carter, you said it was just going to be the two of us," she hissed.

"What? It's just dinner," he chuckled. "I promise, it'll be fun."

Tori stepped up to the table. "Mind if we join you?" Without waiting for an answer, she sat in the booth next to Hannah, nudging her closer to the wall. Carter slid over to make room for Phillip.

"Hannah." Tori beamed widely. "I don't know about you, but I'm still on cloud nine. I'm constantly pinching myself just to know I'm not imagining that Carter is home." She slapped the tabletop. "I was thinking. Wouldn't it be fabulous to have a party to welcome Carter home in style?" She looked from Carter to Hannah. "Do you want to help plan it?"

Hannah groaned. Even if she wanted a party to welcome Carter home, Tori would do whatever Tori wanted to do anyway.

"So," Tori looked at Carter. "Is this going to be an engagement party too?"

"No," Hannah said sharply.

"It could be," Carter said.

Hannah glared at him. "No."

"Oh please, Hannah," Tori whined. "The two of you never had an official party, and I would love so much to throw it for you."

"No," Hannah repeated with a scowl. "There will be no engagement party. Do what you want to welcome him home, but that's it." Her harshness surprised her, and Tori's wide-eyed stare and the frown on Carter's face indicated that they were surprised as well.

"I don't understand." Tori's gaze bounced between Hannah and Carter, then settled on Hannah's face. "Don't you want to celebrate your love?"

Hannah clenched her jaw. Carter met her gaze with an innocent shrug. She turned to Tori and fixed a smile. "We don't need to do that."

"Why not?" Tori cocked her head.

Hannah smiled genuinely. "Because we're—"

"We're still catching up from all the time we missed," Carter interrupted with a hand on her forearm.

Tori frowned and tipped her head to the side, then glanced at Carter. A knot formed in Hannah's stomach. Given the way Tori's expression calmed, there was no doubt in Hannah's mind that they were up to something.

"Are you sure that's all this is about?" Tori's voice dripped with syrup.

Hannah nodded slowly. "Why?"

"I wonder if it's more your kind and caring nature not wanting to hurt someone else." Tori's smile broadened. "And I think we all know who I'm talking about. And I honestly don't know why you're so worried about hurting Quinn's feelings."

Hannah sat back into the cushion of the booth, relaxing the muscles in her face despite the anger bubbling inside. At this point, the best thing she could do was let Tori continue talking. She'd eventually make her point, and then Hannah could decide how to react.

Tori glanced at Carter. "You didn't tell her about the dare?"

"We don't need to talk about that," Carter said.

Tori waved Carter's words away with her hand. "I really don't know how you could even go out with Quinn after that." She stared at Hannah, waiting for a response.

"Tori . . ." Carter said in a warning tone.

Hannah was confused. "What dare? And what does it have to do with Quinn?" she asked.

Tori giggled. "I can't believe you don't know. Quinn dared Carter to ask you to the prom."

Anger coursed through her veins. Carter had asked her out on a dare? All these years, and she'd been played a fool. She'd been a game to him. Had the friendship they'd developed in college been a game? Had the engagement been another dare? No wonder he'd left her for the Navy. Nothing between them was real. Her hands were shaking in her lap, and she clenched them into fists.

"Tori, none of that really matters now," Carter said. He reached across the table and held out his hands to her. "It worked out for us in the end."

Hannah stared at his fingers as if they were snakes.

"Of course it does, Carter," Tori said. "Hannah should know what really happened. Quinn dared Carter to ask you to the prom because he didn't think Carter would actually do it."

Hannah clenched her fists until her fingernails dug into her palms. Could she believe Tori? She glanced at Phillip, who was biting his bottom lip as he avoided making eye contact with her. She side-eyed Carter and saw the slight uptick of his lips as he stared at Tori.

"Quinn didn't think you were good enough for Carter," Tori said. "He didn't think Carter would do it."

A smile flashed across Carter's face. "Tori, that was years ago. None of that matters now."

Tori scowled at him. "Of course it matters now, Carter. She's confused about her feelings for you because of him. She needs to know what he really thinks of her." Her emotions shifted from offended to overly concerned. "Hannah, you shouldn't worry about hurting Quinn. I'm honestly shocked that he even went out with you, given his opinion of you in high school."

"I don't believe a word you're saying," Hannah hissed at Tori, never breaking her icy stare. "Quinn is not that kind of person. But you know who is? You." Then Hannah pointed to Phillip. "And him." She scowled at Carter. "And you."

Hannah grabbed her bag and slid so hard into Tori that she forced her out of the booth. She could feel the heat burning her cheeks. "But Carter was right. None of that matters now. Now, if you'll excuse me, I've lost my appetite." She stormed away from the table.

She stepped into the cool night air and pulled her phone out of her pocket.

"Hannah, wait," Carter said as he ran up behind her.

Hannah spun on her heel and glared at him. "What?"

"What just happened in there?" He ran a hand through his dark hair, his brown eyes hard as stone. "Tori was trying to be helpful. She doesn't want to see you get hurt."

"Bullshit," Hannah spat. "Tori doesn't care about anyone but herself. She'll say or do whatever she has to do to get her own way."

"She's telling you the truth. I was there, I heard him say it." Carter threw his hands out to his sides. "You just don't want to hear the truth because you're still hung up on him."

"You're really going to stand there and lie to my face?" Hannah rolled her eyes. "I know what he's really like. I've known Quinn since we were five."

"You have?" He fell back a step.

"I *know* that he would never think someone wasn't good enough. Don't stand there and continue to tell me bald-faced lies. Especially if you think it helps your cause." She pointed her finger in his face. "Because I can assure you, it will not."

"Okay," he mouthed more than verbalized as he took a step backward. "I'm sorry. I'll ask Tori not to bad-mouth him anymore. Just come inside and eat."

"No, Carter. I'm going home." She pulled her keys from her pocket. "Enjoy your evening out with *your* friends."

She turned and strolled to her car.

"They're *your* friends too!" Carter shouted.

"No," she said over her shoulder. "They're not. They never really were."

She slid into the driver's seat and started the engine. She looked over and saw Carter staring at her. With a shake of her head, she backed out of the parking space. Once she pulled out onto the road, she called Dani.

"Hey," Dani answered.

"Meet me at my place."

"Everything okay?" Concern filled Dani's tone.

"I need a place to crash. Most of my clothes are packed, but I need help gathering other things," Hannah said as she exhaled a long, cleansing breath. It felt surprisingly uplifting to have made a decision about her future.

"Gladly," Dani said with a laugh. "Be there in fifteen."

Twenty-Nine

Hannah sat at the table in the library and listened to her team discuss their Odyssey of the Mind problem. It had been a long day following a busy night. She and Dani had collected all her clothes, jewelry, and everything else Hannah valued in thirty minutes, then stopped for dinner on the way to Dani's place. Hannah would probably crash there for a few days before she went to her parents' house. Dani's home was closer to the school, so it worked better for the remainder of the week.

She was leading the team that had picked the drama problem. Quinn was guiding the balsa-wood building team across the room. Her team was fairly experienced—three of the seven members had been on her teams for the last two years, so she let her thoughts drift. She stood and strolled to the wall of windows, close enough to answer any questions they might have, but far enough away to have some time to herself.

Looking at the burgundy carpet between her feet, she thought about Quinn for the umpteenth time today. He'd greeted her when he arrived, but they hadn't really had much opportunity to talk since the kids had gathered. It was probably for the best. She still wasn't sure where she wanted things to go with him now that Carter was out of her life. At the end of the day, Quinn had his own life to live, and that involved starting his career and moving to another state.

Maybe she should just accept that a future wasn't in the cards for her and Quinn. Her heart ached at the thought.

"Miss Murphy," a fifth-grade student called out. The girl pointed to the library door.

Mr. Keller stood in the doorway and motioned for Hannah to join him. She reluctantly walked over to him.

"You have a visitor," Mr. Keller muttered. "I've asked him to wait in the teacher's lounge."

Hannah groaned inwardly. She knew who was waiting for her.

"Can you sit with my students?" she asked. There was no point trying to avoid the conversation to come, no matter how much she wanted to.

"Sure," Mr. Keller said. "Anything I need to do?"

Hannah shook her head. "Just let them talk about the problem and guide them to their own answer to any question they have. You know you can't tell them what to do."

He chuckled. "I remember."

"Thanks." She glided past him. "Hopefully I won't be long." She rushed out of the library.

She strolled down the hall toward the teacher's lounge, half wondering what Carter wanted, half considering what she would say to him.

As she walked into the lounge, she closed the door behind her. Carter was standing next to the tall, narrow window, tucked into the corner of the room. He stood tall with his hands clasped together behind his back.

"What are you doing here?" Hannah asked.

"Do you have something after school every day?" Carter took a few steps toward her.

"Pretty much," Hannah answered with a shrug. "Why?"

"Just wondering if there's time in your schedule for me." He stopped in front of her and shoved his hands into the pockets of his jeans.

Hannah tamped down the frustration bubbling in her chest. She moved farther into the room and squared her feet. "There wouldn't be time in my schedule for you if I didn't have something every day. Carter, it's not going to work. Please accept that."

"Where did you go last night?" he asked.

"None of your business."

"You promised me a week, Hannah," he snapped. He closed his eyes and swallowed once. Then he pinned her with a stare. "At least tell me if you were with him."

Was he jealous? Did she care? Of course she cared. She wasn't trying to hurt him, but she had to make him understand. She wasn't going to marry him, and no amount of time would change her mind.

"Why are you here, Carter?" she repeated.

"You're not going to answer my question?"

"You answer mine first," she countered.

"Can't a man come see his wayward fiancée?" He gave her a sly grin that made her jaw tighten.

"Enough," she hissed. She silently counted to ten. It wouldn't do her any good to let her anger show. "What will it take to make you understand? We're not engaged anymore. We're not going to get married. This relationship is over. It ended when you died."

"But I didn't die," he said. "So it didn't end."

The vein in her temple pulsed. "As far as I was concerned, you did."

"All the more reason for you to keep your promise and give me a week to prove we belong together," he argued. "You promised you'd try." His eyes narrowed on her face.

"No, I didn't promise anything. I said you could stay for one week until you found another place to live. As you've proven, you don't play fair." Her voice rose with every word.

"I am playing fair."

"Hardly," she scoffed. "Last night's ambush was not fair. Not by any stretch of the imagination is it fair to have your friends lie about Quinn."

"Tori wasn't lying!" Carter let out a low growl. "And why do you keep calling them my friends? They're your friends too." He paced between her and the window, keeping his gaze averted.

"No, they're not." She walked to the table and gripped the back of one of the chairs. "Tori only speaks to me when she needs me for something, and she rarely needs me. And the guys . . ." She laughed. "They only ever spoke to me when you were around, if they had no other choice. I can count on one hand, with one finger, the number of times they've spoken to me in the past year."

"Now who's lying?" He scowled at her.

Hannah raised a brow, daring him to continue.

"You always loved hanging out with them before." He threw his arms out to the side. "We always had a great time together with them."

"Doing what?" Hannah asked, even though she remembered exactly what they always did with his friends. He shrugged, as if he didn't understand the question. "Parties, bowling alley, pubs, and parking lots. None of which were my choice, and none of it very much fun for me. I don't drink and I find hanging out and doing nothing in parking lots a waste of time." He opened his mouth to argue, but she held up a hand to silence him. "As for bowling, while I don't hate it, I hate doing it with your overly competitive cronies. Watching you all make a competition out of everything got super old, super quick."

His friends in college had been a different breed. They'd been pleasant to be around, but his friends in Rocky Creek never seemed to grow up.

He frowned. "You never told me that."

"Yes, I did." She fought to keep the whine from her voice. "You just never listened, and you dismissed any idea I had when I suggested we do something else."

The look in his eyes softened. "I would never do that," he murmured. "I always listened to you."

She tilted her head to the side. "Except on Sunday, when I told you I'd be at the store after school yesterday. Or yesterday, when I agreed to have dinner with you, *if* it was just the two of us."

"Okay, those are bad examples." He waved a hand, brushing her words away. "Those have happened since I returned, and I'm sorry. I've just been so excited to be home, sometimes I can't help myself." He gave her a dashing smile. "But I always listened before. I'll bet you can't name even one time that I didn't."

Hannah growled under her breath. She could name several times he hadn't considered her suggestions or feelings, not because she kept track of everything he'd done wrong, but because those had been the worst offenses. "Christmas break our junior year," she began. "I wanted to go to the Trans-Siberian Orchestra concert, you promised you'd buy the tickets, but on the night of the concert, you told me we were going to do something else with your friends. You never bought the tickets, and we spent the night in the game room at the pub."

"They have Christmas concerts every year," Carter said, his cheeks turning red. "If it had meant so much, we could have gone the next year."

"And if you'd just let me buy the tickets myself, we could have gone," she said. "My grandmother's seventy-fifth birthday party the summer after we got engaged. You knew how excited I was about that, and how much I wanted you to meet her. But the day before the party, you told me you'd made plans for us to spend the day at the lake with your friends."

"I don't remember that." Carter shrugged.

"Of course you don't. You were always at the lake with your friends in the summer, the days probably all blend together." Hannah moved her hands to her hips. "You made up some story about it being Eric's last day in town, and I went to the party without you."

"Oh yeah." Carter said. "I remember, it was his last day before he went back to his campus."

"It was July, and I saw him in town three days later."

Carter's mouth fell open.

"You joined the Navy without talking to me about it," Hannah said.

"This again?" Carter rolled his eyes. "Seriously, Hannah. Let it go." He glared at her. "Or are you saying you didn't want me to serve our country?"

"Puh-lease," Hannah sneered. "You know darn well that it's not about that, Carter. It's the fact that we were supposed to be planning a wedding and a life *together*. You made a decision that affected us both without talking to me, your future wife, about it first. You brushed off my concerns after the fact like they were nothing, and you were perfectly okay with waiting for a wedding to be convenient to your schedule."

"You could have set a date without me," Carter said. "I would have been there."

"I tried setting a date," Hannah growled. "Three times. And all three times you said it wouldn't work for you because of training."

"Then that wasn't my fault." Carter's grin broadened.

"No, it never is," Hannah muttered.

Carter remained quiet for several minutes. "Who are you?" he said, breaking the silence.

"Sorry?" Hannah lifted her eyes to his face.

"I don't think I know who you are anymore," Carter said. "You've changed. You're not the woman I left when I went to boot camp, and I'm not entirely sure I like this new you."

Hannah pressed her lips together.

"You used to be so sweet and easy to get along with." He shoved his hands into his pockets. "Now . . . you're not. You're stubborn and hurtful, and don't consider anyone else's feelings when you say and do things. I want my considerate, kind, loving fiancée back, Hannah."

"It's not going to happen. Carter. Get it through your head. We're. Not. Getting. Married. And I'm not going to be the pushover you were engaged to again either."

"But—"

"No!" she said. "Carter. It's over. There's nothing you can say or do that will make me change my mind."

Anger flashed across his face before he blanked his expression. "Okay," he said softly. "I understand." He turned toward the door, then stopped and looked over his shoulder at her. "Will you be at the party on Friday night?"

"Carter," she groaned.

"It would mean a lot to me." He pouted a little and gave her an innocent, wide-eyed stare. "Please? Just one last thing."

Hannah held his stare as she considered his request. It finally seemed like she'd gotten through to him that things were over between them. She could attend the party in his honor and then wash her hands of him. Her mind raced about the next steps: packing everything up and moving out, finding a new place to live, and getting on with her life without Carter for the second time.

"Okay, I'll go as a courtesy to you." She turned back to the window and looked out.

She heard the door close behind him, but she remained where she was, replaying his final argument in her head. Was she really so different? She hated hurting anyone's feelings, but it was better than pretending their relationship was something it wasn't. And something it could never be again.

"Hannah."

"Hm?" She turned and saw Quinn standing on the other side of the room, still in the alcove of the door. "Sorry, I'll be there in a second." She pushed away from the wall.

"No need," he said. "The last student just left."

"Just left?" She glanced at her watch. How long had she been alone in the teachers' lounge? "Sorry. I lost track of time."

"Everything okay?" He strolled toward her.

Hannah shook her head. "Am I a horrible person?"

The fury that flashed through Quinn's eyes took her breath away. He turned and glared at the door. "Did he say that?"

"Not in so many words," she said with a laugh. "He did say that I'm not the same person I was when he left for basic training." She wrinkled her nose at the memory of his words. "And that he's not sure he likes the new me."

Quinn stood next to her and stared out the window. "Are any of us the same person we were two years ago? Does it bother you that he said that?"

That he doesn't like the new me? She stared out the window at the expanse of the green lawn. Just below the rise of the hill, an occasional car drove by.

"I feel like it should," she began slowly. "And I think if it were anyone else, it would." Quinn's eyes were so full of compassion and concern, they drew her toward him. It took everything in her to fight the pull and remain where she was. She inhaled a deep, shaky breath and slowly released it. "With him, though, I couldn't care less."

"That doesn't make you horrible." He reached out his hand, and she laced her fingers through his. "I can't say the same for him."

She laughed lightly and covered her mouth with her free hand. The tension that had infused her muscles a moment ago eased from her body. Quinn always had a way of putting things into perspective. For as long as she'd known him, he was pretty even keel. He had a way of making problems seem smaller with his feedback and support. After Carter's death, she'd become more sure of herself, Quinn had simply helped bring that to the forefront, even when he wasn't with her.

She realized now that she loved him. But this sense of comfort and love wasn't new. It felt more like easing into her favorite pair of jeans. She wondered how long she'd actually been in love with him.

As they stepped into the hallway, she sighed. Unlike with Carter, she knew now that while she could physically live without Quinn, she was no longer sure she wanted to.

Thirty

Quinn pulled his truck into the driveway of the stable and searched the dark for Hannah's car. When he saw Carter at the pub with Tori, he realized Hannah would be alone and thought it would be the perfect opportunity for them to finish their conversation. He needed answers that he could only hope she'd be willing to give.

After stopping by her townhouse and her parents' house, this was the last place he knew to look for her. If she wasn't with Dani, he wasn't sure where else he might find her. When the beam from his headlights landed on her compact car, dwarfed by Dani's truck, he breathed a silent cheer and steered his vehicle in that direction.

He parked next to Hannah's car. As he climbed out of his truck, she came out of Dani's camper, sliding her arms into a heavy coat. In the dim light shining through the camper's windows, he could read the question in her eyes.

"How did you know where I was?"

Quinn smiled. At least now he had an idea of what her priorities were. To stay hidden. Most likely from Carter. He hoped not from himself.

"I looked for you," he said.

"Oh." She gave him a wide-eyed stare. She'd stopped at the back of his truck, just behind the wheel.

"I just wanted to talk to you." He balled his hands at his sides. He wanted nothing more than to wrap his arms around her and hold her tight against him while they talked. He was more than a little tempted to toss her into the cab of his truck and drive her to his house. They could talk in the warmth of his vehicle and, provided the talk went the way he hoped, make up in the warmth of his bed.

Then he'd never let her go again.

She gave a small smile as she moved past him to the door of the barn. When she slid it open and walked inside, he shuffled after her as a light illuminated the walkway in front of him. He stepped over the threshold and followed Hannah up to the hayloft.

She sat down on the haybale chair he'd created for her and wrapped a blanket around her shoulders. She turned her head, bathing her face in the blueish light of the nearly full moon. She inhaled, and he expected her to say something, but she remained silent.

Ever since she'd confessed that she was being dishonest with people, he'd wondered what she was talking about. His mind had run the gamut of possibilities over the last twenty-four hours. All of them had to deal with Carter. Some possibilities made him want to take the job and leave for Atlanta tomorrow. Some made him want to stay and fight tooth and nail for her.

Whatever she answered, he knew it would impact his decision. He just wasn't sure how.

"Yesterday, in your father's office, you said you'd been dishonest with people for the past year. What were you dishonest about?"

Hannah pulled the blanket around her tighter. "Why do you want to know?"

Quinn strolled toward the open door. "So I know what to do with my life, I guess. I don't know." He stared out over the moonlit pastures and rolling hills. It really was beautiful here, and it suddenly hit him how much he would miss views like this.

"What do you think it might be?" she asked.

"I think it has something to do with Carter. Maybe that you'd been secretly married? Or that you had been faking your engagement. I don't know."

Her shoulders rose with a deep inhale. "I'm more than willing to tell you right now, but first I need to know. Has something changed?" she asked softly.

He shook his head.

"You still have a job offer in Atlanta?"

Quinn nodded.

"And the reasons you applied for the job are still important to you?" She tipped her head. "You still want the challenge? The notoriety? The money? Whatever it is, does it still matter to you?"

Quinn's mind raced as he pondered her questions. Until recently, he hadn't understood that Alexa had been behind his motivation to apply for those jobs in the big cities. One of his recent conversations with Rachel had helped him realize that. But he couldn't see why it really mattered what his motivation was or where it came from.

"If those reasons still exist, then you should follow your dream." Her gentle tone, though it was meant to soothe, only deepened his frustration. "Nothing I say or do should have any impact on that."

Quinn's stomach turned to lead. She wasn't going to give him an answer, and he wasn't sure what that meant for him. Or for them. The look in her eyes relaxed, and she glided toward him, her hand stretched out from under the blanket. He slipped his fingers against hers and pulled her toward him.

"What about us?" he spat as the words came into his thoughts.

"Right now," she shrugged, "there really isn't an 'us.'"

He opened his mouth to argue but realized she was right. They may have been fighting when Carter showed up, but he'd ceded the battlefield by leaving her with Carter. He hadn't given her the support she needed or fought for her when she'd needed him to. Now he saw that he may have lost her forever because of it.

"But if there was, I would tell you the same thing." She smiled sadly. "I want you to succeed in whatever you do. I want you to do whatever job is going to make you happy."

Her words planted a tiny seed of hope in his chest. Maybe things weren't so bleak after all.

"You make me happy." He felt the truth of that at his core.

"That may be true, but whether you go or stay is entirely up to you. It's what you want for your life independent of me." She slipped her hand out of his and a chill went through him. "You can't decide to stay or go because of something I might say or do." She held his stare, and he got the sense she was bracing for something. "But you can't decide to stay or go because of your ex either."

He didn't move, but he felt like she'd just pushed him out of the open door. "I'm not," he said.

"Are you sure?"

The quiet words stopped him in his tracks. "Why do you ask?" he said.

She moved toward the other side of the window. "You bought a house here and were content to live in Rocky Creek. Content to settle down with Alexa here," she said. "So, what changed?"

His decision to move had come so gradually, he wasn't sure when he'd first had the thought. For almost a year, he'd tried so hard to push Alexa out of his thoughts, but he couldn't argue with Hannah's theory. After his break-up with Alexa, he'd been so overwhelmed with a need to prove that he could be better than the man she'd chosen. He'd never meant for Alexa to know about his success, he'd never planned on seeing her again, but could she have really been the driving force behind his desire to move?

A warm hand on his biceps drew his attention out of his thoughts. Hannah was looking up at him, her eyes wide and her heart open.

"You need to decide what you want to do," she said.

Quinn gently pulled her into his arms, and she leaned her head against his chest. He closed his eyes as he inhaled deeply, sweet pear and magnolia wreathing his sinuses. This was all he really wanted when he arrived at the farm tonight. He never wanted this to end. How could he leave her?

He lowered his lips to her ear. "What will you do if I leave?" he whispered.

He felt her shrug. "I'll figure that out when the time comes."

As they stood there, an idea began to form. Maybe they *could* both have what they wanted.

Thirty-One

Hannah was sitting at her desk, grading the most recent math test, when there was a rap on her door.

"Come in," she called, not lifting her pen or her eyes from the paper in front of her. Once she was finished with the test, she looked up to find Mr. Keller staring down at her, his hands fisted on his hips. "What can I help you with?"

"I believe we need to have a discussion about your guests," Mr. Keller grumbled.

Hannah rose to her feet as she thought about who might be visiting her now. Quinn would be at work, and even Carter would know better than to come see her during the school day.

"Lighten up, Keller. I can assure you my visit is strictly professional," a husky voice said as Seth walked into the room. "Besides, I don't think my wife would appreciate anything else."

"Hi, Seth," Hannah laughed as Rachel's husband stopped beside her desk, subtly positioning himself between her and Mr. Keller.

"Five minutes," Mr. Keller stated as he trudged toward the door. "And I want to see you in my office after school." With that final warning, he left Hannah's classroom.

Hannah's laughter died as she looked at Seth's suddenly serious face. A sense of dread washed over her as she plopped into her chair. "You're bringing me bad news, aren't you?"

He pulled over a chair and sat down. "Did you think there would be any other kind?" he asked.

Hannah took a deep breath. She had been dreading this conversation ever since her meeting with Seth. "What did you learn?"

"Straight to the point?" Seth asked with a grin, a dimple appearing in his right cheek.

"You heard my boss," Hannah answered. "Five minutes," she said in the deepest voice she could muster. "Besides," her voice returned to normal, "my students will be back from the library in about ten minutes."

"Ah." Seth nodded. "In that case, the news isn't great."

Hannah frowned. "What did Carter do?"

"He was actually court-martialed fourteen months ago and received a bad conduct discharge from the Navy after about eight months of jail time." Seth pulled some papers out of the case he had placed on the floor beside him.

Hannah's eyes widened. She took the papers and looked them over. "This happened around the time I was told he was dead."

The list of charges was long. There were numerous derelictions of duty, a few unauthorized absences, and a general disobedience thrown in several times. The civilian charges were even more numerous. Three DUIs, five drunkenness in public offenses, two bar fights, and two reckless driving charges.

As far as she knew, he'd never driven drunk or had a bar fight. But there had been times in college when he and his friends had gotten rowdy enough to be asked to leave the bar they were in or the party they were attending. In all of their time together, he'd never reached the point of being in trouble with the law.

She finished perusing the list. "So, where has he been for the last six months?"

"Under house arrest in Wichita Falls, Texas, for some of his crimes." Seth pointed to one of the papers at the back of the stack in Hannah's hand. "Seems the local cops didn't want him skipping town right away."

Hannah flipped through the paperwork. "I'm surprised they wanted to keep him around longer than they had to," she said.

"I think it was more about making sure he had paid his monetary dues, not the fact that they liked having him around," Seth answered.

A numbness settled in her chest, and she released a long sigh. "There's more?"

It wasn't really a question; she could see the answer on his face.

"You said Carter was in Officer Candidate School?" Seth asked.

She nodded. "That's what he told everyone."

"He was never enrolled in OCS. He nearly flunked out of basic training, and his assignment after graduation was an A School in Texas for vocational training. That's when his behavior seemed to spiral out of control. He was arrested and jailed six weeks into the three-month program."

Her jaw dropped, and the icy numbness spread like fingers through her body. Closing her eyes, she began to rub her temples.

"One last thing."

"You can't be serious," she grumbled.

"You weren't listed as his next of kin," Seth said slowly, pulling one more paper from his case.

"So?" Hannah took the paper and glanced at it. It was Carter's entrance paperwork with all of his personal information. He had written his mother as his next of kin. "We weren't married yet, so that's not surprising."

"True," Seth said. "But what is surprising is that you were notified of his supposed death."

"I don't understand," she said.

"His parents would have been the only people the Navy would have notified in the case of his death or disappearance. As far as the Navy was concerned, you didn't exist in Carter's life."

Hannah's shoulders slumped as her fingers went slack. The application in her hand fluttered to the floor.

"I've searched the Naval database, and the men in the picture you gave me were not from the Navy." Seth's voice sounded like it was coming through a tunnel.

Hannah was familiar with the sound; it usually happened when she was on the verge of throwing up because of a migraine. She was having a hard time catching her breath. She'd known Carter wasn't being honest. She'd been suspicious of his stories. But hearing it and seeing it in black and white was still overwhelming.

She glanced at the clock over Seth's shoulder. Her students would be back any minute, and she needed to pull herself together. She could fume about this turn of events later.

"But I think you figured that out already." Seth laid his hand on her forearm and gave her a comforting squeeze.

She stood to see Seth out. As they stepped out into the hallway, he smiled sadly at her.

"Don't do that," she said.

"Don't do what?"

"Don't pity me or feel bad for me. I'm actually glad you've told me all of this. I just need to process the information." She grinned at him. "I will be fine. And I appreciate you doing this for me."

"Anything for a friend," he answered. "Now, if you'll excuse me, I have a lunch date with my wife."

Hannah laughed as the tiny voices of her students grew louder behind her. She waved to Seth as he walked toward Rachel's classroom, then turned to greet her students and ushered them back into the room. She suddenly couldn't wait until she saw Carter again.

Hannah swiveled on her father's desk chair as she read through the inventory and purchase lists one more time, then glanced at the security monitors. Her sister was walking toward the office. She turned to face the door as Kailee strolled in.

"Why aren't you at home?" Kailee plopped down onto the sofa.

"Because I have things to do here." Hannah waved her hand at the computer monitor. "Why aren't *you* home?"

Kailee shrugged and stared at her fingernails. Hannah waited for her sister to say more, but she remained silent, staring at her nails. Hannah turned back to the computer screen and began preparing the order.

"I heard there's a party for Carter on Friday," Kailee said.

Hannah's fingers froze on the keys. She wasn't sure where Kailee had heard that news, but she knew what she was about to ask. "No."

"No?"

Hannah turned to face her. Kailee's eyes were blazing with anger.

"There's not a party?" Kailee clarified.

"No." Hannah laid her hands in her lap. "You're not going."

Kailee's face reddened and she bounced to her feet. "I wasn't asking your permission."

"I don't care. I don't want you—"

"It's not about you," Kailee scoffed. "He's my friend and future brother-in-law. I want to be there."

Hannah stood and squared herself to her sister. "He's neither of those things. You aren't his friend. You're an admirer, and he loves to collect those. He feeds on your attention and will keep you around for his ego."

Kailee took a step back. "That's not true. How can you say those things?"

"Because I know him better than you do," Hannah said.

"Stop it," Kailee said. "You're just being mean."

Hannah tried not to laugh. "You're not listening. Who knows him better, you or me? Which one of us has lived with him? Which one of us was engaged to him?"

"Are you still mad that he joined the Navy?" Kailee said.

Hannah relaxed her expression. "Put yourself in my shoes for a moment."

Kailee glanced at Hannah's blue flats. "Ugh, no thanks."

Hannah walked over to the door and closed it. "Imagine this: You're engaged to be married, weeks away from graduating from college. You're ready to start planning your wedding, but your fiancé has other plans. Do you think you should have a conversation about something like, oh, I don't know, joining the Navy before it actually happens?"

Kailee's brows came together. "Of course."

"Me too," Hannah said. "Do you know who didn't think we needed a conversation?"

Kailee slowly shook her head.

"Carter. Without even a hint that he was thinking about it, he just came home one day and announced that he'd joined the Navy. No conversation. No consideration for what I thought. He just did what he wanted. He always did what he wanted."

Kailee fisted her hands on her hips. "Well, maybe if you weren't always taking care of everyone else, he wouldn't have felt the need to leave."

"Excuse me?" Hannah's chest tightened and her teeth clenched.

"Dani needs help, so you run off to the farm. Mom can't cook, so you

prepare meals for us. Dad needs help at the store, so you're here all the time."
Kailee's features hardened. "Have you ever wondered what you could have
done to make him want to stick around."

"First of all, I did all those things after he disappeared. Secondly, when
we were together, I did everything he asked me to do," Hannah shouted. "We
went where *he* wanted to go. We saw who he wanted to see. Yes, he brought
out an adventurous side of me and I enjoyed it, but I still put all of my needs,
wants, and dreams on the back burner, just to make him happy."

A wave of nausea rushed through Hannah. She couldn't believe she'd
done all of that for him. She'd loved him, and that was all that mattered at
the time.

The redness in Kailee's face faded.

"Look," Hannah sighed. "Carter's not a bad guy, when he puts in the
effort." She wanted to tell her sister everything she'd learned from Seth.
She wanted to warn her sister that if she went to the party, she'd see a side
of Carter she may not like. But mostly, she wanted to protect Kailee from
the hurt that would come when she learned that people, especially those
she looked up to, weren't always as they appeared. "We've both seen that
goodness in him, but his friends are not good people. I don't want you around
them." Kailee opened her mouth to argue, but Hannah held up her hand.
"I don't trust them. But I do trust you." She'd never said those words to her
sister, but when they passed her lips, she knew they'd come from her heart.
"I'm asking you not to go to the party, but you do what you think is best."

Kailee was silent. Hannah could almost see her thoughts, could tell
she wasn't sure how to respond. After a few moments of silence, Hannah
returned to the desk.

"I need to finish this up for Dad." She lowered herself to the seat, then
looked over her shoulder at her sister's back. "I'll talk to you later."

Kailee left the office and closed the door behind her. Hannah watched
her sister's progress through the store on the monitors. When the front door
closed behind her, Hannah put her face in her hands and let the tears of
frustration, anger, and years of bottled-up anguish fall.

Thirty-Two

From his vantage point at the back of the room, holding up the corners of the wall with his shoulders, Quinn surveyed the room, doing his best to keep his eyes off Hannah. Finnigan's party room was crowded tonight, and she and Dani had claimed the first table in the front corner by the door. Not surprisingly, they both had glasses of water and were refusing drinks and conversation from almost everyone who'd approached them.

The only people he'd seen stop at Hannah's table, and receive a warm reception, had been the newly married Kerri Harris and the three women who were with her. As he pushed away from the wall, intending to go speak to Kerri and her group, a cool breeze chilled the right side of his body as a blonde head rushed past him.

Kailee.

As Hannah's sister sidled past Kerri's table, Quinn followed at a cautious pace. He had a strong suspicion that Hannah didn't know Kailee was here by the way Kailee was ducking through the crowd.

As Quinn approached Kerri's table, he kept an eye on Kailee, who was currently trying her best to blend in with the crowd as she cast frequent glances in her sister's direction.

"What's gotten you so enthralled?" Kerri asked.

"Nothing much." Quinn shrugged. "I'm surprised to see you here tonight."

Kerri sighed. "Well, Jackson and the band are practicing. Since Charlie works so closely with Carter's father, he thought someone should be here to represent the company, and we had nothing else to do."

Quinn looked at each woman in turn. Two of them were Kerri's sisters-in-law. The third woman, who was very pregnant, was a local celebrity.

"Quinn, you know Mason's wife, Charlotte." She waved toward the redhead beside her. "And Nathan's wife, Janelle."

Quinn gave them all a nod of acknowledgment.

"And that's Janelle's sister, Kelsey." Kerri motioned toward the pregnant woman across from her.

Quinn smiled at Kelsey. "It's good to see you again."

Kelsey and her husband had been integral in getting the pub back up and running. They had single-handedly, and anonymously, paid for all the new equipment in the kitchen.

"I'm surprised to see *you* here, Quinn," Kerri said.

"Why?"

Kerri glanced over at Carter, who was talking to a small crowd of people. "He is the competition. Celebrating his return is the last thing I thought you would be doing," she said.

Quinn clenched his jaw. There wasn't much of a competition, but he'd decided to make an appearance to support Hannah if the need arose.

"He was a friend," Quinn mumbled.

Kerri's head bobbed once in acknowledgement, then she smiled. "How did your meeting with Charlie go?"

Quinn's heart raced with excitement. He'd met with Charlie earlier in the day to talk about his future after graduation. The conversation had been a good one, and he couldn't wait to finish their discussion on Monday.

"It went well," Quinn answered.

"Still not going to tell me what it was about?"

Quinn chuckled. "Nope, you'll just have to wait."

Kerri pouted, and he laughed harder. He lifted his gaze to the room and looked around. His laughter died abruptly when he saw Kailee.

"I gotta go." With a squeeze of Kerri's shoulder, he walked toward Hannah's sister, who was now surrounded by three of Carter's friends.

"I said I'm not interested." Kailee's shrill voice was his first warning that something was wrong. As he got closer, the flush on her cheeks was the second.

"C'mon, sweetheart," Phillip cooed. "I just want to show you a good time."

Quinn's skin tightened as he clutched his hand into a fist.

"No." Kailee's wide-eyed stare met Quinn's.

Phillip, Eric, and Will laughed as they watched Kailee scurry away toward Quinn.

"Where you going, baby?" Will called, chuckling as his gaze met Quinn's glare.

Kailee hid behind Quinn.

"Seriously," Eric laughed. "We're all twice the man he is."

"And she's sixteen," Quinn said. "You think your cellmate will appreciate your manliness?"

Their laughter died abruptly. Behind Phillip's back, Eric and Will exchanged a look of surprise.

"Sixteen, huh?" Phillip smirked. "She's too young for you too, then. Or is she a consolation prize? You can't have her sister, so you get the next best thing?"

Kailee's inhale hissed past Quinn's ear, and his nostrils flared. He took a step toward Phillip.

Phillip chuckled as he moved toward Quinn. "I don't know why you're surprised. You were always a loser, especially when Carter was around."

Quinn tightened his fist as he remembered the years of torment at Phillip's hands before he'd become a part of their group. Then there was the teasing that he'd put up with when he'd finally been accepted as a part of Carter's crowd. It had started out as good-natured ribbing, at least to Quinn's thirteen-year-old mind. But by the time they were seniors, he'd seen it for what it was. Outwardly, they'd accepted him as one of them, but within the group he was still the unpopular, chubby nerd. And they'd never really let him forget that.

"I thought we'd finally proven that at prom," Phillip continued, his sneer growing. "When Tori dared him to ask your crush before you could."

Quinn's nostrils flared and he clenched his teeth. As soon as she'd issued the dare, he'd known trusting Tori had been a mistake. Until now, he hadn't realized she'd shared his secret with others.

Phillip hooted. "Did you really think you could trust Tori? She disliked you almost as much as we did. She was just better at hiding it."

Quinn noticed the mean-spirited glint in Phillip's eyes.

"You were never good enough," Phillip scoffed. "Maybe you finally—"

Quinn drew back his fist and slung it as hard as he could at Phillip's face. His fist made contact, silencing Phillip as he fell back into the arms of his shocked friends. Eric and Will stared at Quinn, their eyes wide and mouths agape, then looked down at Phillip's limp body in their arms. Phillip's eyes were closed, his mouth slightly open, his teeth bloodied, his cheek already swelling and turning blue.

"Oh my goodness," Kailee gasped as she tugged on Quinn's loose arm. "I can't believe you just did that."

He couldn't believe it either. He'd wanted to do that so many times in high school, and if Carter hadn't stepped in to stop him, he would have.

"You should probably get out of here," Kerri said as she appeared in front of him.

As Quinn's vision came back into focus, he realized a crowd was growing around the unconscious Phillip and the others. Kerri was pushing him backward, away from the crowd, as Kailee tugged on his arm.

"We'll handle this," Kerri's sister-in-law said. Quinn nodded and turned toward Kailee and the door.

"Thank you so much." Kailee moved to his side. "I shouldn't have come. Hannah told me not to, but I wanted to celebrate Carter's return. She'd warned me about his friends, but I thought she was just being selfish and mean."

Quinn let Kailee's words wash over him as he tried to calm his racing heart.

"Is . . . Carter like his friends?" Her brown eyes, just a little darker than her sister's, were full of innocence and sadness.

He forgot all his anger and focused on Kailee. "Hannah asked you not to come, right?" They continued the slow walk through the crowd toward the door. "Don't you think she had a really good reason for that?"

They stepped outside. Kailee's shoulders drooped. "I do now." She stopped short and looked up at him. "You won't tell her I was here, will you?"

"No, I won't tell her," Quinn said. "But maybe you should?"

Kailee nodded.

"Would you like a sundae?" Quinn asked.

"Hot fudge?" Kailee asked as she slipped through the open door.

Quinn smiled. "Is there any other kind?"

"I can't thank everyone enough for coming tonight," Tori announced to the crowd to much applause.

Hannah watched Quinn slip Kailee out the back door of the pub and breathed a sigh of relief. She had a feeling her sister would show up, even after their argument in their father's office.

"I told you he'd handle it," Dani whispered.

"It is so hard to believe that ten weeks ago we were here to memorialize our dear, dear friend." Tori's eyes shone with adoration as she looked at Carter. Hannah swallowed her disgust and looked away.

"Can we leave now?" Dani asked.

"After this little show." Hannah flourished her hand toward the center of the room where Tori and Carter commanded the crowd's attention. The room was packed, almost shoulder to shoulder. Far more than had attended his memorial party. She guessed a resurrection was a bigger deal. "Thank you again for letting me crash with you for a few days. And thank you for coming to this. I know how you feel about Tori."

Dani grimaced. "This isn't about her. I couldn't let you come alone. Who knows what they might be up to." She waved her hand at Tori and Carter. "Besides, it may be the last of her parties either of us ever get invited to, so we may as well enjoy it."

"I'm actually counting on that," Hannah laughed. She'd always hated Tori's parties, both when Carter was around and even more when he wasn't.

"So, let me turn it over to the man of the hour himself." Tori held her hand out toward Carter, who took it as he moved closer. "Carter Elliot."

The roar of the crowd was deafening as Carter took the microphone from Tori and turned in a slow circle to wave at everyone. When his eyes landed on Hannah, he smiled seductively, causing her to squirm.

"He's up to something," Hannah muttered under her breath.

Carter stood next to Tori, relishing the applause, until the crowd quieted down.

"Want to leave?" Dani stood and grabbed the strap of her purse off the back of her chair.

Hannah started to slide off the barstool as she tried to listen to Carter's words over the sound of the room.

"The last year has been rough for me," Carter said. "I thought I would die when they captured me, but knowing how much I was loved helped me get through the torture."

The crowd applauded again as Hannah's feet hit the floor.

"But there was one person in particular that I couldn't wait to get home to."

Hannah froze, one hand on the back of her chair, the other under the strap of her purse on her shoulder. Carter's catlike grin widened.

"I honestly could not have made it through a year of captivity if it hadn't been for the love of my beautiful and patient fiancée, Hannah Murphy." He stretched his arm toward her, holding out his hand for her to take. "The Buttercup to my Westley. Come up here, my darling."

Hannah's knuckles turned white around the back of the chair. That had been their Halloween costumes the year they started dating, and she'd hated the nickname ever since. She'd even told Carter she hated the nickname, but she'd smiled and nodded every time he'd used it anyway. Her molars ground together, and her eyes narrowed on his smug smile. But she remained still, fighting the urge to do as he asked and join him. She didn't want to be that woman anymore. The one who did as she was asked just to make everyone else happy.

"Hannah, come on." Carter motioned for her to join him.

She held her ground. She wasn't marrying him, and she knew that if she did as he asked, it would be that much harder to persuade him, and the rest of the town, of that fact. Her chest grew tight, and she could feel her pulse in her temples. She'd come here for one reason and one reason only: to say goodbye to Carter and move on with her life. She realized her mistake too late.

"Hannah, let's just go," Dani said, slowly prying her fingers off the back of the chair. Hannah focused on the feeling returning to the tips of her fingers as Dani released them from their death grip.

"She's just shy," Tori called out. "Let's give her a round of applause." Tori began clapping, the crowd joined her, and the mischievous spark in Carter's eyes grew malicious.

"Hannah," he said again, coolly. "Sweetheart."

Hannah slipped her purse off her shoulder and handed it to Dani. If Carter wanted her by his side, she'd go. But she was doing this on her terms, and he was about to regret forcing her hand. She'd hoped to be able to tell him what she'd learned from Seth in a private conversation, but he'd avoided her all night.

Now she knew why.

"I'll be right back," Hannah growled as she stepped around the table.

She made her way through the crowd and stomped toward Carter. His smile faded as she glared at him, and he took a step backward as she approached. When she stopped in front of him, he was no longer grinning. The malice had disappeared and was replaced with an uneasy shaking of his head. He reached for her, but she smacked his hand away.

"What do you think you're doing?" Her tone silenced the room, and she felt all eyes focused on her.

Carter's eyes widened, but he kept the tight smile on his lips.

"See, I told you she was shy," Tori said through a nervous giggle.

Hannah ignored Tori and kept her eyes on Carter. "I have told you repeatedly, and I thought you understood, but maybe the problem was that I didn't have enough witnesses. So, now that we do, let me make this clear: we are not getting married."

Carter chuckled and looked around the room, shaking his head and trying to wave off her words. "Can't we talk about this later?" He gave Hannah a small shrug.

"Clearly, we cannot. You apparently don't listen when we're alone. Maybe now you'll hear me." Hannah glanced around the room and swallowed the nervous lump in her throat.

Everyone in the crowd was zeroed in on her. Most of their faces were frozen with surprise, and some mouths even hung open. What had she done? No one here knew this side of her. Maybe this was a mistake.

Carter reached for her again, but she took a step backward. "This past year in the POW camp, you were the only thing that got me through. I couldn't wait to get home and marry you. I regret not doing it sooner, but the anticipation of our wedding helped me survive."

"Oh, I'm sure," Hannah said. "Would you mind telling the crowd again where you've been the past year?"

Tori laughed. "I'm not sure anyone really needs to know that. We're here to celebrate his return, and that's all that matters."

"Last chance to come clean," Hannah said just loud enough for only Carter to hear.

"I've told you everything," he announced to the room. "I've been a prisoner of war for the last year, more or less. I don't know what else you want to hear," he said through clenched teeth.

The lies. The dare. The smug look on Tori's face. Carter's deception. Enough was enough.

"So, where were you being held as a POW? Kandahar? Kirkuk?" Hannah pulled back her shoulders. "Or maybe Wichita Falls?"

Carter's face paled. "How?"

"How?" Hannah repeated, her eyes narrowing on him. "How did I find out?"

Carter's nostrils flared, and he turned to Tori. She shrugged as she mouthed the words, "I didn't."

Suddenly, it all became clear. Tori had known Carter was alive. Hannah wondered now if Tori had been keeping tabs on her for Carter. And for how long?

"How did I find out what, exactly?" Hannah said. "How did I find out you were actually in jail?"

Those in the crowd closest to them gasped.

"How did I find out that you were never at Officer Candidate School?" Hannah's voice grew louder so those farther away could hear. "How did I find out you were kicked out of the Navy? Don't worry, Tori didn't tell me you were alive."

Tori's cheeks turned a bright red.

A low murmur rolled through the crowd. Carter grabbed for her again with a shaky hand. She stepped out of his reach as Tori tried to calm the crowd, whose restless energy was becoming angry.

"That's enough," Carter hissed, a fearful look in his eyes as he looked around the room.

"How many more lies have you told since you came home?" Hannah asked.

"How could you do this to me?" Carter snapped.

"Do what to you?" Hannah countered.

"How could you make up these lies in front of my friends?" Carter took a step toward her, his pale cheeks now flushed with anger.

"What did I lie about?" She reached into her pocket and pulled out her phone. "I will call Seth right now and clear this up. He's the local Navy recruiter." Hannah quickly searched for Seth's information as adrenaline coursed through her veins. "He's also a chief petty officer and has been in the Navy for over thirteen years. He has all kinds of ties to higher-ups and can verify everything."

"Who?" Carter fell back again.

"Quinn's brother-in-law," Tori answered, her face pale to match Carter's.

"I should have known," Carter scoffed. He turned to the crowd. "Relax, everyone, everything she says is false."

"Everything she says is true," someone shouted.

The crowd gasped as people turned and looked for the voice. Then the crowd parted, allowing Seth to move forward.

"Thank you," Hannah murmured to Seth.

"You did good." He gave her a warm smile.

Tears pricked the back of her eyes. She had done good. She'd stood up for herself. In a very public way. She didn't allow Carter to dictate how things would be. She stood a little taller and swallowed the tears of her triumph.

"Are we done, Carter?" She raised an eyebrow as she waited for him to respond.

With a clenched jaw, and after a few seconds of silence, Carter finally nodded.

Hannah turned on her heel and stormed toward Dani. Her friend handed Hannah her purse, and they walked through the crowd and left the pub.

"I don't know about you, but I'm starving," Dani said.

"I could eat," Hannah agreed, then with a smile added, "and I think we deserve to celebrate."

Dani laughed as they left the pub for their favorite Chinese restaurant.

Thirty-Three

Hannah looked out at the dark, empty street below and pressed her forehead against the cold windowpane. Despite the pink walls and décor in her attic room, she felt anything but cheery. She'd woken up this morning hoping that a day at the farm would lift her spirits and help her forget about what had happened last night. For the most part, it had done both, but as Dani had relived the confrontation between Hannah and Carter, embarrassment had taken all the relief she'd felt and stomped all over it. After they'd finished up with the horses, she and Dani had met up with Hannah's father and removed the remainder of her things from the townhouse. Any lingering embarrassment had disappeared, leaving her to wallow in her regret and self-pity.

She shouldn't have humiliated Carter the way she had. As someone who had always taken care to consider everyone else's feelings, she'd done a horrendous job of it. She would never forget the look of fear and betrayal in his eyes. She could have let everyone know he hadn't been a POW without divulging everything he'd told them was a lie. She probably should have stopped with that, then talked about the rest in private. Would Carter ever forgive her for the way she'd acted? Did she really want him to?

When they'd gotten her things out of the townhouse, they'd found a few of Quinn's things. Everything of his reminded her of their time together and pulled at her heartstrings. She hadn't had the chance to speak with him since he'd come to the farm Tuesday night, five nights ago. He'd said that he wouldn't move if she asked him not to. She wanted, more than anything, to ask him to stay. She loved him, and now that Carter was finally out of her life, she was free to be with Quinn. But he needed to follow his dreams, and she wanted to stay in Rocky Creek. Those two desires weren't compatible, no matter how much she wished them to be.

"Knock, knock."

Hannah lifted her head and slowly turned toward the entrance into her hideaway. Kailee stood silhouetted by the light from the stairwell. Her hands were wrapped around a large bowl of popcorn.

"Come on in," Hannah murmured, her voice cracking. She wasn't sure she'd said a word to anyone since she'd gotten home several hours ago.

Kailee crept closer, hugging the bowl as she stopped at the entrance of the alcove. "I see you've decorated," Kailee said, her voice barely above a whisper. She pointed to the photographs Hannah had brought from the townhouse that afternoon.

Including the landscape she'd meant to give to Quinn as a birthday present.

"You've been up here before?" Hannah asked. Her sister had never shown any interest in her attic room.

Kailee's cheeks turned a pale pink. "A few times since you left for college."

"Why?" Hannah asked, curiosity getting the better of her.

Kailee took a step closer and lifted her eyes to Hannah's face. "I was missing you."

Tears stung the back of Hannah's eyes, and she blinked a few times to try to hold off the onset. Her sister had always seemed indifferent to Hannah's absence, and to hear her express her feelings now, on top of everything else, was almost too much. Hannah slid closer to the wall and patted the bench seat beside her. Kailee strolled over and lowered herself to the seat.

"I often thought about calling you to talk," Kailee continued softly, "but wasn't sure you would want to talk to me."

"Oh," Hannah sighed, pressing the palms of her hands together, then between her thighs to keep from putting a hand around Kailee's shoulder. They were in new territory, and Hannah didn't want this exploration to end yet. "I would have welcomed a call from you, Kailee. I've always wished we were closer than we are."

The corner of Kailee's mouth quirked upward. "Me too."

Hannah leaned her back against the cool window. They sat silently for a few minutes, the only noise in the room the rhythmic sound of their breathing.

"So, why aren't we?" Hannah finally asked, a question for both of them, as she searched her own memories and feelings.

Kailee shrugged. "Maybe because I've always been jealous of you."

"Jealous?" Hannah said. "Really?"

"Yes, really." Kailee set the popcorn on the bench between them. "Is that hard for you to believe?"

Hannah was confused. "You're so outgoing and popular. Everyone likes you. I don't know why you would be jealous of me."

"Because everyone loves you," Kailee said.

"Not anymore," Hannah scoffed. Not after her outburst at last night's party.

"I doubt that," Kailee said. "Everyone who knows you will understand you would have only acted like that if pushed to it. The rest will simply forget about it in a day or two."

Hannah studied her sister's face, saw the twinkle in her eye, and laughed lightly. "Which category do you fall into?"

"The first," Kailee said. "Do you know what it's like following in your footsteps in school?"

"What do you mean?"

"For a while, especially in elementary school, it was always the same," Kailee began. "The teacher would recognize me as your sister and maybe mention in passing how much they'd loved teaching you, and how much they looked forward to teaching me as well." The light in Kailee's eyes faded a little. "And then I would make a small mistake, or I'd get a bad grade or misbehave, and they never treated me the same after that."

"Oh, Kailee, that's awful." Hannah sighed sadly. As a teacher, she would never compare siblings that way. She and Kailee were evidence enough that brothers and sisters weren't always alike when it comes to . . . well, anything.

"When I was in middle school, my teachers verbalized their criticisms a little more. At least to me. And it's even worse in high school," Kailee said.

Hannah took her sister's hand, giving it a squeeze.

"I'm so sorry to hear that. I can't imagine how awful that feels," Hannah said sincerely. "Mom and Dad don't compare our behavior, do they?"

Kailee shrugged. "No, not usually. Although, lately, I think Dad sometimes wishes I was a little more like you. I don't have any interest in helping at the store, and I don't help around the house as much as I could—"

"Because you're afraid you won't do it right?" Hannah interrupted.

Kailee smiled. "Or do it to your standards."

Hannah looked out the window. It would seem that she and her sister had more in common than either of them had ever realized. Hannah had always felt insecure in her own skin in middle school and for most of high school. She'd always thought Kailee was much more confident in herself. Apparently, she'd been wrong.

"Hannah, I have to tell you something," Kailee whispered, the worry seeping out of her voice.

Hannah gave her sister's fingers another squeeze. "Go ahead."

"Promise you won't get angry?" Kailee frowned, and Hannah nodded. "I went to the party." Kailee's words rushed out. "But before you get mad, hear me out."

Hannah's stress melted. She knew Kailee had been at the pub, but clearly Kailee didn't know she knew. If Kailee was confessing, though, she must have a reason.

"I'm not going to get mad." Hannah's words were slow, and her eyes softened. "I asked you not to go, so why did you choose otherwise?"

"Because I didn't think it was fair," Kailee whined, pulling her hand away and folding her arms over her chest. Her lower lip pouted. "I still thought Carter was my friend, and I wanted to celebrate his return."

Hannah studied her sister, trying to decipher what Kailee might be thinking. "Fair enough," she answered.

"I learned a lot last night. About both of you," Kailee said. Hannah pressed her shoulder to the window as she gazed at the empty street. Kailee had left the party before Hannah's outburst, so Hannah wasn't sure what her sister could have learned about her. She wasn't sure she wanted to know.

"I know you think I had a crush on him," Kailee started.

"I'm not sure that's what I thought. I know you looked up to Carter and wanted to be popular and well known like him. At least, I hope you didn't have a crush. He's eight years older than you."

Kailee smiled and shrugged. "Maybe a small one. But you're right, I did look up to him. He was everything I wanted to be. And the best part about it was that no one looked down on him for it."

Hannah relaxed as Kailee's words sunk in. Carter was so opposite from Hannah that it was almost natural for Kailee to want to emulate him. She was twelve when Hannah and Carter had started dating. She was just starting to discover who she was, and probably starting to tire of always being compared to Hannah. While Hannah had seen the idolization, she now understood better why it had happened.

But as much as she hated to admit it, her sister's admiration for Carter instead of her still stung.

"I get it," Hannah muttered, looking out the window again.

"But last night changed that for me," Kailee said. "I understand now that popularity isn't anything if you're not really a good person. Carter ignored me every time he walked by me last night, and the things I heard him say about almost everyone there were awful. And his friends are even worse."

Hannah zeroed in on her sister. "What happened?" she asked.

Kailee sighed. "Nothing, but if Quinn hadn't stepped in, I don't know what might have happened."

"Where did you go after you left the party?" Hannah asked hesitantly. She and Kailee were just starting to bond, and she didn't want to do anything to jeopardize that.

"We went for ice cream," Kailee answered.

Hannah thought about her first kiss with Quinn outside of the pub after she'd escaped one of Tori's parties. At least now Hannah would never be invited to another one.

"Quinn seems to think you've been deceiving people since Carter died," Kailee blurted, then covered her mouth with her fingers.

Hannah considered her sister's comment. She'd avoided telling Kailee the truth about her relationship with Carter because of how much her sister adored him. She hadn't talked about Carter with Quinn because she didn't want to live in the past. She'd kept the truth from everyone else simply because it was easier to let them believe whatever they wanted.

"The truth, and what I've kept from almost everyone, is I was ready to end things with Carter before he died."

Kailee gasped. Hannah waited to see the judgment or disapproval form in her sister's eyes.

"Why?" Kailee asked.

Hannah thought about the answer. If Kailee knew how weak Hannah had been, would she think less of her?

"I think you said it yourself," Hannah carefully chose her words. "We were just too different. And I wasn't confident enough at that time to end the relationship. Carter was the only thing I knew, my first boyfriend. He'd swept me off my feet and made me feel alive. But things slowly started to reveal themselves over the years, and I realized how different we were as people. Especially after he went to boot camp and I was alone with my thoughts and feelings."

Kailee's lips pursed. "But you were always different. Why did you start dating him to begin with?"

Hannah laughed. "Well, when the most popular boy in school asks an unpopular nerd to prom, apparently it's not okay to tell him no. The funny thing was that I wasn't even in love with him like all the girls were. I mean, I knew who he was—everyone knew who Carter was—but I didn't get wrapped up in all the hype."

"But why did you start dating him if you knew you were so different?" Kailee asked.

"Why are you so curious?" Hannah narrowed her eyes. "Did Quinn put you up to this?"

"No." Kailee vigorously shook her head. "He didn't ask, but we did talk about you and Carter last night."

"Oh really?" Hannah said. "And what did you talk about?"

"How odd the two of you were as a couple."

Hannah laughed as the day's tension eased from her body. She and

Kailee had never had such a lengthy, relaxed conversation. Even if she wasn't fond of the topic, it was a relief to be so open with her sister.

"I liked being the wallflower at the party," Hannah admitted. "Because, without Carter, I wouldn't have been at the party to begin with."

Kailee grinned. "You liked being part of the popular crowd."

"I did," Hannah said. "But it became tedious going to the same places, with the same people, always doing the same things. And that was the problem. They were always the places Carter wanted to go, with the people he wanted to hang out with, doing the things he wanted to do. I had no say."

"Oh," Kailee said. "So, why did you say yes when he proposed?"

Hannah remembered the night he'd proposed. He had taken her to her favorite spot on the parkway overlooking the city after a nice dinner out. It was the spring of their junior year in college, and he'd gotten down on one knee. The ring was beautiful, the night was a bit warm for early spring, and she'd been swept away in the moment. She couldn't have wished for a better proposal.

"He wasn't so bad when we were away from home," Hannah answered, her voice soft and meek. "He encouraged me to try new things. He was fun and could be attentive and kind when he wanted to be." She sighed and looked out into the darkness. "I think I mistook his need for me as love. I liked being needed. He made me feel useful and desirable and loved."

He had tried, on occasion and usually after a fight, to be more aware of what she wanted. But in the end, even in those rare times, they ended up back where they started, following his plans for the evening.

"There were times he could be nice, or humble, or supportive, and I guess I hung on to those few times more than I should have. I held out hope that he would become the person I saw glimpses of, the one I knew he was capable of being, instead of always being the arrogant, self-centered brat he was when we came home."

Kailee nodded. "So, what changed?"

Hannah smiled to herself. "I did."

Kailee cocked an eyebrow, and Hannah chuckled.

"When he left for the Navy, I was finally able to live life my way,"

Hannah said. "I was so much happier without him than I was with him, and I promised myself I would end things the first chance I got."

They spent a few moments in silence. Hannah reflected on everything she'd just told her sister. It was the stark truth—a truth she'd ignored for most of the last two years, but one she started to fully realize since Carter's return from the dead. Her relationship with Quinn had helped her understand her past with Carter and how happy she could be with the right person.

"Can I be honest?" Kailee asked.

"I should hope so." Hannah took a handful of popcorn.

"You've always been a people pleaser. I think you were more afraid of what people thought of you, not what they thought about Carter."

Hannah was learning that her sister saw more than she had ever given her credit for.

"But I think you underestimate people's opinions of you," Kailee said. "I think you overestimate what people thought of Carter. I think people would have empathized with you if you told them he had joined the Navy without asking. It sucks that you felt like you couldn't break it off with him."

"I guess I wasn't strong enough to find out." Hannah sighed. "I was a coward."

Kailee frowned. "How so?"

"If I were stronger, I would have told everyone the truth a year ago instead of allowing them to pity me every time they saw me," Hannah said.

"You never asked anyone to take pity on you," Kailee argued. "They did it because it made them feel better about themselves. So they could pat themselves on the back for giving you comfort when they only really wanted it for themselves."

Hannah's mouth fell open. "How can you say that?"

Kailee shrugged. "Because I did that."

Hannah stared at her sister in silence. As happy as she was at the honesty they were sharing, she was beginning to wonder if she ever really knew anything about Kailee. Her sister was much more mature than Hannah had thought.

"And when you didn't give me the sympathy I wanted, I began to hate you. At least a little." Kailee's face became sheepish, and she withdrew a little.

"I was angry that you weren't showing the grief I thought you should, and I started to think you didn't deserve Carter. And I'm ashamed at some of the things I said to you this past year, and to Quinn too. I was unfairly comparing him to Carter because if you weren't going to feel grief, I wanted you to feel guilt. I was so wrong. About all of you. I'm so sorry." She shook with sobs.

Hannah moved the popcorn bowl off to the side, then draped an arm over Kailee's shoulder and pulled her sister closer.

"It's okay, Kailee," Hannah cooed, hugging her sister, letting her cry. "I get it. We weren't close to begin with, and you latched on to Carter because he puts on a good face. We both fell for it." Hannah rubbed her sister's arm, hoping to soothe her.

Kailee sat up. Her eyes were red, and she had a runny nose.

"And I imagine you've already apologized to Quinn?" Hannah asked.

A small smile touched Kailee's lips. "Yes. Over ice cream sundaes."

Hannah laughed and tugged her sister closer. "Hot fudge?"

"Of course."

Hannah rested her chin on the top of Kailee's head as she chuckled. At least they had one thing in common. "Then everything's all right. We can just put this behind us and move on."

Kailee pulled away and wiped her cheeks with her sleeve. "So, it's officially over with Carter?" There was a serious look in her eyes.

"It was over well before he disappeared," Hannah said. "The biggest problem I had was convincing him of that."

Kailee's eyes filled with a light of hope. "So, does this mean you and Quinn will get back together?"

Hannah searched for the words she wanted to say. How could she tell her sister it wasn't as simple as that? And why did Kailee suddenly seem so interested in her love life?

Hannah rose to her feet, stretching her legs. She grabbed the fluffy throw pillow sitting in her glider rocking chair, then hugged it to her chest as she began to pace.

"I don't think Quinn and I will get back together," she said as she passed the opening of the gable.

"Why? You're not with Carter anymore, and if what I've heard people say happened last night is true, Carter finally understands that. So the door's wide open for Quinn now."

Hannah cringed. She knew that everyone would be talking about what she'd done at the party. She studied the excitement on Kailee's face, a stark contrast to only moments ago when they had been talking about Carter.

"Why do you want me to get back with Quinn?" Hannah asked. "I thought you hated him almost as much as you hated me."

"You know I don't hate you," Kailee said. "I've just been really confused, you know, with Carter's death. And then what's been going on with Mom."

Hannah bit her lip. "I know. Mom's stuff hasn't been easy on any of us. Maybe I should have been around to help more."

"You did what you could," Kailee said. "I could have done more. I've been kind of a brat through her whole treatment process. But I'll do better. As for you and Quinn, I think what matters is that you were happy with Quinn, and you deserve to be happy." Kailee paused for a moment, then said, "But more importantly, I liked who you were with Quinn more than who you were with Carter."

Hannah shuffled over to the chair, then sat and hugged the pillow to her chest. "How was I with Quinn? And how was I different with Carter?"

"Well, for one, you were much more confident with Quinn. And, second, he stood up for you when he needed to, and stood beside you when he didn't. When you and I argued, he stayed silent, but I still noticed the small signs of support he gave you, or how attentive he was to what was going on."

Hannah was surprised. She'd also recognized these things but thought no one else had seen them.

"Carter never did that. He always walked away when you and I argued. He never seemed to pay attention when you were stressed," Kailee added. "Not like Quinn."

"You're right," Hannah said. "You're more observant than I realized."

Kailee broke into a smile. "Did I hear you right? What did you say?" she teased.

Hannah laughed. "You are right."

As the sisters laughed together, for the first time in a very long time, a peace settled over Hannah. If nothing else came from her short relationship with Quinn and the turmoil of Carter's return, at least she and Kailee were on speaking terms. The seed was now planted, and Hannah hoped that one day their relationship might be what she'd always hoped for.

Thirty-Four

On Monday afternoon, Hannah walked into her father's store and waved to the customer at the register as she walked to the drink cooler. She'd gotten back into her usual routine, going to Dani's barn and helping with the horses on Sunday, then working on Monday. She appreciated the normalcy but hadn't been able to shake a tingling feeling of anticipation all day. She needed to talk to Quinn, but she had been putting it off since her talk with Kailee. His birthday present was still in the back seat of her car because she hadn't yet been able to work up the courage to take it to him.

"Good afternoon, Miss Hannah," Donna called out from behind the register.

"Hey, Donna." Hannah placed a bottle of water and a bag of M&Ms on the counter. Donna greeted her with a wide smile and a twinkle in her eye. Hannah inwardly groaned. "You heard about the party."

It wasn't really a question. She'd gotten similar looks from some of the teachers today. Luckily, they hadn't asked questions.

"So, why are you smiling? It was awful," Hannah said.

"Maybe in the moment." Donna shrugged. "But those of us who know the two of you are just happy you finally stood up to him. You're such a sweet young lady, and no one liked seeing him run roughshod over you."

"Yet no one said a word while we were together." Hannah laughed lightly as she slid her items across the counter so Donna could add them to her tab.

"Of course not. Everyone knows not to meddle in others' affairs of the heart," Donna said as she wrote the items in her notebook.

Hannah respected the adage, but it didn't help the feeling that she'd been doing something wrong all along.

"But if you must know, in my honest opinion, he was never good enough for you," Donna said.

"Well, I wouldn't have minded hearing that," Hannah chuckled. "What a wasted few years."

"Were they?" Donna tilted her head as she stared at Hannah. "I think even bad experiences have something to teach us."

"You have a good point. Thanks." Hannah held up her candy and water, and waved as she began to move toward the office.

"Hannah, wait."

Hannah turned toward her sister's voice, and her eyes widened with surprise.

"What are you doing here?" Hannah asked.

"I have no idea." Kailee shrugged. "Dad texted me as school was letting out and asked me to come by. He didn't tell me why."

How odd. Hannah slid her arm around her sister's shoulder and continued toward their father's office.

"How was your day?" Hannah asked.

"It was awesome," Kailee laughed. "All anyone could talk about was what you did at the party. So many people asked if what you'd said about Carter was true."

"Ugh, I hate that for you."

"Why? It was amazing. Even the teachers were curious," Kailee said in a chipper voice. "Turns out, not many of them actually liked Carter either. They just pretended because his mother was such a pain in the butt." Kailee laughed.

"That doesn't surprise me at all," Hannah said.

They fell into step and continued on to the office side by side.

"You know, I don't think it surprises me either," Kailee said, her tone surprised and full of awe. "I guess everyone but me knew who he really was."

"Kailee, I doubt you were the only one. People see what they want to, especially when it comes to other people."

"So, the people at the party? Do you think they all thought he was Mr. Perfect?"

Hannah's mind scrolled through the faces of the people who had been at the party. "It's hard to say. Maybe half of them know the real Carter but pretend not to just to see what happens or what he'll do next."

They reached the open door to their father's office, and Hannah rapped her knuckles on the doorframe.

Her dad turned and gave them a wide grin. "Come in," he said as he rose to his feet. He hugged them both, then motioned them toward the couch. "Have a seat."

Kailee bounced over to the couch and plopped down as Hannah hung up her coat on the rack. Her father was unusually chirpy, and she wondered what was going on to make him so happy.

"Hey, Dad, I thought you'd be home." Hannah lowered herself to the sofa next to her sister.

"I will go home soon, but I wanted to talk to you girls about something first." Her father sat in his desk chair and rolled it closer to his daughters. "I got a call from your cousin last week."

"Which cousin?" Kailee asked.

"Colin."

Hannah smiled. "How is he?" The last time she'd talked to Colin, he had been growing weary with his job at a large investment firm, and his coworkers had started to get on his nerves.

"He's good." Her father nodded. "He's actually unemployed right now and called me about a job."

"You're kidding," Hannah said.

"A job?" Kailee tipped her head. "Here?"

"Yes, here. In the store." He turned to Kailee. "Kailee, I know you've just started showing an interest in learning how things are done here, and you still can, but he can start right away and has the degree to help."

"That's cool," Kailee said with a giggle. "I just wanted to help out like Hannah does. I didn't think I'd inherit the store one day."

Her father's face broke into a soft, warm smile that made Hannah's heart flutter. After their heart-to-heart, Kailee had been more open to talking. They'd all learned a lot about each other in the past thirty-six hours. Hannah felt they'd all finally turned a corner and things would be easier for everyone in her family going forward.

"He'll be here next Monday." He turned to Hannah. "I thought you could help me train him in running the store."

Excitement washed over her. If Colin were serious about taking over for her father, that would be one less thing she would have to worry about. And Colin's interest, along with his degree in finance, would make him an excellent replacement. But she was getting ahead of herself. First and foremost, it would be nice to see her favorite cousin again.

Her father tapped her on the knee. "Are you okay with this, Hannah?"

Hannah smiled. "Of course. It makes the most sense. I have a career, and Kailee isn't sure yet what she wants to do."

"That's true," Kailee agreed with a vigorous nod of her head. Her father chuckled and patted his younger daughter's hand.

"And it would give you some relief and a little extra free time. Well, once we get him trained anyway," her father said.

"True," Hannah said. "But we can tag-team that, and you can probably do most of it while I'm at school. And best of all, if this works out, the store will stay in the family, and you can stop worrying about that."

His smile widened. "I was never worried about that. We would have found a way."

"What way would that have been?" Hannah laughed. "Did you plan on living forever?"

Kailee giggled beside her, and her father shook his head.

"Just long enough to train a grandchild," he said with a wink at Hannah.

Hannah's cheeks grew hot. "You have a long wait for that," she muttered as she rose to her feet. "Don't you need to get home to Mom?"

"Subtle," Kailee teased.

"You're right." He got up and took his coat off the rack. "I've finished the payroll for the day, but if you want to show Kailee how things are done, you could always get started on the order for the week." He slid his arms into his coat. "Otherwise, I guess I will see you both at home soon?"

Kailee strolled across the small office and gave her father a hug.

"I'm so glad you're here," he said as they embraced.

Hannah didn't hear her sister's response, but she saw her father's smile widen. After a quick hug for Hannah, he left his daughters alone in his office.

Hannah sat in her father's chair, pulled up the week's payroll spreadsheet on the computer, and showed Kailee how the information was collected and entered. After fifteen minutes, they moved on to the spreadsheet for that week's orders. Hannah was in the middle of explaining what items were ordered from which companies when Kailee backhanded her upper arm.

"Ow." Hannah glared up at her sister, who pointed to the security monitors. Hannah's heart skipped in anticipation as she lifted her gaze to the screens, then sank like a rock to the pit of her stomach when she saw Carter coming toward the office. "Fudge," she muttered under her breath as he knocked on the door.

"What do you want?" Kailee snapped.

Carter stood in the doorway holding a large cardboard box. Hannah didn't want to pity him, but the look in his eyes was foreign to her. At least where he was concerned. She'd seen the look of remorse many times on her students' faces often enough to recognize it. And her visceral reaction was always to show them pity and leniency.

Neither of those would do in this situation, but her own regret washed over her like a bucket of ice water.

Carter cleared his throat and stepped into the room. "I found these things in the townhouse. I thought you might like them back."

Kailee took a step toward Carter, but Hannah grabbed her sister's arm. "I got it," she murmured as she stood.

Hannah moved toward Carter with cautious, measured steps, trying to see into the box, keeping her eyes away from his face.

"Think your watchdog can give us a minute?" Carter said with a smirk.

"Was that supposed to be funny?" Kailee barked from the desk.

Hannah held up a hand to her sister and heard Kailee grumble as the springs on the chair squeaked. "She stays where she is. Anything you need to say, she can hear."

Carter turned his focus to Hannah. "Fine," he mumbled, then lowered his stare to the contents of the box. "I don't know if you meant to leave this stuff, so thought I would bring them to you." He held out the box to her.

She glanced at the items inside the container, mostly knickknacks that she had spread throughout her former home. She reached into the box and shuffled some of the items around to get a good look. It wasn't anything she couldn't live without, but it touched her that he thought it was important enough to return to her.

Unless . . .

"Why did you bring them?" She couldn't help the suspicion in her tone.

He sighed and set the box down on the floor. "I honestly just thought you might want them back. If not, I'll just throw it all away."

She glanced at the open box again and noticed a few picture frames and other memories she'd made over the last few years, without Carter. "No, I'll take them." She met his stare. "Thank you," she added.

They stood silently, staring at each other, as Hannah fought the urge to wring her hands in front of her. After a few silent minutes, Kailee cleared her throat, breaking the uncomfortable spell.

"Was there something else?" Hannah asked.

"Yeah," he answered, then took a step back toward the door. She followed him, and they stepped out of the office. Hannah pulled the door closed.

"I just wanted to say that I'm sorry for everything I've done to you."

Hannah's eyes widened.

Carter chuckled. "I know. I didn't say that often enough." He gave her a self-deprecating smile. "If ever," he added. "I'm sorry for that too."

Hannah focused on his face and nodded slowly. "Why did you lie to me?"

Carter's smile faded. "After everything, that's your question?"

"Yeah. Everything else that happened between us is irrelevant. It won't change anything. I just want to know why you lied about your death."

Carter shoved his hands into the pockets of his coat. "I went to jail," he murmured. "I didn't want you to know that." He lowered his gaze to the floor. "I didn't want anyone to know."

"So, faking your death was the answer?" Hannah leaned against the wall and tucked her hands behind her. "What was your plan for when you were released from jail?"

"I thought I'd ride into town, sweep you off your feet, and we'd resume our lives as planned."

"And you expected me to be happy about your return and go along with your plan after being lied to?" Hannah asked softly, feeling an emptiness in her chest. She wanted to feel hurt, she waited to feel angry, but instead she felt nothing. After years of a throbbing in her head or a tightness in her chest when he was around, she was comforted by the absence of both.

He nodded. "I guess I did."

"Why?"

"Because that's who I thought you were." Carter lifted his eyes to hers, and her frown deepened.

"You think I'm a pushover." She wasn't asking. After their years together, she felt certain that was exactly how he saw her. And that was exactly how she was with him.

His mouth opened and closed like a fish out of water. "No. I don't think you're a pushover," he mumbled. His cheeks turned a deep shade of pink. "I thought you would be faithful, and I thought you'd never be able to get over me. I thought you'd be relieved I was home, and we'd be staying in Rocky Creek."

"Carter," Hannah said. "Be honest with me. You thought I would go along with whatever you wanted. That's who I always was."

Carter's eyes were full of sadness. "Not to me."

She inhaled deeply. "Really?"

He remained silent as he nodded.

"You asked me to prom on a dare, which I only just found out," she stated bluntly, and his cheeks colored again.

"I did," he agreed. "But I stand by what I said the night I proposed. You were the purest, most innocent person I'd ever met. Nothing you ever did was for personal gain. You never had an ulterior motive." He gave her a small smile. "Even at eighteen, I knew what that looked like. My mother is a social climber and has always surrounded herself with the same. My life was always filled with people—at school and at home—who used me or my family to better their standing. I had a lot of phony friends."

Hannah opened her mouth to argue but remained silent. He was right; it was one of the first things she'd noticed after they started dating. Everyone around him, at least those in Rocky Creek, used him to make themselves look good. Maybe that was why his behavior in college, away from the people he grew up with, had been so different. But had she been any different than everyone else in their hometown?

"I wasn't much better," she admitted, the truth of her words burning the back of her throat. "I liked being with you so I could experience things I never would have otherwise."

"That's not true." His smile widened. "I know you liked the parties, and you're probably right, you wouldn't have gone to them without me."

Hannah nodded once.

"But we had good times by ourselves too." His smile faded. "At least, I thought we had. That's how I knew you were different. You and I didn't always have to go out, and you still wanted to spend time with me. We talked about things outside of sports or movies, or other people."

She searched her memories and thought of the times when it had just been the two of them, laughing and talking, enjoying each other's company by simply being together. She had forgotten those quiet times.

"Being with you—just with you—let me relax. You had no expectations of who I needed to be or what I needed to do." Carter sighed. "Yet I still screwed it up."

Hannah's chest hurt and her eyes stung with tears.

"You were the best thing to happen to me, but I look back and see that I wasn't always fair to you. I didn't always consider your feelings or wishes." The corner of his lip lifted. "And we did go out way more than we stayed in because I just couldn't resist."

They stared at each other, his brown eyes boring into hers, filled with sadness and regret.

"I don't know what to say," she quietly admitted. "Except I am sorry for the way I acted at the party. I should have told you everything I'd learned in a private conversation, not blast it in front of all of your friends."

"Thanks," he said. "If I remember correctly, you tried to tell me ahead of time, but I didn't want to give you another chance to tell me it was over." Carter stepped toward her. "But I've finally heard you." He reached out and cupped her cheek. "I'm sorry I wasn't the right one for you, but you were good for me. Believe it or not, you did keep me grounded from time to time."

Hannah smiled. "You were good for me too. I learned a lot about myself, about what I like and what I don't. I think you brought me out of my shell when I needed that."

Carter lowered his hand and opened his arms. "One more? As friends?"

Hannah looked at his face, looked for the telltale sparkle he always got when he was up to something she wouldn't like. But it wasn't there. Hannah couldn't remember the last time he'd looked this sincere. She stepped into his open arms.

"Thank you," he sighed and held her for a few heartbeats. When she stepped back, he let her go. "Goodbye." He walked away from Hannah with a brief wave, then disappeared into the store.

Hannah walked into the office and closed the door behind her.

"Who was that?" Kailee asked.

"That's who he was when it was just the two of us."

Hannah floated toward the desk, she felt so light. An enormous weight, larger than she'd realized, had just been lifted from her shoulders. Carter finally understood that their relationship was over. Even better, he finally saw what she had known for several years. They'd never been right for each other, but they'd each gotten something they deeply needed from the other. She'd never wanted to hurt him, and he'd never realized how much he hurt her. She doubted they could be friends and remain in each other's lives, but at least they parted on good terms.

"I had forgotten that version of Carter existed." She relished the lightness in her chest, then looked at her sister's worried visage. "It doesn't change anything. He's out of my life now." She smiled, knowing that the words were true at last.

"Good," Kailee said. "Now what are you going to do about Quinn?"

Hannah's smile faded and she exhaled a slow breath. "Good question."

Thirty-Five

When Quinn pulled into his driveway, he was surprised to see the familiar car sitting in front of his house.

He'd heard what had happened at the party after he left with Kailee. While he and Hannah's sister were having a peaceful, eye-opening conversation over ice cream, Hannah had apparently put Carter in his place and made it clear that they were over.

He hadn't seen Hannah since the party on Friday night. He hadn't spoken to her since the Tuesday before that, which was a week ago. He'd like to use his meetings with Charlie as an excuse, but the truth was, he'd been avoiding her. He'd been busy putting a business plan into place with Charlie that would keep him in Rocky Creek and allow him to put his architecture degree to good use. He was surprised at how much more excited he was by this new turn of events than he had been about the idea of moving away. For the past few days, he'd been planning on how he would tell Hannah, but he wanted to have everything in place first.

It looked like the time to tell her had arrived.

Quinn parked his truck next to Hannah's car and climbed out as her driver's side door opened. He slung the strap of his laptop bag over his shoulder, closed his door, then strolled to the front of the vehicles. She was opening her back door and reaching into the back seat.

"I wasn't expecting to see you today." He shoved his hands into the pockets of his navy blazer and rocked back on his heels.

She closed the car door and gave him a weak smile. "I was surprised you didn't come to OM today."

"Sorry, I was in meetings all day." He forced his hands to stay in his pockets as he looked her over. She wore black dress slacks, typical for school, a blue polo shirt, and was bundled up in a gray hooded peacoat. His eyes landed on the package in her hands, and he wondered what it might be. "I told Rachel I wouldn't be there. Didn't she tell you?"

Hannah took a step closer. "She did better than that. She filled in for you."

Quinn chuckled. As much as his sister loved teaching, she equally hated extracurricular activities. It wasn't because she disliked spending the time with her students, but because she didn't like missing the time with Lily.

"Important meetings?" Hannah asked as her eyes traveled his body. She met his stare with a smirk. "Don't you look fancy."

"Hardly." Quinn scoffed as a cool breeze blew between them. Hannah's shoulders tensed, and he nodded toward the front door. "Why don't we go inside where it's warmer?" She agreed, and he let her lead the way to the door as he got the key ready.

Once inside, he set his laptop bag on the console table as she set down the package on the steps. He helped her with her coat and hung both of their coats on the rack behind the door.

When he turned around, she was holding the brown paper package out to him.

"I know it's late, but happy birthday." Her smile was cautious, and there was nervousness in her eyes.

"Only by a week," he tried to joke. "But you were kind of busy."

She watched as he opened the gift. He gasped when he uncovered the photograph. The landscape of the sunrise over the mountains and pond. He could vividly remember the first time he'd seen it and thought about everything that had come afterward.

"It's my favorite," he whispered.

She beamed. "I knew you liked it," she said. "I thought you could hang it in your new home and think of Rocky Creek."

"I know just where to hang it." His eyes drifted to the bare spot on the wall over the fireplace.

"You already have a place to live?" The excitement in her voice had disappeared. Her eyes darted over his features, and he couldn't help but wonder what she was thinking. Her shoulders rose as she inhaled.

"Quinn—"

"Hannah," he said at the same time, and they both laughed. "You go first." He waved toward the kitchen. "Maybe after we get something to drink."

"That's a great idea." She turned and glided toward the kitchen, then froze in the doorway.

"Oh," she said as she took in the renovations in the kitchen. The cabinets, frames, doors, and countertops had all been replaced, and a new island stood in the middle of the floor. The sink, stove, and refrigerator were all brand new, stainless steel, and positioned in the traditional work triangle. The sink still sat under the window, but the stove had been inserted into the island, and the fridge now sat against the wall.

"You've been busy."

"I've been motivated." Quinn's voice held more than a little bit of laughter.

A new kitchen would be a huge selling point for anyone looking to buy his house. Tears stung her eyes, and she looked away.

"Do you like it?" He strolled past her to the refrigerator, where he pulled out two bottles of water and tossed one to her.

Hannah caught the bottle and looked around the room. It was beautiful. It was exactly what she would want in a kitchen. They'd never talked about his kitchen, but when they cooked together at her parents' house, she had mentioned what she liked about their kitchen.

"It looks amazing." She took a sip of water, then tried to swallow around the lump in her throat.

He strolled toward her, and her heart began to race. "You sure?"

Despite her apprehension, it was clear that he was still planning to sell his house, but she wanted to be in his arms. She needed to tell him the real reason she was here, and she wanted to do it soon. Her anxiety was causing a throb in her temples.

"Yes, I really do love the kitchen."

"Then why the glum expression?" He reached up and rubbed the spot between her eyebrows.

She relaxed at his touch. "Just thinking of all the potential buyers who would love a kitchen like this."

"Ah." He nodded a few times. "About that—" The doorbell rang, and Quinn blew out a frustrated breath. He lifted his finger to her lips. "Hold that thought, I'll be right back." He disappeared into the living room, and Hannah stepped farther into the kitchen. She could hear Quinn at the door but couldn't see who was there.

"Tori?" Quinn said.

Hannah stepped closer to the wall, making sure she was out of sight.

"Hi, Quinn. I have some wonderful news for you." Tori's words were rushed, and Hannah could picture her bouncing on her toes. "I found the perfect buyer for your house."

Hannah's heart dropped to her stomach.

"But—"

"It's a couple with two small children, but they're open to possibly more. I've shown them pictures of the completed rooms and told them you are working on the kitchen and some other areas. They are so excited to move in—"

"Tori," Quinn's voice boomed.

Hannah peeked around the frame of the open doorway, just enough to see Tori and Quinn standing just inside the room, at the base of the steps.

"Yes?"

He shook his head. "Why would you get their hopes up like that?"

Tori tittered and touched his forearm. "Why wouldn't I? You won't even have to put the house on the market. I could have the contract drawn up and everything taken care of by tomorrow afternoon."

"I told you last week that I wasn't selling," Quinn grumbled.

Hannah covered her mouth as she gasped. Was he still planning to move if he wasn't selling?

"Why would you tell them otherwise?"

Hannah noticed the pity in Tori's eyes. She'd seen that look before, always when Tori was about to spin the situation to sound like it benefited the other person but really only helped herself.

"Quinn," Tori began slowly. "Look, I know you're hoping that Hannah will come back to you—"

Quinn turned his face toward the kitchen just a fraction. If Hannah hadn't been watching, she wouldn't have noticed. Tori completely missed it.

"But we both know that's not who she is. That's not how she works. She may be mad at Carter now, but they will work it out because that's what's expected of her."

Hannah's blood heated in her veins. *Who does she think she is?*

"And then where will you be?" Tori pouted. "You'll be in this huge house, all alone. What's the point in that, Quinn? This house is too much for one person, you know that. I don't even know why you bought it in the first place."

"Enough, Tori," Quinn grumbled. "You have no idea who Hannah is. And why are you so invested in their relationship, anyway?"

Tori's laugh tinkled nervously. "I have no idea what you're talking about."

"No idea?" Quinn folded his arms over his chest. The muscles under his shirt flexed with the movement. "When you dared Carter to ask Hannah to prom, after I'd told you that I wanted to ask her, what did you think would happen?"

Hannah's heart skipped a beat, and butterflies filled her stomach. Quinn had wanted to ask her to prom? She'd had no idea. Why hadn't he done it?

Tori took a step backward toward the door.

"Why did you dare him, anyway?" Quinn's calm voice was betrayed by the tension in his shoulders.

The surprise in Tori's eyes was replaced by an angry glare. "Why do you think? She was a nerd and an outsider. She didn't belong in our group. If you had asked her, then she would have ruined our prom."

"*Our* prom?" Quinn scoffed. "Did you think I would have gone with you all as a group if she had agreed to be my date?"

"No, I didn't," Tori snapped. "And that would have ruined everything."

"What was there to ruin?" Quinn asked.

"We were supposed to go as a group. You . . . you were supposed to want to go with me."

Confusion was written on Quinn's features.

Tori paused for a moment, then said, "This may come as a surprise to you—and I'm utterly embarrassed to admit it—but I had feelings for you when we were in high school. I honestly don't know what I was thinking. I just didn't want you to go to the prom with Hannah. I thought for sure she'd turn Carter down, and then you'd see how she wasn't like us. She didn't deserve either of you then, and I'm not sure she deserves either of you now."

Hannah stepped out of the kitchen and slowly strolled toward them. She was halfway across the room before Tori noticed her.

"Then why so much interference in my relationship with Carter?" Hannah stood by Quinn's side. "And why did you keep his secret for so long?"

Tori gasped and took a step back. "H-Hannah . . . I didn't know you were here."

"What secret?" Quinn asked.

Hannah kept her focus on Tori. "She knew Carter was alive." She wasn't sure if that was true, but Tori hadn't denied the accusation at the party.

Tori sputtered and her cheeks turned pink, like she had at the party, and that was all the confirmation Hannah needed.

"She knew Carter was alive, and I'm pretty sure she probably kept him updated on my life." Hannah looked at Tori, then turned to Quinn. "She'd call me once a month or so, ask to go out, and always managed to turn the conversation to whether or not I was dating." Hannah looked at Tori again. "You reported back to Carter, didn't you? So, was the memorial party a test of sorts?"

Tori scoffed. "You're being ridiculous. I don't have to answer any of these questions." She turned toward the door and reached for the knob.

"No, I think you do," Quinn said as he stepped between Tori and the door.

Tori froze and her hand slowly fell. She turned to look at Hannah.

"Why did you do it?" Hannah questioned. She had been foolish to trust Tori, even a little bit.

"You made him happy," Tori answered softly. "He was a different person when he was with you. A better person."

Carter had told her the same thing, but after everything that had happened, Hannah still had a hard time believing it. "That still doesn't give you a right to interfere. You manipulated me for years, almost as much as he did."

"But—"

"No," Hannah cut her off, surprising herself as much as Tori. "No more buts. You and Carter were both wrong to use and manipulate me the way you did. It's time you learn that you can't control everyone. We are not your puppets."

Tori's hand flew up to her chest, and she shook her head.

"Get out of my house." Quinn opened the door. "I'm not selling. Hannah's not getting back with Carter." He looked at Hannah and smiled, then turned to Tori. "And we don't need you in our lives."

With her head held high, Tori glided out into the darkness. After Quinn closed and locked the door, he turned to Hannah.

"You're not moving?" Hannah asked as she stared into Quinn's eyes. He shook his head. "Why?"

"Don't you want me to stay?" he said.

"Of course I want you to stay. But I don't want you to stay just for me. I want you to go to Atlanta if that's what you really want."

"I know," he said quietly.

She bit back tears. "I've given it some thought. If you want to go, you should go."

His jaw tightened, and he strolled past her toward the kitchen. His obvious disappointment knotted her stomach. She turned to watch him but didn't follow, even after he disappeared around the wall. This wasn't how she'd imagined this conversation would go, but everything Tori revealed had flustered her.

"And if you and I are still together," she rushed through the words, "then at the end of the school year, I thought I might move there too." She couldn't believe those words left her mouth, but she meant it.

Quinn emerged from the kitchen and stared at her. The crinkles in the corners of his eyes were gone. "What?"

"I said that I'm willing to move with you," she repeated. "If that's what you want."

He took a slow step toward her. "Why?"

"Would you believe me if I said it's Kailee's fault?" Hannah said. The conversation with her sister had opened Hannah's eyes to a lot of things.

Quinn took another step closer. "Not really."

"The truth is, I was making excuses. It doesn't matter where my classroom is—there will always be kids to teach."

He crept closer. Her heart rate sped up with every step he took.

"And my friends and family will be there for me, no matter where I am," she continued.

He stopped in front of her, and she pressed her palms on his chest. Her fingers itched to move further up, to his shoulders, to thread through his hair, but she willed them to remain still. She stared at her fingertips.

"But none of it matters if I'm not with the man I love." She slowly lifted her gaze to his. "If I'm not with you."

Quinn's eyes lit up before the grin spread across his face. "Really?" He wrapped his arms around her waist and lifted her feet off the floor. "I love you too." His words brushed across her ear, and she squeezed him tighter.

He lowered her feet to the floor and bent his head toward her. Their lips met, and the spark that skittered down her spine was warm and welcomed. As the kiss deepened, she relished the comfort of being in his arms, and the spark settled low in her belly. Reluctantly, she broke the kiss and eased back. There were still things they needed to discuss.

"You won't have to move away because I'm going to stay here," he whispered.

He took her hand and led her to the couch, then motioned for her to sit. Once she was situated, he lowered himself to the cushion beside her. She turned her knees toward his as he took her hands.

"You were right." Quinn's thumb brushed back and forth across her knuckles. "I hadn't realized just how much Alexa's words influenced me. I hadn't even realized that I wanted to leave Rocky Creek because of the things she'd said when we broke up. She left me with this need to prove to myself that I could be that guy. That I could pull in six figures. That I could be successful."

"That you could be like the guy she was going to marry?" Hannah squeezed his fingers.

"Yes," he sighed, and his shoulders relaxed. "And in trying to do that, I lost track of what was important to me. I forgot how much I loved Rocky Creek and how much I love what I do here."

She leaned toward him. "You're going to stay on with Charlie after graduation?"

"Not exactly." His smile widened and he slid closer. "Charlie and I are going to become partners."

Hannah's eyes rounded.

"We're changing things up a little. We're going to start getting into new construction as well as renovations and remodels." Excitement lit his features. He looked so happy; she knew this was the right decision for him. "We even met with Mr. Elliot today to discuss a partnership."

"Really?" she gasped. She couldn't disagree with that move. Carter's father was one of the best businessmen in Rocky Creek. He always did whatever he could to help the community and other small business owners.

Quinn chuckled. "He's going to help us out by directing renovation business to us as we work on building our new construction reputation. He's going to work with me on new housing designs and eventually will send people our way for those as well."

Hannah's mouth fell open.

"He wants to retire at some point and doesn't have anyone to take over for him." Quinn shrugged. "So, he's sort of tapping us as his successors."

Hannah threw her arms around his neck. "Oh my goodness. That's wonderful. I'm so happy for you."

He pulled her close, and she was content to stay in his arms. Then he leaned back, dragging his hands down her arms to her hands, leaving a wave of heat in their wake. She grasped his fingers and held them in her lap.

His fingers lifted to her chin, and he raised her stare to meet his. "I don't need six figures. I don't need to make a name for myself in the big city. All I need is you. And right now, I need to make sure you and I are on the same page."

All she needed was him, wherever that might take her. "What page might that be?" Hannah asked.

"You." He leaned closer until their foreheads were pressed together.

"Me." He peppered a light kiss on her cheek and a current raced through her body. "Together?"

She pulled away slightly, trying to keep the excitement hidden. "I thought I'd made that clear." He shrugged his response, and she swallowed a laugh.

Hannah rose to her feet, giving his hands a tug so he followed her up. "I love you," she said. She took a few steps backward, pulling him with her. "I am sorry I let you think otherwise." His lips parted, but she silenced him with her finger pressed to his mouth. "I want to be with you." She let go of his hands and turned toward the staircase. Looking over her shoulder, trying not to laugh, she added, "Right now." She took off at a run, giggling as he chased her.

When Quinn caught her at the top of the steps, Hannah threw her arms around him and met him in a kiss that filled her with more joy than she'd ever felt. As he backed her toward the bedroom, their lips still pressed together, she amended her statement. She wanted to be with him.

Forever.

About the Author

Born and raised in Virginia, Kathryn Ascher enjoyed writing poetry and fiction in high school, but put it all aside when she went to college. After graduating from Virginia Tech (Go HOKIES!) with her degree in communications, she married her college sweetheart and went to work for a local radio station. After their first child was born, she became a stay-at-home mom and began spending her free time crafting and reading.

Just before her third child turned three, Kathryn decided to give writing another try. When she picked up her first romance novel, she immediately knew that was the genre for her. She was drawn to the strong lead characters and quirky secondary characters, the settings, the humor, and most importantly the feelings of falling in love for the first time. She hopes that her readers enjoy these aspects in her writing as well.

Kathryn lives in Florida with her husband and three children, now two adults and a teenager.

Other Books

in the Rocky Creek series
by Kathryn Ascher

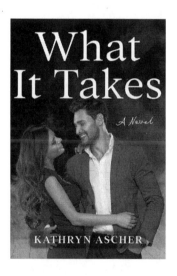

After graduating college, Kelsey Morgan left her small-town Virginia roots to make it in LA. After years slogging in commercials and music videos, her movie career is finally taking off. But she's still miles behind her current costar, and Hollywood playboy, Patrick Lyons.

Kelsey does everything she can to avoid Patrick off-set, hoping to not become fodder for the supermarket tabloids that scour the streets for Patrick, trying to get an exclusive look at him and his alleged woman of the week. Kelsey has successfully kept Patrick at a distance, and her reputation intact, until her drunkard brother-in-law Richard threatens to ruin everything by selling her darkest secret to the highest bidder.

Now the victim of blackmail, Kelsey has nowhere else to turn but to Patrick's arms. But, can he be trusted? Or will the past destroy them all before she can find out if he's the hero she needs?

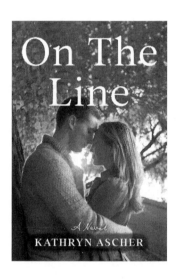

Janelle Wagoner kept a lot of secrets for her husband, but the one she tried hardest to protect was her own. She never suspected he knew or that he would choose to reveal it in such a dramatic way.

Now that he's gone, leaving behind her and two children, Janelle is left to pick up the pieces and try to put her life back together before it's too late.

Nathan Harris has only ever loved one woman, despite the fact that she was married to someone else. After learning that she has been hiding something from him, he's faced with a tough decision: With everything at stake, will he walk away from her for good, or will he lay it all on the line to win her back?

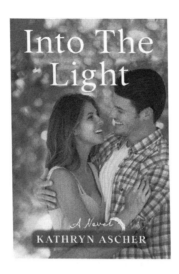

Jackson Harris fell in love with his best friend's sister, but at her brother's request, he stepped out of her life to clean up his act. When he was ready to declare his love to her, she rejected him, sending him back into a tailspin of bad behavior.

Four years later, he's focused on his struggling band, the women who want him, and still trying to forget the one who didn't. When she suddenly shows up as his band's new manager, he realizes that, despite his best efforts, his feelings for her haven't changed a bit.

Kerrigan Dodd has spent the past four years living in Europe, trying to forget that Jackson, the only man she's ever loved, walked out of her life six years earlier. After returning home, the last thing she expected was that her new job was to manage his failing band. To make matters worse, she barely recognizes the boy she fell in love with in his band persona, and the prospect of spending so much time with him has her questioning her ability to do her job.

As Jack and Kerrigan work to turn the band around, they struggle to overcome the secrets that have kept them apart. Just when they're coming together, on both fronts, other forces conspire to keep them from reaching their goals. Will they be able to put the past behind them and clear the way for their future? Or are their current differences too much to move beyond?